To Charm a Scarred Cowboy

Brides of Bethany Springs
Book One

Charlotte Dearing

The right of Charlotte Dearing to be identified as author of this Work has been asserted by her in accordance with sections 77 and 78 of the Copyright, Designs and Patents Act of 1988.

Copyright © 2023 by Charlotte Dearing.
All rights reserved.

No part of this book may be reproduced in any form or by any electronic or mechanical means, including information storage and retrieval systems, without written permission from the author, except for the use of brief quotations in a book review.

This is a clean, wholesome story of love and family
set in late 19th century Texas.

It is the story of Amelia Honeycutt's oldest son, Daniel,
and the woman who doesn't seem to notice
the scars on his face.

Chapter One
Rejected at the Mercantile

Molly Collins

Molly stood at the shop counter, her heart sinking. Her hopes of selling her work at the mercantile, and of earning the money her family desperately needed, were disappearing fast. She hadn't even begun to explain the level of her workmanship or the time she spent perfecting each detail.

She'd brought her best sewing samples, but the shopkeeper's grimace let her know her efforts would amount to nothing. Not one penny. The woman was surly and rude. She peered at the work, wrinkling her nose as she scrutinized the seams.

She turned the shirt over, squinting at the cuff. "Seems a tad fancy. My customers don't give a fig about fine stitching. They want clothes that last."

"My garments are very durable."

The woman raised her eyes above the rim of her glasses, disdain darkening her eyes. Mrs. Nellie Pittman ruled her husband's mercantile with an iron fist and sharp tongue. She occasionally treated some customers with courtesy, but only if they were notable townsfolk or wealthy ranchers.

Molly pressed on, "I can make any sort of shirt you like. It's no trouble."

The woman yelled over her shoulder. "Junior!" Her shout blasted across the mercantile.

Molly very nearly jumped out of her boots. A small cry of surprise fell from her lips.

The shopkeeper didn't notice. "Junior, you'd best not be napping. I told you to sweep the porch. I don't hear a broom."

Mrs. Pittman scowled as she went back to scrutinizing the shirt. A moment later, the sound of sweeping drifted through an open window.

"About time," she grumbled before muttering under her breath, comments about dirty mining families looking for a handout. Molly bit her tongue. The last thing she wanted was charity, especially from Nellie Pittman.

The woman ran her finger along the hem.

"Those backstitches took considerable effort." At once Molly regretted her words. She prayed she didn't sound boastful. A moment before, she'd been about to explain how young brides often traveled from several towns over to get fitted for a gown. She remained silent, however.

"What's this?" the woman demanded, pointing to the tag sewn into the collar.

"I always attach a tag. I want people to know who made their garment. I take a great deal of care with everything I sew, whether it's a man's shirt, a baby's christening gown or a wedding dress. I do my best, regardless."

"Regardless?"

"Yes, ma'am. Regardless of the price I charge, I always take a great deal of care even if I do the work at no cost."

Molly winced, wishing she could stop herself. The woman's expression made it impossible to hold her tongue. The contempt was too much for her to bear.

"For example," she said, "I never charge for christening gowns or children's clothes. It's a habit of mine. I don't like to take money for something so precious, but I make certain to take the utmost care. I especially enjoy working on children's garments and pay close attention to every detail, sometimes adding whimsical elements."

The woman gave her a hard stare.

Molly restrained the urge to explain more of the whimsical details. Inwardly, she groaned at her foolish blathering. Why on earth did she feel the need to explain? Clearly, the woman did not intend to order shirts or anything else. All Molly needed was four dollars to pay next month's rent. Four measly dollars. It might as well be a thousand dollars. The shopkeeper wasn't going to give her a penny.

"Seems to me you're putting on airs with that tag at the back of the collar. What does it mean, *Made with Care by MAC*?"

"My middle name is Anne. MAC is nothing more than my initials."

The woman blinked.

"My name is Molly Anne Collins which is too long to embroider on a tag. That would be a great deal of stitching." She laughed awkwardly. "So many stitches..."

Her words faded. Warmth rose to her cheeks. Goodness, this meeting was not going well. She'd agonized over the prospect of speaking to Mrs. Pittman and things were even worse than she'd imagined.

Mrs. Pittman didn't find her comment humorous. If anything, she regarded Molly with suspicion. One of her children trudged down the aisle, carrying a good-sized box to the back of the store, clearly struggling with the weight. He nearly dropped the box. It slipped from his hands, but he managed to squat quickly and trap the box against his legs.

"What do you have there, PJ?" said Mrs. Pittman. "That better not be the candy delivery you're sneaking around with."

"No, ma'am." The boy froze, his eyes wide. "It's a box from the saddle shop."

He winced, shifting the bulky box in his arms. He was breathing heavily under the strain.

"The saddle shop?" his mother grumbled. "I don't recall ordering anything from those rascals."

The boy paled. He swallowed hard. "I believe you ordered some spurs and bits for the McCord Ranch. A couple of lariats and bullwhips too if I recall rightly."

"Go on then," his mother snapped. "No point in standing around."

He gulped, nodded, and staggered to the back of the store.

The bell on the front door rang as a man and woman entered the store. The woman browsed the kitchen wares. The man approached the counter. He nodded politely and doffed his cowboy hat.

"Good morning," Mrs. Pittman said, her voice a cheerful singsong. "How lovely to see you, Mr. Richards. And Mrs. Richards as well."

Molly's heart fell. She knew this signaled the end of the meeting. Mrs. Pittman would dismiss her to take care of her wealthy shoppers.

Mrs. Pittman lowered her voice. She swept aside Molly's sewing with the palm of her broad and callused hand, nearly sending the linen shirt sailing off the edge of the counter. "Go on," she sneered. "I'm not running a haberdashery."

Molly folded the shirt neatly and tucked it into her bag. Hurriedly, she left the shop, grateful to escape any more humiliation.

When she stepped outside the shop, she paused to consider her options. Perhaps she should tear out the tag and go back. She could wait until the wealthy rancher and his wife left. Despite her desperate circumstances, it pained her to consider such a thing.

After a moment, she decided against it. Things weren't that bad. Yet. Her reputation and livelihood depended on the quality of her work as well as her name. If she couldn't make an income from her sewing, how would she care for her ailing father? With a renewed sense of purpose, she left the mercantile, casting aside the memory of the disagreeable Mrs. Pittman.

Somehow, someway, she'd earn the money to pay the rent. She'd rely on her skills and plenty of prayer. With God's help, she was sure she could manage, and with a little more of the good Lord's help, Papa would soon heal from the mining accident.

Chapter Two
Sworn to Protect

Daniel Honeycutt

Daniel rode along the riverbank. He headed for an oak grove, a cluster of giant trees sprawling across the gentle bend of the stream. The Bethany River glittered in the midday sunshine. One of his fellow volunteer lawmen waited in the shade of the oaks. He'd come to report to Daniel, to explain the latest concerning an outlaw who preyed on families living around the town of Bethany Springs.

Daniel and several others, including his two brothers, were members of a secret brotherhood. Lawmen of sorts, although not in the traditional sense. They worked without pay. None were appointed or deputized, nor did they wear a badge like the Rangers did.

The Bethany Brotherhood was a secret group sworn to protect the vulnerable.

Some people called them vigilantes, but that word did not describe who they were or what they did. Their purpose was to protect those who could not protect themselves, and to do it in a way that was fair and just for all.

The Bethany Brotherhood, twelve men from the small town and surrounding lands, met every two months. Usually, they met in the home of the eldest member. Trouble didn't keep a schedule, though. It showed up any time, any day, stirred up by men who considered their wants and rights were more important than others.

A junior member of the group had asked to meet with Daniel. The man wanted Daniel's approval on a matter of concern.

As Daniel drew close, the man stepped out from the dappled shade. He nodded and lifted a hand to wave. Daniel put his horse into a lope, closed the distance quickly and dismounted a few paces from his brother-in-arms.

"Andrew," Daniel said. "Good to see you."

"Same," Andrew said with his usual quiet manner. "Good to see you, sir."

"The family's well, I hope?"

Andrew gave the barest hint of a smile, a rare occurrence. "Yes, sir. The baby's learning to walk and we've got another one on the way."

Daniel felt a pang squeeze his heart. "Give Katie my best."

Andrew had taken the secret oath just a year before. It was clear by his words and posture that he regarded his commitment to the group with solemn reverence. Daniel appreciated his loyalty. Andrew saw his role as a duty to the father he'd never known, a man who died in the war. He was also a husband and father, and those responsibilities only made Andrew more devoted to the cause.

Andrew spoke. "Found out who was cutting Mrs. Harlow's fence line. It's the same fella who took twenty head from that widowed lady near Sandy Flats."

"Good to know. Have you taken care of things?"

Andrew shook his head. "Not yet. Not till you give me the go-ahead."

At times, Daniel forgot that the younger men needed the approval of the older men. They needed permission to take care of matters, but *how* they took care of things was up to each man's discretion. The unspoken rule was to run troublemakers out of town and use as little force as possible. Sometimes the outlaw could be persuaded easily, other times, a little more effort was needed.

Two years ago, Daniel faced one such man, a man who refused to listen to reason. The showdown happened an hour after sundown when Daniel confronted the cattle rustler.

The thief hadn't taken well to Daniel's charges. He'd gotten belligerent. Drawn a knife. In the ensuing melee, he threatened to cut a ranch servant. Daniel stepped between the outlaw and the young woman. The thug slashed Daniel's face, injuring him gravely.

The outlaw was found guilty of other crimes, not just cattle rustling, and eventually hanged. Daniel got his man but paid a heavy price, the loss of the sight in one eye. His life was forever changed. He pushed the painful memories away.

Almost without realizing, he adjusted the band of his eye patch. "Do you need another man? I could lend a hand."

Andrew hesitated as his gaze drifted to Daniel's eye patch.

Daniel grimaced. He could see fine out of his good eye, but folks acted like he was blind. The jagged scar down the side of his face didn't inspire much confidence either. Folks often recoiled at his hideous injuries. Or considered him some sort of invalid. Daniel wasn't sure what he disliked more.

"Well," Andrew said, "I don't believe I need another man."

"All right," Daniel said from between gritted teeth.

Andrew looked aggrieved. "You've already done a lot."

"Right."

"Besides, this rascal isn't more than 120 pounds, soaking wet."

"Good to hear." Daniel slapped Andrew's shoulder, probably with a little more force than necessary. "A 120-pound cattle rustler shouldn't be too much trouble for you and Roger."

"We'll manage," Andrew said, his tone conciliatory.

Daniel swung into his saddle. "Mind the scrawny outlaw doesn't have a knife in his boot. You hear?"

Andrew paled as his gaze darted to Daniel's injured eye. He replied softly, "Yessir."

Chapter Three
The Crack of the Whip

Molly

Molly made her way from the mercantile to the livery barn. While Mrs. Pittman had wounded her pride, she was determined not to let it trouble her any longer. Nellie Pittman wasn't the only person in Bethany Springs who could pay her for sewing. She had various projects in the works. Somehow, she'd find enough to pay rent.

She tried to put aside her worries.

Instead, she prepared for another good-natured dispute with the livery barn owner. Mr. Armstrong was a friend of Molly's father. He never accepted a single penny for keeping her horse. He said Molly's father was like a son to him, which made Molly an honorary granddaughter.

He saw her coming down the walkway and got her mare. When she came into the barn, he called out a greeting from the back. "I'll have your horse ready in two shakes of a lamb's tail," he said.

"No hurry," she called back.

She eyed Mr. Armstrong's office to the left of the entry. His desk sat beneath a sunny window, piled high with ledgers and papers. A half-eaten ham sandwich sat upon some wax paper next to an apple. He'd likely bought the meal at the nearby lunch counter. The poor fellow had been widowed years ago and ate a great number of ham sandwiches.

"I'm sorry I disturbed your lunch," she said.

"No trouble. The barn's quiet today. I sent most of my men to tend to the haybarn. We're getting a load this afternoon."

He led her horse from the back stall and the mare followed, docile as a lamb. Armstrong Livery was the only place Molly could leave the horse her brothers had aptly named Vixen. Every other livery barn refused. The horse's bad manners were known to all.

Vixen simply didn't like most men. Molly figured her horse had been mistreated at some point in the past. Somehow, Mr. Armstrong had earned the mare's trust, maybe with slices of apple or cubes of sugar. Or maybe it was on account of the older man's gentle demeanor.

He stopped a few paces from Molly. "Here's your girl. She did fine. Didn't draw blood. Not even once."

Molly straightened the mare's forelock and trailed her fingers along the length of her blaze. "That's my pretty Vix."

"She's more settled each time I keep her."

"That's because she knows you have a kind heart." Molly held out a freshly pressed shirt, folded neatly with the sleeve mended and missing button replaced. "This is for last week when you kept Vixen. The Collins family is no charity case."

Augustus Armstrong frowned. "I know that. I don't want your money. Maybe when the mine reopens, and your father goes back to work."

"My father won't go back to the mine," Molly said. "Not if I can help it. Once my brothers join the military, I intend to open a dress shop far, far from the Presidio Mine."

Mr. Armstrong looked aghast. "What will become of your father if you open a dress shop?"

"I'll take him with me, of course. I'll always care for Papa. While I run my shop, he can read his books. Maybe even write one if he's feeling up to it."

Mr. Armstrong shook his head, handing her the reins. "Don't tell me John Collins is going to spend the rest of his days in a rocking chair, sipping lemonade. He's not one for idleness. He'll need to work when he's healed. He's far from elderly."

Molly held out the newspaper she'd picked up at the post office. *The Galveston Guardian.* "If I end up in Galveston maybe he'll take up fishing. That would suit him. Better the wide-open sea than a dark, dangerous mine."

Mr. Armstrong's smile faded. "You're serious about all this?"

"I am indeed."

Silence stretched between them, the only sound came from the horses and mules munching hay in their stalls. Sunshine shone through the slats of the barn. Motes of dust swirled in the soft light.

Mr. Armstrong lowered his worried gaze to the shirt she'd mended.

Molly wondered if he found fault with her work. Rarely did she fret about what others thought of her sewing. She liked to think she was the finest seamstress in Bethany Springs. She'd learned from the best, after all. Her earliest memories were sitting at her stepmother's knee, working on some small sewing tasks. Brigit showed her how to sew small, even stitches, gently chiding her for any less than perfect seams.

Molly knew her work was good, but the look in Mr. Armstrong's eye made her worry, nonetheless. He was a somewhat wealthy man, accustomed to finer things. Maybe he detected some small imperfection in her handiwork. "Is something wrong?" she asked quietly.

He shook his head and turned the shirt over absently. All signs of cheer and humor drifted from his expression, as if sinking under the weight of old sorrow. "The sea can be dangerous, Molly. Oh, she's pretty to look at, but every so often, a storm rolls across the water, barreling to land and taking everything in its path. Those big storms show no mercy."

Molly knew that to be true, but at least the storms offered warnings, or so she'd heard. Mines, on the other hand, collapsed in the blink of an eye. Rocks fell without mercy, burying or crippling men. A shudder rolled along her spine. She winced as she recalled the day, two months ago, when they'd carried her father home, his clothing tattered, his legs badly injured.

Usually, Molly spoke her mind, but for once, she held her tongue. Distantly, she recalled something her father had said about Augustus Armstrong, back when the two men first struck up a friendship. Papa explained that Mr. Armstrong had lived on the Texas coast, somewhere near Indianola. He had lived through one of those great storms and lost much of his family to it.

In the quiet, he tucked the shirt under his arm and turned away to check the mare's cinch.

Molly shifted her weight from one foot to the other as she tried to think of what to say. In the face of another's grief, she always fretted that she would say the wrong thing and make the person's misery even worse.

She was nineteen but had already suffered her share of losses. Her own mother died when Molly was two days old. Several years later her father remarried, a woman as kind as the day was long. Molly adored Brigit. Hungry for a mother's love, she blossomed in her stepmother's tender care. When

Brigit passed away four years ago, she'd taken a piece of Molly's heart with her.

That didn't mean Molly found it easy to say the right thing around others who grieved. Usually she spoke in haste, letting her temper get away from her. When it came to suffering, she was left tongue-tied. It was probably for the best, considering how she had little skill in choosing the right words.

Voices came from the haybarn in the back, two stable hands squabbling over chores. Mr. Armstrong finished looking over the mare's tack. The sunshine returned to his expression as if appearing once again from behind a heavy cloud. His eyes sparked with mirth.

"You'd best stay here in Bethany Springs," he advised, a smile playing on his lips. "Marry one of the cowboys here in town. Raise up a family."

"I'm too busy raising my brothers. I have no mind for marriage or babies. By the time the boys leave for military school, I should have enough saved. I'll pack up our things and move us to Galveston. Lord willing, I'll own my own dress shop, my own home and never pay another dime of rent."

Silently, she added, *especially to the same family that owns the Presidio Mine.* It was best to keep such thoughts to herself, however.

Mr. Armstrong spoke. "You want your own dress shop in Galveston," he muttered. "Who is going to mend my shirts, hem my trousers? What's more, if John Collins leaves town, I'll have no one to play checkers with, or argue with about local goings-on."

She smiled but said nothing.

He took the reins and led the horse to the mounting block outside, a wooden stand he'd built just for Molly, grumbling vigorously all the while. *Can't hardly abide by a gal riding astride. Seems wrong. It wasn't done in my day. Ain't respectable but might as well make sure she can hop onto the saddle with some semblance of decency.*

She'd considered telling him she wore britches under her skirts, but the poor, dear man would probably never again look her straight in the eye.

He held the mare's bridle and fixed his attention at some point down the road. She ascended the steps and with a quick, deft motion, swung into the saddle. She tucked her skirts while glancing around but found that no one paid a whit of attention. Probably because there were more outlandish sights in the roughhewn town of Bethany Springs, a place where men outnumbered women five to one, a town where men often took to brawling in the middle of the street, even on the Sabbath, no less.

She gathered the reins and cleared her throat to signal she was ready to be on her way.

"You give my best to your father," Mr. Armstrong said, squinting at the barbershop two doors down. "Tell him I aim to pay him a visit when he's feeling up to a chat or maybe even a game of checkers."

Molly winced. Her father was in no condition to receive company.

She coaxed a smile to her expression, even though Mr. Armstrong seemed intent on looking anywhere but at her. "I'll certainly pass that on," she said cheerfully.

The mare shook her head and stepped lightly, suddenly energized by some stray wind or scent. Hard to tell with Vixen. Molly tried to soothe the horse, but the mare only grew more agitated. The horse pricked her ears as if trying to discern some distant threat. Mr. Armstrong's features knit with worry.

"It's fine," Molly said lightly. "Vix is just ready to get home to her pasture so she can kick up her heels."

He nodded silently, stepped back and waved her off. Molly put the horse into a trot and set off down the main street of Bethany Springs. Vix moved with her head high, alert for some sign of trouble.

Just as Molly passed the mercantile, two children dashed from the back alley. She recognized the boys as part of the owner's brood. Two of them ran across the road. They shrieked and cavorted, one of them waving a bullwhip overhead.

Molly drew a sharp breath. "My heavens."

"Bet I can make it crack better than you," the smaller boy jeered.

"Nah," his brother scoffed. "You're too puny."

"You're gonna take that back."

"Won't either."

Molly watched in horror as the child twirled the whip. The length of leather whistled through the air. Vixen shied. Molly tried to turn her to escape the sight of the boys' game. The mare reared, only partly coming off the ground, thankfully. If Molly could keep the mare moving forward, it would prevent her from rearing once again. Before she could turn the horse, the boy managed to snap the bullwhip.

The crack split the air. The blast was as loud as a gunshot.

Vixen spooked. Instead of rearing, the mare lowered her head and burst into a gallop.

Molly knew she should be afraid. Instead, she wondered why and how the mare knew about a bullwhip. Molly's eyes stung. She bent low, tucked her head, laced her fingers through the mare's wild, flowing mane and held on for dear life.

Chapter Four
Vixen, The Rascal

Daniel

The sight of a bolting horse galloping toward him struck Daniel as a tad odd. Horses bolted all the time for various reasons, but what struck him as curious pertained to the rider, not the horse. He frowned. Was he seeing things? Sure looked like a female sitting astride the horse. The horse and rider were a way off yet but coming fast.

The town of Bethany Springs stretched across the horizon, no more than half a mile away. Even with just one good eye, he could make out the buildings and dust in the distance. Nothing out of the ordinary there. It was the rider barreling down the road who bewildered him. From the space of about a hundred strides, he could make out the details. The woman, more girl than woman, clung to the horse.

A protective instinct kicked in. He urged his gelding into a lope along the terrain that stretched beside the road. He rode behind a stretch of canebrake, across a dry creek bed and turned back to meet the girl's horse, picking up speed to match the runaway horse. His gelding jostled the smaller horse, a mare if Daniel had to guess. The mare bared her teeth, the little witch.

Daniel grabbed the bridle and slowed his horse. The mare shook her head, trying to wrench free, but Daniel held fast. By and by, he brought her to a halt. Her flanks heaved like bellows. Lather foamed along the length of her reins and across her withers.

When he felt assured that she wouldn't try to bolt, Daniel turned his attention to the rider.

The girl, pale and stricken, set her hand on her midsection as she gasped for breath.

Daniel dismounted, left his gelding ground-tied and circled to the girl's side. Fearing she might collapse, he said a quiet word of comfort and eased her from the saddle. Her knees buckled but he caught her in his arms and carried her to the side of the road where he set her on a flat expanse of rock.

The narrow road, framed by a grove of canebrake, offered shelter. Wind rustled across the reeds. Usually there were people traveling to or from town. Not today. Today the road was empty of travelers. Not a single horse and rider came down the rough road.

Daniel felt a tight pinch of worry. The girl was small and achingly fragile. It was pure chance that he'd met up with her as she raced along the lonely road on the runaway horse. What might have happened if he'd ridden that stretch of road later? The girl might have fallen from her horse and lain on the road for an hour or more. He winced, trying not to imagine all the distressing possibilities. He thanked the good Lord for watching over the vulnerable girl and for giving him the chance to lend a hand.

Crouching before her, he got his first look at the girl's face. She was young. Maybe twenty, if that. Honey-colored, wavy hair framed her heart-shaped face. Strands of soft tangled curls had come loose and blew across her brow, dancing on the breeze. Aside from the freckles, her skin was peaches and cream, which pretty well summed up her scent too. Sweet. Summery.

Daniel reached to brush the hair from her eyes but stopped himself.

He tightened his fingers into a fist. His scarred face and eyepatch frightened womenfolk. He ought to move away but couldn't resist lingering to take in more of the girl's pretty features.

Freckles dusted the bridge of her nose. Her eyes, the color of amber, looked at him with a mix of surprise and defiance, as if annoyed that he'd taken her from the saddle. At least she wasn't recoiling with dismay.

"I'm fine." She tried to insist, but probably didn't realize her voice shook. "Really."

He smiled.

Her mouth tightened. Her brows knit. "I don't see what's so funny."

"You don't look fine. You look a little tuckered out, truth be told."

"I feel perfectly fine. It's my mare. She's a little skittish."

"I'll say."

Looking past him, she bit her lip. "She might run off. I've never taught her to ground-tie. Well, I tried but the lesson didn't take. Vixen's a bit hardheaded, you see."

He saw all right. He'd seen it firsthand. Reluctantly, he tore his gaze from the girl's pretty face and straightened. With a soft word, he approached the mare and gently took hold of her reins. She pinned her ears, reminding him of some dang mule. He ignored her bad attitude and returned to where the girl sat, keeping a firm hold on the obstinate horse.

"I hate to trouble you," the girl said stiffly.

When she tried to rise, Daniel stopped her with a light hand on her shoulder. A jolt of awareness moved across his palm and down his arm. It had been a long time since he'd spoken to a young lady.

Not since Cordelia Pratt broke off their engagement days after he'd been injured. She explained that a girl like her could never marry a man like him. Whatever that meant. When the surprise wore off, he realized that the broken engagement was no great loss. He courted her out a sense of obligation to his mother. As the oldest son, he needed to set an example and settle down. His mother had insisted, cajoled, and threatened.

He'd never yearned to brush Cordelia's hair from her eyes. Never. Something about this stubborn, willful girl stirred a strong yearning inside him. It would pass. He felt certain. It was nothing more than a fleeting desire.

A soft, pink blush bloomed across the girl's fair skin, making him wonder if she felt something too. When she averted her gaze, he was certain she was trying to fend of some sort of response.

The mare pawed the ground, stirring up a cloud of dust. "You quit that," he commanded.

The mare obeyed, but her ears flicked back to make it clear she didn't like to be bossed.

"I'm sure I'm keeping you," the girl said, lifting her chin to level a calm, cool look his way.

He shrugged. "I have a meeting at the bank, but it can wait."

Her eyes grew wide with concern. "In my experience, it's not good to keep bankers waiting. You want to be as polite and courteous as possible."

"That so?" He schooled his features to keep from smiling. Mama owned the bank. She might be a tad miffed if he showed up late, but the bank manager and loan officials wouldn't dare complain.

The girl nodded. "Bankers are awful people. Heartless. Almost as wicked as people who own mines." She folded her hands and gave him a knowing look. "Take it from me. Over the years, I've known a great number of both and they're utterly contemptible. I think it's a job requirement."

"Are they now?"

"Monstrous," she said on a sigh. "Without any redeeming merit."

Before Daniel could reply, the mare nipped his shirt. He waved his hand to shoo her away. The ornery horse was undeterred. Just the opposite. In a flash, she clamped down on the fabric and pulled. The material ripped, tearing the sleeve from shoulder to elbow.

Daniel stared at his bare arm and the tattered fabric, too stunned to say a word. The girl clapped her hand over her mouth. Sparks danced in her eyes. She shook her head and lowered her hand as she struggled to hold back her laughter. "Vixen, you're a very bad girl. How could you?"

The mare sniffed the shirt, nibbling the edges of the ripped fabric.

"You git," Daniel warned.

His tone seemed to trouble the mare. She flicked her ears and side-stepped away with a teasing toss of her head, narrowly missing Daniel's horse. The gelding remained still but eyed the mare with bewilderment.

"I reckon it's your mare that's monstrous," Daniel muttered as he tugged at the remains of his tattered sleeve. "Without any redeeming merit."

"This is terrible." The girl jumped to her feet and let out a small murmur of dismay when she swayed unsteadily.

"You'd best stay put. You've had a fine scare and need to sit a while."

It should have come as no surprise that the girl ignored his demand. Muttering under her breath about important appointments and devious bankers and whatnot, she went to the mare and rummaged through her saddlebag.

"Where did I put it? Thank goodness the shrew at the mercantile didn't care for my handiwork. Though it was probably the tag. Of course. Nellie Pittman must have thought I was putting on airs."

Daniel blinked as he watched her search for Lord knew what. Was she daft? He couldn't hold back a chuckle. Maybe she was daft. Daft, but pretty. Everything about her was achingly feminine. He spent most days with rough cowboys. Not delicate, pretty, stubborn females. He watched her, spellbound.

"Aha!" She tugged a shirt from her bag and held it up like a trophy. "I'm sure this will fit you."

Daniel remained silent, watching her with a mix of amusement and curiosity. She tossed the shirt she'd found over her arm and, to his very great surprise, drew close and began to undo the top button of his shirt. Her scent washed over him, making his thoughts scatter.

Was this girl really going to unbutton his shirt? All the way?

He ought to put a stop to this foolishness, but that was the last thing he wanted.

Bring on the foolishness, he thought with a flicker of rare happiness. He glanced toward the road, grateful that there wasn't a single traveler in sight. He wanted nothing to interrupt the girl's attention, even if it bordered on improper.

She worked diligently, undoing the first button, and then started on the second as a frown furrowed her brow. She was adorable. He would have liked nothing better than to wrap her in his arms and kiss her.

Sadly, the improper moment didn't last long. Her fingers brushed across his neck. Her touch was electric. She seemed to feel it too for she drew a sharp breath of surprise and jerked her hands away.

She blushed once more. This time, her face turned a deeper shade, more red than a rose bloom.

Gazing up at him, her eyes held a startled look. "I can't imagine what came over me."

"S'all right. I didn't mind one bit, truth be told."

Wincing, she moved away. "I'm terribly sorry. You see, I'm used to having to hurry menfolk along when they have an important appointment."

"That so?" He tried to tamp down an unexpected flare of jealousy. A thought flickered across his mind, a bewildering notion that this girl, whose name he still didn't know, belonged to him, or would one day. It was an idea that formed in the furthest corner of his mind. An idea that felt right. Like it had been there all along.

For that reason, he found the didn't much care for her comments about "menfolk."

"How many of these fellas do you have to hurry along?" he asked.

"Just two. Sometimes three but usually just the two."

Daniel scowled as he undid his own buttons. "So, you're married to one of these menfolk?"

Surely not. She was too young. He held his breath. Waited.

A cloud of confusion moved behind her eyes. "Married?"

Distaste edged her tone. He felt a smile tug at his lips. She wasn't married. Good.

She wrinkled her nose. "I'm not married. I have two brothers. Twins. Sixteen years old."

"Who's the third?" This was none of his concern, but he yearned to know just the same.

"My father," she said primly. "I don't usually help him but lately he's needed a little assistance."

Satisfaction unfurled inside his chest. In the days to come, he'd look back and laugh at this moment and all his foolish yearnings. For now, he was mighty pleased to know she wasn't married. He shrugged off his shirt and handed it to the girl. He wore a sleeveless undershirt. He noted her gaze as it drifted across the expanse of his shoulders. He smiled. She cleared her throat with embarrassment and turned her back.

"You're very tall," she said, as if trying to regain her dignity.

He pulled on the new shirt and chuckled at her missish ways. A moment before, she'd unfastened the top button of his shirt, but now she couldn't even meet his gaze.

Standing a half-pace behind her allowed him to take in a little more of the girl's features without her being aware of his attention. Her hair was bound in a knot. A few wisps had blown free of the tidy arrangement. Soft tendrils clung to her neck. He inhaled, catching a hint of her pleasing scent, made that much more pleasing since she was unaware of his mischievous attention.

He finished putting on the shirt as he considered teasing her. Nothing too untoward. Perhaps a request for help with one of the buttons. He held back. The poor girl had been through enough, what with her out-of-control horse and the near calamity of what might have happened.

She spoke about the shirt he donned. "I'd like to point out that I made the shirttails extra-long."

He glanced down. "So you did."

"I added the length to accommodate the cowboys around Bethany Springs. I'd hoped Mrs. Pittman might want to buy them for her customers."

He was about to ask what she meant but she forged on before he could get a word in edgewise.

"You can rest assured that even though you're tall, the shirt won't come untucked."

"Alrighty."

With what sounded like a touch of pride she went on. "The shoulders and sleeves are generous to allow for roping or whatever tasks a cowboy or rancher might need to do in the course of his day. The white linen is probably all wrong."

She shook her head with regret. "The white fabric will show dirt, of course. Why didn't I think of that? On the other hand, the color will look fine when you go to your bank meeting. Clothes make the man, and I'm certain, in my shirt, you'll be the finest dressed gentleman in the room, and that should earn you a few points with the scoundrels you're meeting. They'll all be in suits and waistcoats but not one will have a shirt with such small, even stitches, although I hate to boast."

"The shirt's fine even if the buttons are a little tricky," he drawled. He'd finished dressing but couldn't resist a small teasing comment. "Not for you, of course. You seemed pretty good at buttons. Probably your small, delicate fingers."

She gave a small murmur of alarm and moved hurriedly to the side of her mare. Giving him a look of silent rebuke, she shoved his ruined shirt into the saddlebag. In the next instant, and with surprising swiftness, she pulled herself up into her saddle.

The mare, the hellion who'd flat-out attacked his shirt sleeve, didn't even flinch but remained quiet and placid. Her ears looked relaxed, not pinned back as they had earlier. Her lower lip drooped. The critter was half asleep, judging from the looks of things. The girl, on the other hand, appeared chagrined. He ought to have kept his teasing comments to himself.

Daniel couldn't help feeling disappointed the girl had managed to mount her horse all on her own. He'd missed his chance to help. He would have dearly liked to wrap his hands around her delicate waist and lift her to her saddle, but that was not to be.

The girl gathered her reins and looked to be ready to leave. Daniel's heart squeezed. Standing rooted to the spot, he tried in vain to summon fitting words. He didn't even know her name. Hadn't given her his. All because he'd been too distracted.

A wave of self-recrimination burned inside his chest. The girl was young, probably ten years younger than his twenty-nine years. When he lost the use of one eye, and Cordelia had broken their engagement, he'd vowed never to marry, never to seek out a woman's affection. Up till now, he hadn't been troubled by the prospect of a life of solitude. With dismay, he noted that his view had suddenly and irrevocably shifted.

Let her go, he told himself.

Forget her eyes, her smile, the way her scent reminds you of a summer morning.

For a long moment, the girl gazed at him, a smile playing on her lips. "The shirt fits perfectly."

He stood silently.

She went on. "As if it were meant for you. You look mighty handsome, if you don't mind my saying."

She grew flustered, embarrassed by her admission. Another splash of color washed over her features. Her eyes sparkled. A soft laugh fell from her lips. Her smile widened. "Thank you for your kind help. Best of luck at your meeting. Don't let them bully you. Bankers are either at your neck or at your feet."

He nodded even though he had no idea what she meant. Bankers were at your neck or at your feet? What kind of bankers had she met? Had she been mistreated? Questions drifted through his mind, but before he formed some semblance of a query, his mind circled back to the word "handsome." Had he heard correctly?

"Goodbye now," she said, her voice lilting. With that she turned her horse and trotted away along the desolate road. He watched, a dozen questions coming to his mind. The road led to the Presidio Mine. The ridge was home to the miners' cabins, most of which were owned by his family. He could find her if he wanted to, surely. But that would lead to nothing. He reminded himself of the thing he'd come to believe. He was better off alone.

With a heavy sigh, he swung into the saddle and urged his horse into a lope, riding to town, trying mightily to push away all imaginings of the nameless girl.

Chapter Five
H is for Henry (Hopefully)

Molly

Molly had to rush to get lunch ready on account of her morning in town. It consisted of a simple stew and buttermilk rolls. Papa blessed their meal and then the family began to eat. A few moments before, when Molly had served the meal, she thought it smelled delicious, but now she hardly tasted her food.

Her brothers sat across the table and bragged about the fish that had slipped off the line that morning. She knew they were trying to goad her into a response, trying to raise her ire and draw her into fussing at them for abandoning their chores and lessons to run off and fish at the nearby stream.

She *ought* to fuss. Someone needed to rein in the unruly sixteen-year-old twins. Papa certainly wouldn't complain. No, he'd only ask them for the precise spot on the riverbank where they'd almost caught the enormous fish. *Was it by the weeping willow, or by the bend close to the crossing?*

Molly hardly followed the thread of the conversation. Instead, she wandered lost in thought. The image of the handsome stranger flashed in her mind, teasing her with the memory of the morning's calamity. She let her memories drift.

If she tried, she could picture the stranger standing before her and could almost see the span of his broad shoulders.

"Doing all right, Molly Anne?" her father asked.

She dropped her spoon. It clattered against the bowl. Papa's voice startled her, especially since her thoughts concerned a handsome stranger and his broad shoulders. A flush of mortification burned her face.

Picking up her spoon, she drew her shoulders back and turned to her father. "Fine. I'm just perfectly, perfectly fine. Why wouldn't I be?"

Her brothers gaped, silent for the first time since they'd sat down to eat.

A smile tugged at the corner of her father's mouth. "You've been mighty quiet."

"Quiet?" Molly asked.

"Twice now, Jack has talked about finding work here in Bethany Springs, so he doesn't have to go to the military academy. Will spoke of signing onto the Honeycutts' cattle drive to Fort Worth in June. He intends to work as a cowboy. The whole time you've been staring off, gathering wool."

"I'm tired. That's all," Molly said hastily. "The boys just like to tease me about attending the academy. The best response is to ignore them."

Will studied her, squinting. "Thing is, you were sort of smiling."

Jack nodded. "Exactly. You were staring off with a dopey smile."

Dopey? The nerve! Molly wrapped her fingers around the buttermilk roll, focusing on Jack's forehead. Her brother's taunt took her to her childhood days when her twin brothers loved nothing better than to make her mad. With a little luck, she could peg him on the head with the roll. That would teach him to mind his own business. She resisted the wicked urge. Setting the roll back on the plate, she made a point of ignoring his infuriating smirk.

She reminded herself that she wasn't a child. Not anymore. She needed to set aside childish ways. Even if her rotten, irksome, smelly brothers tried to rile her, she'd remain poised and calm.

Ever since her stepmother passed away, Papa depended on her to manage the household. She prided herself on her various skills, from preparing meals, getting the boys to do their lessons, and even earning money with her sewing.

If she resorted to flinging dinner rolls, she might as well surrender her hard-won authority.

"Oh, Papa," she said lightly. "I know perfectly well how much my brothers want to get under my skin. They like to tease me about the academy. They dismiss how hard I worked on the applications."

"Even signing our names," Will exclaimed.

His accusation wasn't true, and Will knew it, but the comment always got a good laugh from his brother. She narrowed her eyes at both boys. Their smiles vanished. They held up their hands in mock fright.

Molly turned to her father. "I'm sorry if I drifted off. I have so many sewing projects I need to get done."

Papa eyed her with worry. "It's a lot for you, girl. I'm sorry. If only-"

"Papa, don't say another word. You know I love my sewing projects more than anything. Goodness, I'd sew pretty things for free. One of my next tasks is a christening gown for the little Cartwright girl. Myrna told me they had almost given up having a child. But the good Lord blessed them and answered their prayers. That is what I love about my work, getting to know a little about people's lives. Their struggles and triumphs."

Her eyes prickled.

The boys studied her with a hint of disbelief. Of course, Will and Jack thought her ideas were absurd. Neither of them cared one whit about the sorts of things that mattered to her. Once more, she considered sacrificing her buttermilk roll for the satisfaction of bouncing it off the head of one of her brothers.

Her father's expression held a tinge of worry. He winced as he shifted in his chair. "I haven't checked the coffee tin but meant to ask if we have enough for rent. You know it's due week after next."

Molly nodded. "Why, you're right about that. I'd almost forgotten."

Papa looked dismayed. "Molly?"

"We're fine, perfectly fine. Did I mention that Mr. Armstrong sends his regards? He wants to come visit."

Her father's eyes lit. "You saw Augustus in town?"

"I did indeed. Vixen isn't allowed at any of the other livery barns. She's on the naughty list. Good thing she likes Mr. Armstrong's hospitality."

"Does he still have all his fingers?" Will asked.

Jack scoffed, joining in. "What about his hair? Did Vix yank a chunk of hair from his head? Is he walking around with a bald spot?"

The two boys chuckled and eyed her with sparks of mirth dancing in their eyes. Her father shook his head disapprovingly. Despite his best efforts, Molly clearly saw that he struggled to keep from laughing along with the boys.

Molly sighed.

There was a time, before Brigit had passed away, when Molly had a staunch ally against her brothers and father. Her stepmother insisted she and Molly needed to stick together like bread and butter. There was strength in numbers.

Molly could almost hear her stepmother's conspiratorial giggle. She recalled all the times she'd sat beside Brigit, next to a sunshiny window, working on a sampler. Brigit always said the two of them needed to forge a battlefield alliance against the menfolk. She claimed that the females would exemplify civility and decorum in the face of male obstinance and ornery behavior.

The memory faded. In its place was the recollection of Brigit's final words. *Take care of our boys.*

A surge of emotion welled deep inside. Her father clasped her hand and gave her a squeeze. "You two boys quit. Molly loves her mare. There's no need to talk about Vixen's particular ways. Not when it upsets Molly."

The boys grumbled.

"Go on," Papa said. "Wash up so Molly can tend to her sewing."

Will and Jack complained at the extra chores. They complied, however, and began clearing the dishes. Papa sat with Molly a spell before excusing himself and limping back to bed for his afternoon nap.

Molly slipped away, retreating to the peace and blessed quiet of her room. She closed the door behind her, wishing for privacy from prying eyes. She searched her sewing corner, a table, shelves, and chair set by the window, and pulled the stranger's tattered shirt from the lengths of muslin and linen.

She held it up to the window. The spring sunshine cast a dappled light through the bough of the pecan tree. Vixen had certainly left her mark. The fabric was ripped from the shoulder seams all the way to the middle of the sleeve. Threads hung from the torn remnants.

The man's scent clung to the fabric.

Unable to resist, Molly inhaled deeply, taking in the pleasing fragrance of soap, a sort of piney smell mingled with a masculine scent. Clean and strong. For the hundredth time, she recalled the way he looked. His eyepatch made him appear fearsome. A jagged scar ran down the side of his face. He'd suffered a grave injury somehow, but she'd seen far, far beyond his injured countenance and glimpsed a quiet nobility. A gentle nature. A kindness he likely tried to hide.

As she held the shirt up, she noticed an inside pocket, a deftly, hidden pouch. She draped the shirt across the corner of her bed and ran her fingers inside the pocket. She found a swath of material, edged with threading, a gentleman's handkerchief. Her heart skipped a beat. Ever since she'd parted ways with the stranger, she'd tried to imagine who he might be. The handkerchief offered an intimate glimpse of her rescuer.

The edge was embroidered with a delicate stitch. A small rose adorned each corner. Beneath the bloom was the letter H. She sank to the edge of her bed, trying to imagine the man's name. Hollis? Harvill?

She wrinkled her nose. Neither Hollis nor Harvill pleased her. Not one bit.

As a schoolgirl she'd known a boy named Hollis. She'd gone to school with Hollis in one of the mining towns where Papa had worked. He was a vile, cruel bully. Hollis enjoyed tormenting animals. Molly showed him the error of his ways. She'd caught him pelting rocks at a poor kitten living under the schoolroom.

He was a head taller than Molly, but she pushed him hard. He fell to the ground. When he sprang to his feet, he dusted himself off and charged. Molly braced herself for his wrath. Lucky for her, the other pupils rushed to her defense. After that, Hollis never dared throw another rock at a helpless animal.

"Hollis is no good for my handsome stranger," she murmured, holding up the handkerchief and eyeing the embroidered letter H. "But I do like the name Henry."

She set the handkerchief on her pillow, then thought better of leaving it out in plain sight. Instead, she tucked it beneath her pillow. She brought her attention back to the man's shirt to see if it could be mended. Her mind kept returning to the man rather than her work, and she ended up contemplating the matter far longer than she should have.

If she repaired the sleeve, it wouldn't be exactly like it was before. It couldn't be helped, however. She also wondered if she'd ever see the man again. Despite her misgivings, she threaded her needle and began to repair the shirt.

Her imagination worked hard that afternoon. She pictured a hundred scenarios, everything from him knocking on their door the next morning, asking if she lived at this house, to him chastising the mercantile shopkeeper and demanding she buy as many shirts as Molly could make. Molly even envisioned the outlandish notion that one day she and Vixen would save *him* when his horse startled into an uncontrolled gallop.

That notion made Molly laugh aloud.

When she finished mending the shirt, she pressed and folded it before tucking it away for safekeeping. She then moved on to her other sewing.

None of her neighbors had much to spare, not with their menfolk out of work. All of them waited for the mine to reopen and made do with what they had. Most of the wives took on extra washing, or whatever they could manage.

After sewing for much of the afternoon, she set her things away. It was time to start dinner. Before she left her room, she tugged Henry's handkerchief from under her pillow. With a gentle touch, she ran her finger over the embroidery. It was fine workmanship, as good as anything she could do herself, and she approved. Henry must have some means, she thought.

What was the handsome stranger doing at that very moment? She pictured him, clad in the linen shirt she'd given him. Who would have guessed she'd give the shirt away to a perfect stranger?

In her thoughts, she saw him. He stood before the bank officials, dashing and handsome, whereupon the bankers would approve his request without a second thought.

She laughed because the entire notion was silly, of course. Still, she liked to think that the stuffy bankers agreed to his demands, quaking in their boots, wondering where Henry had gotten his fine shirt.

Where was he now? She wondered. Her scarred hero. Was he alone? Did he have a wife and family? Perhaps he did and his wife had embroidered Henry's handkerchief. His wife would wonder why he'd returned home wearing a different shirt. The notion left Molly with a hollow feeling deep in her chest.

If the day ever came where Molly encountered her rescuer, would Henry remember her? Would he recall the moments they'd shared on the side of a lonely road?

It wasn't anything she should dream of, she reminded herself. Those sorts of dreams were for others. Not her. She had a duty. Her obligations were to her family. She needed to care for her father. In addition, she had to do whatever necessary to keep her brothers out of the Presidio Mine, even if it meant sending them to the military academy so far away.

Molly prided herself on caring for her family. Come what may, she must not allow her foolish yearnings to wander off to notions of handsome, kindly strangers. The man might have a wife and family of his own. He might not even live nearby.

No. Molly Collins was far too sensible to be led astray by notions of romance. She had responsibilities to the Collins menfolk. Duties. Obligations laid upon her capable shoulders, tasks that she alone could manage. An important promise to keep, the vow she'd given Brigit, the last words they'd shared.

Chapter Six
Amelia Honeycutt

Daniel

Daniel watched his mother preside over the meeting with her usual business-like demeanor. Amelia Honeycutt greeted her employees and ushered the well-dressed men to the huge oak table in the Bethany Springs Bank meeting room.

She took the seat at the head of the table and gestured for the men to sit in the chairs to her left and right. The men, older and overweight to varying degrees, were the presidents of her banks in Bethany Springs, Galveston and Victoria. All three fawned over Amelia, blatantly trying to earn more than a polite nod or comment.

Daniel waited, trying not to show his amusement.

Mama held herself aloof, never showing a sign of approval or friendliness to any of the men who worked for her, which made them try that much harder to get into her good graces. Before he sat down, one of them, the fella from Victoria, presented her with a brooch.

"It belonged to my great-aunt," he said with a hint of groveling.

Mama gave him a withering stare.

"It might look swell with your pretty dress," he suggested.

Daniel muttered under his breath. "Wrong move, my friend."

Mama kept her cool gaze fixed on the man. He looked downcast. He slouched and made his way to his seat. For a long moment, no one spoke. The men shifted uncomfortably. The Victoria man mopped perspiration from his brow.

Mama returned his gift and took her seat. "A lady only accepts jewelry from her husband. Now, shall we get to business?"

"Certainly. I meant no disrespect." The Victoria fella snatched the box and dropped it in his pocket.

Mama ignored him and listed items on the agenda. When she was done, she folded her hands and directed her attention to the various bank presidents. She sat, ramrod straight, hands folded in front of her.

The men took turns presenting monthly reports, and while Daniel should have been listening or at least pretending to listen, he wasn't. His mind drifted to the quiet stretch of road outside of Bethany Springs. He pictured the girl's amber eyes and could almost hear her laughter when that foul-tempered nag tore his sleeve.

He smiled.

From the other end of the table, his mother eyed him with a narrowed gaze. As her bank managers droned on about assets and regulations, she kept her gaze fixed on him. Daniel knew the look well. He offered a slight shrug, giving his best impression of complete innocence.

She pressed her lips together and arched a brow. His mother wasn't buying his innocent act.

Inwardly, Daniel groaned. She'd do her utmost to wring every detail from him. He wondered if he ought to go ahead and tell her about the girl. Mama might have information.

She'd likely know the girl's name. After all, the girl and her family probably lived in one of the Honeycutt rental houses.

Daniel recalled the girl's words about bankers. She clearly disliked them, but she likely hadn't ever met a banker like his mother.

Amelia Honeycutt might look like a society lady, all politeness and fine taste, but on the inside, she was pure steel. Widowed during the Civil War at the age of twenty-three, Mama had to set aside her debutante ways to fend for her family. She had to learn fast, too, especially with two young boys and a baby on the way.

Mama always said those were lean and mean years. She had property, four hundred acres of scrub ranch land, but the land needed improvements, like fencing, cattle pens, cabins for ranch hands. She had no money to invest. The war had left the family destitute. Banks struggled too and refused to lend money to most men, and certainly not to a young, widowed woman.

Somehow, she managed to keep food on the table. Then one day, she had the good fortune of taking on a hard-working, shrewd foreman, a seasoned cowboy who wasn't bothered by the notion of working for a woman. Of course, it didn't hurt matters that, as a young boy, Sheldon Whitson had worked for Amelia's father-in-law. He knew the Honeycutts, and he knew they were good people.

Sheldon built up the Honeycutt herd, rounding up the ornery longhorns that had grown feral during the war years. The critters were wild but hardy. Sheldon and his men drove the animals north to the stockyards in Fort Worth.

With the profits, Mama took on new ventures. A wood mill in East Texas. A small bank in Houston. Another in Victoria.

Her finest moment came when she bought the Bethany Springs Bank, the very one that had denied her loan.

He chuckled inwardly. Maybe Mama and the girl would agree about bankers. Some of them anyway.

Lost in thought, he hardly noticed when his brothers strolled into the meeting.

"Sorry to be late, Mama," Simon said as he bent to kiss her cheek.

"That's no trouble," she murmured.

Zachary gave his mother a kiss but remained silent. Mama's brow arched as she watched the two men sit on Daniel's side of the table. Simon listened to the men finish their reports while Zach gave Daniel a pained look as he pushed a folder across the table.

A few words scrawled across the folder showed it held a report about the mining accident two months prior. Daniel knew little of the incident and did not care to read some long-winded report. He had enough to contend with. He kept himself busy with the family's cattle interests.

After his former fiancée broke things off, he had found solace in the quiet of the family ranch. He was content to live on the outskirts of the land, making a home in the cabin he had built with his own hands. The rough-hewn structure sat high on a ridge with a fine view, overlooking the Bethany River and the vast grazing lands of the Honeycutt Ranch.

The cabin was rustic, but it was home. What was more, it was all he needed. His days were long. The work was honest. Just him, his horses, the cowpunchers, and the surly longhorns. Yes, the cattle were cantankerous, but they could be managed with a good bit of respect and distance. A fast, wily horse did not hurt.

Life was fine. Lonesome, but perfectly tolerable. He answered only to himself. Not even Mama's foreman ventured out to the back pastures. He woke when he wanted, usually in the predawn darkness, and hit the hay when he could not stay awake a minute longer. He spent his days tending to the land and to the animals, a life which pleased him most of the time.

Best of all, he didn't need to crawl down a cramped mineshaft. Ever.

His mother hadn't ever intended to take on a mining venture. It was new territory. The family acquired the mine when the owner defaulted on his loan and left town.

Truth be told, he felt a little sorry for his brother. Zachary had volunteered to manage the Presidio Mine. Since then, it had been a string of headaches. The worst calamity came when the main shaft collapsed at the fore of the mine. The accident involved some mishandled dynamite. Forty wonders no one was killed.

Daniel gritted his teeth. He ought to talk his mother into selling the danged mine to the mining company from Oklahoma. Or better yet, close operations entirely and permanently. Sure, there were folks who made fortunes in mining, but the Honeycutt family did not need a whole new venture.

Zach looked despondent, eyeing the report lying in the middle of the table.

Mama took note of Zach's discontent and began winding down the meeting. At the close, the president of the Bethany Springs Bank announced that he had fired the man in charge of collecting rent on the ridge by the mine.

"We'll need to hire a new man," Mama said. "Rent is due next week, though I don't intend to collect. I had hoped giving families a hardship stipend at the mercantile would help, but it's not enough. We need to let the families know that they do not owe rent. Otherwise, they will leave Bethany Springs. We can't run a mine without workers."

"I'll take care of talking to the mining families," Daniel said, without hesitation.

She looked surprised. "Really? You're willing to leave the ranch and talk with folks?"

Daniel felt the attention of the bank managers along with that of his brothers as he held his mother's gaze. None of them could imagine that he, Daniel Honeycutt, had volunteered to travel the length of the ridge to tell a bunch of downcast miners that their rent payments would be deferred. Daniel was reclusive. He never volunteered to take on extra tasks, especially if it involved dealing with strangers who would stare and ask nosy questions.

All he could think of was the idea of the girl, the pesky girl with the ornery mare. He was certain that he would find her if he had the time and opportunity. His mother narrowed her eyes and he saw the silent, unspoken question written plainly in her eyes. *What is this all about?*

Daniel pretended not to understand.

Thankfully, Mama dismissed the men. A young lady, one of Mama's assistants, came to the door to ask if the family needed refreshments, but Mama waved the young lady away, shutting and locking the door. She fixed her gaze squarely on Daniel.

"What in the world is going on with you boys?" she asked, hand on hip, a smile hidden amidst her words. "Zachary looks like something the cat dragged in and Daniel wants to make a half day trip to visit the mining community."

Daniel shrugged. "Just trying to help, Mama. You always told us we ought to do our part."

Simon glanced at Zach and smirked. "At least no one's got a blackened eye or needs to be bailed out of jail."

Zach scowled at Simon.

"You're offering to do your part, Daniel?" Mama asked. "You realize you'll need to deal with people, not longhorns, right?"

"I'll manage," Daniel said. "It's been a while since I was up that way. I can take a day or two away from the ranch. It would be good to get out. I've got some business to attend to tomorrow, but I'll leave the day after."

Zach and Simon both stared at him.

Mama pursed her lips and studied him as if trying to find some small fault in his explanation. A weakness she could use to her advantage, or some give in his walled defenses. He kept his gaze steady, unwavering, refusing to buckle under pressure.

Zachary grumbled. "Does anyone care about the report?"

Mama strolled down the length of the table. Out of habit, Daniel and his two brothers rose to their feet. Simon offered his chair, holding it for his mother and helping her get situated. He took a nearby seat. All eyes went to Zach as the family waited.

Mama's brows shot up. A smile tugged at her lips. "Well?"

Zach raked his fingers through his hair. "I read the report. Three times now."

Mama's amusement faded. "Three times? That can't be good."

Zach went on. "There's good news and bad news. The reason we didn't end up with any casualties is on account of one fellow in particular, a man who carried the injured men out of the rubble."

"I heard about that, but never learned his name," Mama said.

"The report doesn't list his name, just his initials and that he'd risked life and limb to help others."

His mother paled. "Is that the good news or the bad news?"

Zach looked distraught. "It's bad on account of his injuries and those of the other men. But that's not the bad news."

Daniel's heart squeezed. His thoughts darted to the girl with the wicked, runaway horse, stars in her eyes and mischievous smile. Silently, he offered a prayer that none of her family were injured that terrible day.

Ranching was dangerous. No argument there. But the danger was usually a threat that could be seen beforehand. Stampedes, tornadoes, fires were manageable if a man had time to act. Not so with mining.

Mama waited, her hand trembling over her heart. No one spoke. For a long moment, the meeting room was quiet, save for the tall grandfather clock ticking by the door. Even Simon, the talkative one of the family, remained quiet.

"Every single day," Mama said quietly, "I thank the good Lord that we didn't end things with a dozen funerals or more. Men were injured but no lives were lost."

She closed her eyes and drew a deep breath before opening them once more. "I'm not sure if I should reopen the mine. I would say no if it weren't for the men who desperately need work. I'm not looking to make an overnight fortune but would like to make some money back on the investment."

Mama looked crestfallen. For a moment, Daniel wondered if his mother might back away from a challenge. Maybe she would sell the mine after all. Fine by him, just so long as he found his amber-eyed girl first. Not that he had designs on the girl. No, he just wanted to make sure she was provided for and would not scurry off to the next mining town.

Mama's shoulders slumped. She could always manage pretty much whatever came her way, just so long as no one suffered or, God forbid, *died*. She'd lost her beloved husband too early, and despite priding herself on a steely constitution, Mama could hardly bear the thought of someone dying before their time.

Young folks dying was far too cruel. And wrong. Every time she caught wind of a tragedy that took the life of a young person, she'd retire to her room to grieve in private. Most folks would never suspect Amelia Honeycutt had such a tender heart.

Daniel remembered the look on his Mama's face the day he walked in with most of his face bandaged, and one eye completely covered over. His mother begged him to explain what had happened, but the Bethany Brotherhood was a secret group, known only to the men in the group. Zach and Simon knew what had happened, and why, but their mother knew nothing.

In the end he had to tell her, not the details, and certainly nothing about the brotherhood and its mission, but that the injury had been an accident that happened in the service of a good cause. After that, she relented. The only time she spoke of her heartbreak was when she prayed at family meals, asking God to watch over her boys.

He watched her trying to remain strong in the face of the near tragedy of the mine. She drew a deep breath and spoke quietly. "So, what's the bad news?"

Zach ran his fingers along the edge of the folder, looking thoughtful. He didn't hesitate more than a moment. He spoke, his tone resolute, forging on as if trying to get the hard part out of the way as fast as possible. "The bad news," Zach said with grim determination, "is that the accident was due to negligence. We've determined that the foreman used twice the explosives he needed."

Daniel leaned forward, resting on his elbows, rubbed his brow and tried to piece together how someone could cause an accident that resulted in the collapse of the front shaft of a profitable, established mine.

"How do you know?" he asked.

"Folks said the mine collapsed after an explosion. My men discovered orders for dynamite delivered the day before. There should have been enough material for a week, but the storage shed was empty."

His mother straightened and lifted her chin. "The foreman disappeared the day of the incident."

Simon shot a worried look Daniel's way.

"I want to find that so and so," his mother said quietly, "and have him thrown in jail."

"Dang," Simon muttered. He gave a mischievous smile to lighten the mood. "That's *just* what we need. Mama chasing after the dad-gummed rascal who went and blew up her mine."

Daniel couldn't help but think... Three family members in the Bethany Brotherhood was plenty. Mama would have to start her own secret brotherhood... well, sisterhood.

Chapter Seven
A Dress for JoJo Ward

Molly

Molly woke in the predawn hours with remnants of sweet dreams fading into the darkness. To her utter dismay, she'd dreamt of the stranger. Henry.

The man had dwelled in her mind ever since the encounter on the road. Thoughts of him came to her at odd moments each day, but this was the first time she'd dreamt of him. In her dream, she was helping him with his shirt buttons. Heavens! What had she been thinking? Never had she been so forward.

She pushed the dream aside as she cringed with embarrassment.

Henry meant nothing to her, she told herself. Nothing.

She said her morning prayers and requested help to better herself, an ongoing effort to improve her character. Each week, she came up with a list of flaws that she wanted to address. Her rule was to avoid troubling the good Lord with more than three flaws at a time.

Last week, she'd narrowed it down to one single fault.

Envy.

Not just your garden variety envy, like she felt when her friend, Gemma, wore her new summer dress to church, or when another friend, Annie, announced her engagement. No.

She was praying for help to end her deep, singular jealously of Josephine Ward. Josephine, or JoJo to all the other girls in Bethany Springs, had been accepted to a girl's music school in Georgia. She made the announcement after church a few weeks ago, telling the small crowd in the church courtyard that she planned to visit the music school in a few weeks.

"I intend to accept their offer in person," she proclaimed to the parishioners. Her mother watched adoringly and led the small group in a round of applause.

As Molly listened to the sundry details, the acceptance, the trip and all the other exciting particulars, she'd been struck by a mortifying surge of fierce envy. To her dismay, this transgression occurred while she stood atop the church steps after Sunday services.

Almost at once, shame assailed her conscience. She had no right to resent JoJo. No right to be envious. Envy was a sin. It went against the Tenth Commandment. And to think she'd committed such a transgression not five minutes after Pastor Jones blessed them and urged them to uphold high Christian ideals.

Her shame hadn't diminished the ugly feelings. She didn't really know JoJo very well aside from singing together in the Christmas choir. On the long walk home and over the course of the next few days, she suffered more bouts of wicked envy when she imagined JoJo flouncing off to her fancy school.

"JoJo's old dresses are so drab," her mother complained a few days later when Molly met her on the road. "I can't have my little music prodigy looking as plain as a mud hen, now can I?"

Molly hadn't known what to say or what to think when Mrs. Ward hired her to sew a dress for the trip. While Molly needed the money desperately, she hadn't missed the way

Mrs. Ward spoke about the work, acting like she was doing Molly a favor.

Molly shook off her petty resentment and thanked God for the blessings He'd bestowed upon her and her family. Last night, she'd finished JoJo's dress, which meant she was that much closer to having what she needed for rent.

Even better, Papa's injuries had improved. He was walking without a cane for part of the day. He didn't wince when he rose from his chair, or groan in his sleep. He still had a long way to go but seemed encouraged.

The boys were doing well too. They seemed resigned to attending the academy in the fall which meant she had a real chance of leaving Bethany Springs and starting her shop once they were settled.

She tied her ungovernable hair with a faded ribbon and put on her wool socks and boots. Shivering, she hurried to the kitchen, lit the stove, and made tea. Next, she kneaded the dough for breakfast, plopped the loaf in a pan and shoved it in the oven. She tucked the candle in her lantern and, with a shawl around her shoulders, she hurried down the thin mud trail.

Her mind drifted to the stranger. Henry had touched her shoulder. The memory of his touch came back to her as she eyed the first hint of sunrise, a crimson ribbon on the eastern horizon. She couldn't hold back a smile. Henry was fast becoming a secret indulgence. A small private moment where she allowed herself to imagine what it would be like to be courted by a gallant, kind-hearted gentleman.

Inside the coop, the chickens clucked drowsily. Molly moved quietly from nesting box to nesting box, speaking gently to each sleepy chicken as she gathered the eggs.

"Thank you, Peppermint. Very kind of you, Rosemary. Much obliged, Nutmeg. Very grateful for your service, Cinnamon." Basket in hand, she neared the last nesting box and warily eyed the final chicken, a surly black beauty who held herself apart from the rest of the flock. "Are you going to be a well-behaved chicken this morning, Pepper? Or are you feeling broody?"

The bird cocked her head, black feathers shimmering in the candlelight. Pepper could be sweet-natured one day, and irritable the next. Both boys were afraid of Pepper. Molly didn't mind her moods. The hen simply didn't like to be jostled or treated unkindly. Flattery never hurt.

Molly took a step closer. "You're a very pretty girl. I admire you greatly and think your eggs are the finest in the coop. Don't tell the other girls."

Pepper ruffled her feathers.

Slowly, Molly edged near, cooing softly as she reached into the warm, fragrant hay. The black chicken flapped her wings but didn't fuss or peck. To Molly's surprise, the ornery bird even shifted a little as if to get out of Molly's way. When Molly found not one egg but two, she praised Pepper, telling her what a fine, upstanding bird she was. A paragon of her kind.

"Thank you kindly, my lovelies," Molly said as she paused before the low doorway. "I will return with your breakfast just as soon as I've fed my menfolk."

Later that afternoon, she walked the short distance to the Wards' home to deliver JoJo's dress.

While most of the houses in the area were rectangular cabins, some built with a dogtrot and constructed of once-sturdy, squared, cypress timbers, the Ward home was a frame cottage with a fresh coat of snow-white paint. The windows had six panes on both the upper and lower sash. A brick chimney poked from the steep, gabled roof. Gingerbread lattice woodwork adorned the corner porch, a pretty sight despite the forgotten flowerpots.

The Ward family was the only family in the mining community who owned their home. They also owned twenty acres of scrub land, thanks to an inheritance from one of Mrs. Ward's uncles. Molly grimaced, trying not to think of how much she lacked to pay rent that month. While Mr. Ward had lost his job, the family more than made ends meet with the garden and livestock.

The Wards doted on JoJo, their only child. She never had chores or helped her parents and liked to say as much. She boasted about her carefree days. Mrs. Ward claimed that chores would only take her little darling away from piano practice.

Usually, Molly heard JoJo's piano from the road. Today, the house was quiet.

She knocked on the door and waited. JoJo opened the door. She wrinkled her nose at first but smiled when she saw Molly had her new dress. Her demeanor changed from disdain to a close approximation of friendliness.

"Come into our humble abode," she said airily.

Molly followed her through the small parlor, down a narrow hall to the kitchen where Mrs. Ward and two other women worked. In the center of the table sat a basket full of ripe strawberries. One of the women hulled the berries. Another stood by the stove, stirring a large pot.

Jars of strawberry preserves lined one side of the table and the far counter. The aroma of stewed fruit made Molly's mouth water. A breeze blew through the open window, carrying the scent of fruit blossoms drifting from the Wards' peach orchard.

A memory of Brigit came to mind. Her stepmother loved peaches, more than any of the other Texas fruits. She'd always wanted a few peach trees and had planted several dozen over the years, but the family moved before the trees had time to mature. The Collins family never stayed put for long. Papa always wanted to chase the next big money mine, hoping he'd finally get ahead, or perhaps a chance to run things.

It was funny how smells could bring back the old days before Brigit passed. Molly shoved the memory aside.

The two women glanced up, pausing their work. Molly could see they were Mrs. Ward's kin. They had the same deep-set eyes, the same downturned mouth and wore their hair in the same tight arrangement.

Molly hung back, hugging the dress tight to her chest, wondering if Mrs. Ward would approve of her work. Rarely did she suffer from a lack of confidence about her sewing. If anything, she was a tad prideful. That's what Papa had pointed out a time or two. Or more.

JoJo wandered around the kitchen, yawning loudly, with exaggerated disinterest.

"That was mighty fast," Mrs. Ward fussed, drying her hands on a rag. "Let's hope you took enough time to do a good job."

The other women set their work aside, waiting to see what Molly had. JoJo picked up a jar, turned it over and set it atop another jar. With a bored expression, she folded her arms, and waited for Molly to show them the dress.

"Go on, girl," Mrs. Ward chided. "We don't have all day."

Molly shook off her hesitation and unwrapped the frock from the delicate tissue she'd wound around the dress to keep it clean. She held up the dress for Mrs. Ward's approval.

"I did as you asked, giving the dress a little extra room in the shoulders so that JoJo would be comfortable on her travels. I added wool braid to the hem and trimmed the sleeves with velvet."

Mrs. Ward peered at the collar and then examined the cuffs. The women murmured a few words of admiration. Even JoJo looked pleased, her eyes sparkling with delight.

"Not bad," Mrs. Ward said. "I suppose it's true what they say about your abilities. Strange that a girl of your age could do such work. I figured folks exaggerated because they felt sorry for you."

Molly wasn't sure what she meant but had some definite opinions about whether folks exaggerated. A sharp reply was at the tip of her tongue, but she recalled her father's gentle rebuke and his words about pride coming before the fall.

"Thank you, Mrs. Ward," Molly said from between gritted teeth.

"I like the fabric. And the color." JoJo marveled.

"Thank you. I picked the blue fabric because I was certain it would look pretty on you." She laughed, suddenly feeling awkward.

JoJo drew a sharp breath of surprise. "Thank you, Molly."

Molly smiled, drew a deep breath, and felt the tension in her shoulders ease. JoJo could be tiresome, and Molly admitted to feeling envious of the girl. But deep down, she knew that JoJo loved music with all her heart. She deserved her hard-won chance to go off and study music.

"You did a fine job matching the grain of the material," one of the women said.

"It'll do," Mrs. Ward sniffed. "I'm glad you did the work so quickly. Don't let your father have any of the money you've earned."

Molly's heart thudded. She felt the women's keen attention fixed upon her with curious stares. Molly didn't respond. Instead, she slowly folded the dress and tried to bundle it back into the tissue. JoJo waved off her clumsy attempts and took the dress. Even JoJo seemed shocked by her mother's harsh words. She kept her eyes averted to avoid Molly's gaze.

Mrs. Ward opened her purse. "I'd hate to think my charity would end up paying for the man's whiskey. Everyone knows he was drinking right before the accident."

The blood drained from Molly's face. It wasn't true. Papa had indulged in spirits since the accident, but never became inebriated. He'd have a few drinks in the evenings with some of the other men. Papa said it was to pass the time as they waited for the mine to reopen. Part of her suspected that he suffered from melancholy since he'd never indulged before the accident.

Shock and embarrassment burned inside her heart. She refused to argue. She refused to dignify Mrs. Ward's words with any response whatsoever. What was more, she refused to let Mrs. Ward offer any so-called charity.

"I don't want you to pay for the dress," Molly said quietly.

Mrs. Ward knit her brow.

JoJo's eyes widened.

"I won't take a penny." Molly backed away, stopping at the door of the kitchen.

JoJo regarded her with shock and dismay. "What about the fabric? The trim and the buttons and the lace around the cuffs?" JoJo sounded incredulous. "You have to let Mother at least pay for your materials."

"The dress is a gift," Molly said to JoJo. "I wish you all the best at your music school."

No one spoke. JoJo's eyes filled with worry. She shifted her gaze from her mother to Molly and back to her mother. Mrs. Ward remained silent and stony-faced.

Molly wanted nothing more than to escape the judgment she saw burning in the woman's eyes. She lifted her chin, squared her shoulders, bid the women good day, and showed herself out of the Wards' cottage.

While she desperately needed the money for the dress, she wouldn't allow Mrs. Ward to speak badly of her father. He'd overindulged a time or two and had burst into song when the McCampbell child was baptized, which turned a few heads in the church, but he was hardly a habitual drunkard.

Mrs. Ward liked to think herself superior to others and to rub their noses in their misfortune. There were rumors that circulated about Papa and now she knew where they'd started.

She clenched her jaw. "I'll remember this, Trina Ward. I hope your strawberry preserves grow a thick layer of mildew."

She stepped outside and marched up the road. Now she understood why JoJo was at times so disagreeable. Who wouldn't be disagreeable with a mother like Trina Ward? Poor JoJo. At least she'd escape her mother's clutches when she went off to school. Perhaps that was the real reason JoJo was so pleased, and who could blame her?

Just a few steps past the Wards' home, a small, grubby child darted from their orchard. A girl. Little more than a child, really. One of the children of the mining families who lived along the ridge. The girl's face was gaunt, her eyes round and fearful as she clutched a pail of strawberries. They were likely stolen from the Wards' gardens.

A moment before, Molly had been full of indignation and a deep sense of injury. Mrs. Ward had insulted the Collins family, after all, but her resentment melted like morning dew in the early rays of sunshine. Her self-pity faded away. The girl was hungry. Clearly.

Molly considered how she and her family might be struggling but they hadn't gone hungry. Not once. She drew a deep breath and noted a sense of profound gratitude.

Despite difficult circumstances, there were always others who suffered more. She had no money, of course. Not after storming out of the Ward home without payment, but if she had any money in her pocket, she'd have offered all of it to the slight, frightened, and hungry girl.

Before Molly could offer a friendly, encouraging word, the girl darted down the road and vanished beneath the shadowed depths of a narrow trail.

Chapter Eight
Word Comes of Two Young Outlaws

Daniel

After the bank meeting, Daniel and his brothers returned to their mother's house. Mama had asked them to stay the night. They spent an enjoyable evening together, catching up and reminiscing. Daniel had intended to set off for home at first light. He needed the day to talk to his ranch hands about his trip and what he expected them to do while he was gone. All he wanted was to begin his search for the girl he'd come to think of as Mack, but he couldn't just leave without a word. His mother seemed reluctant to let them slip away so early in the morning. First, she made a fine breakfast. Then she insisted they linger to talk about various notions that were *important* and *pressing*. Daniel and his brothers listened politely. When they finally managed to excuse themselves from the table, Mama asked them to stay just a short while longer so she could show off the newest foal.

The three men exchanged a look as they followed her to the corral. They knew it was pointless to argue. It was best to go along with her requests, since they so rarely gathered as a family.

Sheldon Whitson, the Honeycutt foreman, worked patiently to coax a halter on a month-old foal. The youngster shook off his attempts and tried to escape but Sheldon persisted. Finally, he succeeded. Daniel and his brothers, standing nearby, offered a few words of congratulations.

Amelia Honeycutt took the lead line from her beleaguered foreman.

Daniel offered a good-natured jibe. "Sheldon, the wild broncs are no match for you, but the foals always have a passel of tricks."

Simon chimed in. "Pretty sure the little rascal took a bite from your collar. You'd best check. He might have taken a chunk from your shoulder too. Might need stitches."

Sheldon made a show of checking his collar and running his palm down his neck. He shook his head, flashed a wry grin, and grumbled good-naturedly about the obstinate youngster. "Dang foal is as wily as they come."

Daniel's mother waved off his words. She led the foal around the perimeter of the corral, praised him and told him how very pretty he was and how he'd make a fine cow pony in a few years' time.

Mama loved working with the youngsters. She kept several broodmares, but Mandy, a pretty, dark bay, was her favorite. Mandy's foals grew to be the finest horses on the Honeycutt Ranch.

The mare grazed in a nearby pasture, belly-deep in thick grasses. Every so often, she lifted her head to make sure junior was doing all right and then went back to grazing. Plenty of mares would fret if their little one was too far off, especially if folks were around, but Mama liked to say she and Mandy understood each other.

The three brothers, Daniel, Zach, and Simon, stood at the rail, watching, and offering compliments while she led him around the corral.

"She's a beauty," Zach called out.

Sheldon strolled across the corral, his smile flashing beneath his Stetson. "Now you've done it."

"What did I do?"

"It's a colt, not a filly."

Mama was too busy to notice, however. She stroked the foal's glossy coat, stopping for a moment to allow Mandy to sniff the top of his head. Mama petted the mare and tried to go on, but the foal planted his hooves and shook his head. He didn't care for his lessons. Not one bit. Especially if he needed to part from his mother. He pawed his tiny hoof and swished his tail.

Daniel's mother spoke to him gently and after a spell, the youngster allowed her to lead him.

"Been meaning to talk to you boys," Sheldon said quietly, resting his elbow on the top rail. "Probably nothing much but wanted to mention it just the same."

Sheldon's tone didn't seem to suggest much in the way of urgency. Daniel didn't pay too much attention to the old-timer. For the past few days, his mind had wandered off, as distractible as a colt with a new halter, always drifting to the girl on the runaway horse.

While Sheldon spoke, Daniel wandered, lost to his thoughts, imagining how he'd find the girl. Soon, hopefully. He wasn't sure how, but he knew he'd find her, nonetheless. He remembered the name of her horse, Vixen, but he didn't know the name of the girl. His only clue came from the tag in the shirt she'd given him.

Crafted with care by MAC.

MAC?

After he glimpsed the delicate tag, he resolved to call her Mack, just so he'd have a name for the girl who refused to leave his thoughts. The memory of her smile was the last thing he saw when he closed his eyes at night, and the recollection of her pretty eyes was his first thought when he woke. He told himself it was just a little harmless flirtation. The girl warmed his hard heart, but she also stirred a protective instinct.

I'll find you, Mack. Not that it'll amount to anything, but I need to know you're all right... that's all. After I know, I can go back to my quiet life...

"It might have been a one-time deal," Sheldon said. "Maybe I'm reading things wrong."

His thoughts of Mack faded. He tried to pick up the thread of the conversation running between Sheldon and his brothers. Sheldon's tone had changed and now held a note of urgency. What had he missed?

Simon looked aggrieved.

"Some of those families are barely getting by," Zach said.

"What's the trouble?" Daniel asked. "Something amiss on the ridge?"

Sheldon nodded. "One of my men got held up the other night. He traveled the road that leads up to the mine just before dusk. Couple of young fellas held him up and took a month's pay, money he intended to give his uncle and aunt."

Zach muttered under his breath.

Simon spoke. "Hate to think the men are from around these parts."

Sheldon winced. "It sounded like a couple of youngsters, but you never can tell. Might be a pair of full-fledged outlaws."

The three brothers shared a knowing look. Daniel knew Zach and Simon both asked the same, unspoken question. Was this a matter for the Bethany Brotherhood?

Daniel's chest tightened, his worried thoughts rushing to the girl he rarely managed to get out of his mind. Now he had a new passel of worries. Was she safe? A shiver of cold dread trailed down his spine. Some of the miners could be a rough bunch under the best of circumstances.

If only he knew the girl's name. If he knew who she was, he'd get on a horse and find her so he could protect her from criminal elements. He pictured her face, her wide eyes, imagined whisking her away from the ridge and the rough mining community. And then what? Take her where exactly?

He didn't care. He just wanted her off the ridge. Sooner rather than later. He curled his hands into tight fists, suddenly grateful that his eyepatch and scars often frightened people. If his fearsome appearance kept his girl safe, then it was worth it.

"Lots of folks are packing up," Sheldon said. "They figure they'd best look for work since no one knows when the mine will open again."

Sheldon waited, looking expectantly at the men.

"We're working on that." Daniel didn't want to say too much. They still didn't know the extent of the damage or when it would be safe to reopen.

His thoughts turned from the troubling subjects to something else entirely, or perhaps it was better said, some*one* else. Mack. He fretted about her. The girl with the amber eyes and runaway horse.

When Sheldon left, Daniel turned to his brothers. "No need to trouble the boys with this problem," he said gruffly. "I'll take care of matters on my own. You two are heading out of town. If I need help, I'll send word to the other fellas."

Zach and Simon nodded. He suspected they were relieved that they didn't need to change their plans. Which made him suspect they traveled on business that their mother wouldn't approve of. Both of them had grumbled about the mine foreman. They wondered if he'd set off the extra dynamite deliberately. They'd spoken of questioning him.

Daniel didn't think it necessary. The man would never work for the Honeycutts again. That was enough for him. He shrugged off his brothers' complaints. Let them do as they pleased. He had his own plans.

Chapter Nine
Mr. Armstrong's Generous Offer

Molly

With the rent payment weighing even more heavily on her shoulders, Molly spent every spare moment sewing. She had come up with a new plan. Instead of shirts, she sewed bonnets. Perhaps the hats would impress Mrs. Pittman.

After she made the first hat, she got the idea to make a matching one for a little girl. Hopefully, Mrs. Pittman would approve. Just to be safe, Molly didn't add her customary embroidered tag.

Skipping the tag was a sure sign of her desperation.

She was about to finish the smaller of the two bonnets when she heard people talking on the porch. Her brothers and father spoke to a man who sounded like Augustus Armstrong.

She set aside her work and went to the door where she found Mr. Armstrong chatting with her father. The boys were both absorbed in a pamphlet, sitting on the bench, quietly reading.

"It would do us both some good, John." Mr. Armstrong gestured to the boys. "Your children might enjoy it as well. They've got a couple of cooks they hired out of San Antonio, a couple of German gals. Two sisters, very pretty. I've heard the food's the best this side of the Red River."

Papa pressed his lips together to form a grim line. "I don't know if I believe in healing mineral springs."

"That's why you need to come see for yourself. Folks travel from all parts of Texas to take the water baths." Mr. Armstrong turned to the boys. "Tell your father what sorts of ailments the waters can treat."

Molly stepped out the door, shutting it quietly behind her.

Mr. Armstrong grinned. "Morning Molly. I was trying to convince your father to take the family on a little excursion. Just for a few days."

Molly drew a sharp breath. An excursion? She and her family hadn't ever had the means to take trips. While Mr. Armstrong likely traveled wherever and whenever he pleased, the Collins family wasn't accustomed to such luxuries.

"Before you say no, let me explain that the mineral waters do wonders for my rheumatism," Mr. Armstrong said. "I go to Bethany Hot Springs twice a year and the baths make me feel half my age. I got to thinking about your father, how taking the water might help his injuries."

Mr. Armstrong looked sheepish. Molly knew exactly what he was up to. He wanted to find a way to keep the Collins family from leaving Bethany Springs. She glanced at her father, a pang of sympathy squeezing her heart. He looked uncertain. No one had ever offered to take him on a trip.

"Where are the wells?" Molly asked Mr. Armstrong.

"About fifteen miles from here. On the other side of the mine. The wells form the headwaters of the Bethany River."

"I don't know about any of this, Augustus," her father said. "It doesn't sound like my kind of place."

The boys grumbled. They thought the trip to the hot springs would be a tremendous adventure.

Jack got to his feet, holding the pamphlet. "The springs might help you heal your bad leg. They've got a long list of things they can cure, everything from scurvy to opium addiction."

Molly shook her head. "Oh, my."

"What's opium?" Will asked, coming to his brother's side, and peering at the pamphlet. "And lookie, the waters even cure *female complaints*."

He grinned at Molly, a teasing gleam in his eye. "We'd better take you and leave you there a spell."

"You hush," she replied.

"You might stop complaining," Will added.

"I don't complain," Molly snapped.

She waited for someone to agree. When no one replied, she huffed softly and folded her arms.

Papa limped to the bench and sank heavily. "It sounds pricy, Augustus. I don't feel right accepting."

Mr. Armstrong crossed the porch and took a nearby chair. "That's the thing. My nephew is part owner. I never pay a penny. He puts me up in his finest rooms on the third floor, overlooking the wells and the pretty scenery."

"It sure sounds nice," Jack said, reading more of the information. "The water gets to 110 degrees."

"And it cures baldness, Papa," Will exclaimed.

The two boys hooted with laughter. Papa chuckled as he ran a palm across his thinning hair. Mr. Armstrong grinned as he pointed to his thick crop of hair as if presenting proof of the water's healing powers.

"I wouldn't mind getting a little of my hair back," Papa said. "Brigit always said I was a handsome fella."

Molly couldn't hold back a small smile. She remembered Brigit complimenting Papa on his fine looks. Who would have thought John Collins held some small bit of vanity? She could almost hear Brigit's laughter.

"So, can we go?" Will asked.

"What's St. Vitus Dance?" Jack looked up from reading the pamphlet. "Some sort of disease? Or some sort of dance?"

"Who cares?" Will replied. "Maybe me and Molly will dance along with St. Vitus." He darted across the porch and swept Molly into a jaunty two-step. Molly protested, but he wouldn't relent and soon he had her laughing at his antics. He led her down the porch, spun and brought her back the same path.

As they danced merrily, Molly recalled the dance instruction Brigit arranged years before. Back then, the boys had been a head shorter than her. They'd grumbled vigorously, claiming they had no use for dancing. Now her brother stood a head taller than her, and instead of scowling, he wore a broad smile as he twirled her around the porch.

"Don't you want to go, Molls?" he asked.

"I can't possibly go along. I have so much work to do."

Jack groaned. "You always have work to do. Have a little fun. You've gotten boring lately."

Will laughed as he spun her in a twirl. "That's not true, Jack."

"Thank you," Molly said, breathlessly.

Will added, "It's not true that she's gotten boring lately. Molly's *always* been boring."

Jack chuckled and nodded with agreement.

"You two are incorrigible," Molly managed to say. "Papa, make them stop teasing me."

"We can't leave Molly here," Papa said. "Doesn't seem right."

Will slowed his dancing and kissed her cheek. "Thank you for the dance, Miss Molly. Your lovely St. Vitus dance has cured me of my hectic fever."

She pushed him away, trying her best to look stern. "Oh, hush already."

"It would be good for your father to go. It would help him heal," Mr. Armstrong said quietly, his gaze fixed on Molly. "A man needs to work. Even if it's not in the mine."

The group grew quiet. Molly had to admit Mr. Armstrong was right. Her father didn't tolerate long days at home. Ever since the accident, he'd suffered bouts of despondency where he spoke of his doubts, wondering if he'd ever recover or lead a useful life. During those times, his pain seemed far worse, and he'd languish in bed and hardly eat a bite.

Maybe it would suit all of them if the Collins menfolk went to the hot springs. Her father might get some relief from his pain. The boys would have fun. With the house to herself, she'd have fewer chores. She'd only have to cook for herself which would mean she could spend her days sewing. Why, she might have a wealth of sewing samples to show Mrs. Pittman.

"Can't bear to leave you behind, Molly Anne," her father said.

The boys watched her intently, their expressions solemn. Mr. Armstrong looked thoughtful, gently drumming his fingers on his knee.

"You should go on, Papa," Molly said. "The waters will do you a world of good."

"It doesn't seem right. We're a family. We do things together."

A flicker of dismay flitted through her thoughts. It was true, they were a family, and they were always together, but those days were ending soon. In the fall, the boys would travel to Virginia to attend the academy. With them gone, it would be just her and Papa. The boys would begin a new life. The family would be forever divided. The prospect troubled her but at least they wouldn't work in a mine.

Silence hung heavily. She could tell her father was about to change his mind and tell Mr. Armstrong he didn't care to go. The boys both shifted their gaze to Papa as if sensing the same thing.

"Don't worry about me," Molly said lightly. "I'll be perfectly fine. I'll be able to sew to my heart's content."

Her father looked skeptical.

Molly forged on. "By the time you get back, I'll have a dozen new dresses, in a dozen different colors, all trimmed in velvet and lace."

The boys smiled. Mr. Armstrong nodded. Papa, however, wasn't convinced.

She twirled, curtsied, and waved a make-believe fan. "You Collins men will return from the springs full of pep, with stories to tell about all the wonderful adventures."

"She's right, Papa," Will said.

Her father's expression softened.

Molly laughed. "And when you see me in all my finery, you'll wonder what happened to your plain, humdrum, boring Molly."

Chapter Ten
A Baby Changes Everything

Amelia Honeycutt

Amelia said goodbye to her three boys, trying her best to appear cheerful. Daniel explained that he'd set out for the ridge the next morning, claiming he might be gone a few days and would bunk at the foreman's cabin by the mine if need be. After that, both Simon and Zachary left, riding off the opposite direction, claiming some business west of Bethany Springs.

The Honeycutt home always seemed especially lonesome after the boys left. She wandered the house, expecting to find them, listening for their voices or footsteps even though she knew perfectly well they were gone.

While she felt proud of the men they'd become, she missed them something fierce. She worried too. Sometimes she thought they got up to no good when she wasn't looking. If only they'd settle down and marry. Then she'd stop fretting about them.

Sitting at her vanity, she brushed her hair and arranged it into a tidy knot.

An old tintype photograph caught her eye. It was a picture of her husband taken before she met him. Tall, strapping, and handsome, the picture always made her wistful.

"George, I know they're grown men. I suppose a mother never stops worrying."

She studied the old picture, wishing it had captured her husband's startling gray eyes. When they first met, she'd made the mistake of saying he had pretty eyes. He'd burst out laughing and told her she shouldn't say such a thing to a man.

"I miss you, George. Especially when our boys leave."

Taking her hat from a nearby table, she set it on her head, mindful of the hair pins. She didn't usually talk to her late husband, or not here in the house. Usually, she saved those talks for when she visited his grave.

"I'm going to pay Sophie a visit," she announced to the small, framed image. "Yesterday, she sent word about a surprise she wants to show me. Probably a new hat from Paris. I'll be sure to tell you if it's anything earth-shattering."

She left the house, grateful to escape the heavy silence.

At the end of the garden walkway, she found Sheldon. Her foreman held the reins of the gelding he'd saddled for her. He hastily took his hat off and offered a polite smile.

"I could ride along with you to keep you company, Mrs. Honeycutt. Might be nice to visit a spell."

Amelia pulled on her gloves. "Visit a spell? Sheldon, you're terrible company. If we rode the five miles to Sophie's house, I'd be lucky to get three words out of you."

Usually, Sheldon chuckled at this sort of comment. He'd worked at the ranch for over twenty years now and his stoic ways were well known to her and the rest of the ranch hands. Sheldon talked with her three boys plenty. Why, he'd taught them how to ride and shoot and probably cuss too, or so she suspected. But with her, he only spoke when necessary, preferring to keep his own counsel.

His wife, Franny, once told Amelia that Sheldon was a little daunted by Amelia's forceful nature. The two women had a good laugh over that. Amelia said she hadn't made her way in life by being shy or reserved.

Sheldon had to be sixty years old, a little stooped but still spry. They had a fine relationship built on respect. But this might be the first time he'd offered to ride somewhere with her to keep her company. It made no sense.

She narrowed her eyes. "What is this about?"

He pressed his lips together, with what looked very much like a petulant refusal to reply. The boys used to do the same thing years ago. They'd get mired in mischief and would do anything to avoid answering her questions.

"You've never asked me this before, Sheldon. Planning on asking for a raise?"

He turned his hat over in his hands and shook his head. "No, ma'am. Nothing like that."

She took the reins and gripped the saddle pommel. "What's on your mind, then?"

"One of my ranch hands had a little scuffle the other night. Clyde, the new hire. A couple of fellas gave him trouble and lightened his wallet."

She paused before getting on her horse. "Is he all right?"

"Yes, ma'am. He's fine. Just a little embarrassed."

With a soft grumble, she swung into the saddle. "I'm sorry to hear about Clyde. But I don't need help."

He shook his head and continued fussing over his hat.

"Now, Sheldon, don't fret. I'll be fine. I'll be back by sundown." Unable to resist a sassy comment, she added, "And if I see those two rascals, I'll make them return Clyde's money."

Knitting his brow, he searched for some reply that wouldn't overstep. Before he could come up with a suitable response, she bid him a cheerful goodbye and set off down the road.

As she traveled past her land, she noted with some pride the fine grazing and the straight-as-an-arrow fence line. The ranch was a sight different then it was twenty years ago when her George passed.

She'd acquired an extra 5,000 acres of prime grazing land, including an additional mile-long stretch of land bordering the Bethany River. Her place was prosperous and beautiful, and she knew her husband would be proud of her and what she'd accomplished, which was worth more to her than all of her worldly possessions combined.

George Honeycutt would hardly recognize the place now. What would he think of the barbed wire? Probably have mixed feelings, just like she did when she'd first heard of the newfangled way of fencing.

Barbed wire was the only fencing that would hold an ornery longhorn. The sharp barbs had helped her earn a living, but she had to admit she missed the open range, too.

The years had passed so quickly, bringing so many changes.

Sheldon's words about a theft near the mine wrapped a thread of worry around her heart. Daniel rode the trail that very day. She should have asked Sheldon if he'd spoken with the boys about the danger.

Another worry tugged at her thoughts. There'd been a time when she suspected her boys took on the role of watchmen, where they'd taken justice into their own hands. It was a troubling thought, to be sure. She especially fretted about Daniel whose eyesight was compromised.

With a fearful heart, she prayed, asking the good Lord to watch over her three boys. "Heavenly Father, keep them safe. I couldn't bear any of them getting hurt. Not again. Daniel's injury broke my heart."

When she got to the McCord ranch house, a ranch hand met her with a polite greeting and offered to tend to her horse. Amelia went to the front door and was about to knock when Sophie opened the door to greet her.

"I knew it," Sophie said, gloating. "If I asked you to visit yesterday, you'd come when it suited you, but if I told you I had a *surprise*, you wouldn't be able to stand the suspense. You'd have to come as quickly as possible."

Amelia's worries about her sons faded to the back of her mind. Sophie always brightened her day. Her sparkling eyes and teasing grin made Amelia smile.

"Can you stay for lunch?" Sophie asked.

"I have to go to town this afternoon."

"What for? Can't it wait?"

"No. I have to go to the mercantile to speak to Nellie Pittman."

"Oh dear. That's too bad. She's such a disagreeable woman. *Comme c'est terrible!*"

Amelia sighed. "It can't be helped. I need to extend assistance to my workers. Otherwise, they'll leave Bethany Springs."

Sophie looked bored. She had no interest in the Honeycutt ventures and often said as much. Amelia could tell she wasn't done trying to make a case for staying for lunch.

"Tell me about this surprise." Amelia eyed her friend's earbobs and pearls. Next, she checked both wrists. Sophie wore jewelry, of course. Sophie always kept herself looking perfectly lovely, but the bracelets and necklace were all pieces that Amelia had seen a hundred times before. "I figured Robert bought you something pretty, something shiny."

Sophie shook her head, a playful smile tugging at the edges of her mouth. She held the door open and beckoned Amelia inside. "Guess again."

"No jewels. Well, you certainly look mighty pleased. A new piano?"

"Not even close," Sophie said lightly.

Amelia followed her down the hallway to the family's parlor. The McCord house had started out as a small cabin and been enlarged over the years. Now, it boasted a second story and a summer kitchen apart from the main house. It seemed that with each addition to the house, the more cramped it became, probably because Sophie always had new projects, along with plenty of company. If it wasn't one of her boys, it was some down on their luck, far-flung relative from Sophie's side of the family.

The pesky Cajuns, her husband called them when Sophie was out of the room. Cousins who don't mind outlasting their welcome. Or drinking till sunrise. The Cajuns, Robert declared, were the reason he had gone gray by age forty.

Sophie and Amelia had attended a girls' school together in Louisiana. When George Honeycutt courted Amelia, Sophie came along to chaperone and had fallen hard for George's friend. Robert went off to fight in the war between the states, but unlike George, he survived the fighting and returned.

Sophie wore a new silk gown that showed off her narrow waist. She was still a tiny thing, despite having given birth to four children, a girl and three boys. Amelia, in her trousers, shirtsleeves and boots, as usual, felt shabby next to Sophie.

Sophie opened the door to the parlor and ushered her in. She held her hands wide. "See anything different?"

Amelia scanned the room. She saw nothing new, probably on account of the sheer volume of books, fabrics, china dolls and various notions piled on the tables and shelves. Even the chesterfield was covered with a half-finished embroidery project concerning a country flower garden.

Ever since Sophie's daughter married a doctor in Victoria, and had announced she was expecting, Sophie had been a whirlwind of new ventures. Sewing. Knitting. Even sketching and painting.

"I don't see anything different," Amelia said. "Why don't you just tell me-"

Amelia's words faded as she caught a soft sound. A baby's murmur. Amelia drew a sharp breath when she glimpsed the cradle. Drawn with a force she could not resist, she crossed the room, weaving between the various chairs and stacks of books.

Lying in the cradle was a heartachingly tiny baby. She lay beneath a soft, pink blanket, gazing up at Amelia with wonder. She gurgled as she stretched out her arms. Her little legs kicked, tossing the blanket aside.

"Oh, Sophie," Amelia whispered. "Little Madeline has come to visit."

"She did. Marie's husband went to a meeting in Galveston, so she decided to stay with us to let us enjoy some grandparent- time. She's resting upstairs, taking a little nap to catch up on her sleep."

For a long moment, Amelia could hardly think or speak. Her recollection of the boys when they were small was hazy. Had they ever been this small? This perfect? Their baby stage was a distant fog. What she remembered more clearly came later when they were older, mischievous boys, not cooing babies.

They'd made her life busy and happy, a welcome distraction from her grief after George passed. A memory of the toad Zachary left under her pillow flashed through her thoughts. Following the toad, she pictured other mishaps, involving molasses dripped on schoolbook pages and rotten eggs tucked in Sunday shoes. Later they'd taken on other outlandish ventures such as trying to saddle a longhorn bull.

No, the baby memories seemed too far off to properly recall.

"I just had pesky boys," Amelia murmured as she gazed wistfully at the baby's halo of golden curls. "I loved them with all my heart. But what I wouldn't have given for a little girl."

Sophie lifted the child from the cradle and put her in Amelia's arms. The girl was impossibly delicate. Amelia felt almost afraid to hold her but didn't want to give her back to Sophie. Instead, she stayed very still and took in the baby's features. Her long eyelashes framed robin-egg blue eyes. Her small rosebud mouth quirked as if trying to curve into a smile. Her hands curled into tiny fists. Her fingers were impossibly small.

Sophie wrapped her arm around Amelia's waist and sighed happily. "My chores aren't getting done. But do I care? Not one bit."

"No," Amelia said softly, gazing at the baby. "Of course not."

"All I want to do is sit and watch her while she sleeps. Robert grouses about ham sandwiches for dinner every night, but I told him he'll survive a few more days. He didn't argue too much, probably because he loves having Marie and the baby here as much as I do. He dotes on little Madeline. Being a grandpa suits him."

"Lucky you," Amelia said. "You're twice blessed with a daughter and granddaughter."

Like Amelia, Sophie had three sons. But she also had a daughter, Marie. Amelia had always secretly envied Sophie for that reason. Sophie's three sons were cantankerous boys who were as wild as they came. Robert McCord blamed his sons' antics on Sophie's Cajun blood. Sophie blamed their antics on her Texan husband and his cowboy ways. She claimed her three boys were born feuding and fighting.

Sophie always said that the good Lord gave, and the good Lord took away. That was how things went. While her boys could try her patience, her mild-mannered daughter made up for her unruly brothers. Marie was her blessing.

Amelia gazed down at the baby and sighed. The child was a treasure. Little Madeline was a tiny perfect angel sent straight from heaven's door.

Her eyes stung with tears that came from nowhere. Her shoulders shook. She tried to swallow the lump in her throat. For the past two months, she'd been overwrought about the Presidio Mine. It was a considerable worry, but it faded from her mind as she gazed at the baby. She knew in an instant, she'd give up every claim to the mine if only she could have a grandbaby.

Sophie eased the baby from her arms and looked at her with dismay.

"I don't think my boys will ever settle down," Amelia said.

Sorrow welled deep in her chest. "Zach got caught up in a brawl in Houston last month. I had to promise the sheriff he'd stay out of town for an entire year. The brawl cost me a pretty penny. I wound up paying the auction barn for a hole in their roof, a matter that I still don't fully understand, and Zach still hasn't fully explained. Something about a fella who outbid him on the sale of a horse."

Sophie's eyes widened.

"Simon has a new sweetheart every month but never bothers to introduce her to me. It seems the moment I ask about his gal, he breaks things off." Another sob threatened. She was mortified by her tears but helpless to stop them. "And Daniel doesn't want a wife *or* a sweetheart. Not since he got the wrong end of a knife and Cordelia jilted him."

Sophie nodded sympathetically. "Daniel's so honorable, never one to brawl. To think he's the one of all our boys that gets hurt collaring an outlaw. Makes my heart ache."

Amelia dried her tears and tried to regain her dignity. Sophie went to a nearby chesterfield and sat down. Amelia sat beside her. The two women's attention drifted to the baby on Sophie's lap. Amelia held out a finger for the girl to grasp. The child clutched it tightly and drew her brows together thoughtfully. The women both laughed softly at the sight.

"You know Marie's husband claimed he didn't want to settle down," Sophie said quietly. "Grover's fifteen years older than Marie. He told his parents he had no time for a wife and was married to his medical practice."

Amelia smiled. "They make a lovely couple. I recall the wedding and the way he looked at Marie as they said their vows."

"Those vows might never have happened if his father hadn't laid down the law. He told Grover that a man needs to come home to a wife and, God willing, a few children. He flat-out threatened to leave his money to charity if Grover didn't find a nice girl to marry."

Sophie chuckled and smiled at the baby. "That's right, my darling, Madeline. You see how grandparents will resort to anything?"

"I wish Grover's father would talk to my boys. At times I wonder if they'd be more settled if only they'd had a father around."

Sophie shook her head. "Hush. Don't torment yourself. My boys are worse than yours, even with Robert's strong hand."

Amelia considered what Sophie had told her about Grover. The father's threat had resulted in a very contented marriage and a sweet, little darling baby.

She pictured her sons one by one. Zach's green eyes, so like the eyes of her own father. She imagined Simon's easy grin and Daniel's quiet dignity. Daniel. Her breath caught in her throat. Her eldest son claimed he didn't want a family and was content living alone, but, of the three boys, she considered him most suited to family life. Her heart skipped a beat. All three of her sons would be fine family men even though they didn't yet realize it.

Turning to Sophie, Amelia smiled. "Maybe I'll conjure up a few threats of my own."

Sophie pouted. "Stay for lunch. I'll help you form a few proper threats that really scare the Honeycutt boys."

"Can I come for lunch later in the week?"

"No." Sophie's cheeks pinked. "The invitation is for today. Just today."

Amelia rose. She wondered what Sophie was up to, insisting lunch had to be that very day. "I can't, Sophie. Not today. Besides, you already said that lately you're only fixing ham sandwiches."

"Fiddlesticks. I had something special planned for you." Her color deepened. "For today's lunch, that is."

Amelia considered asking what Sophie was scheming but little Madeline distracted her. Amelia gave the child one last, lingering gaze. "I'll come pay you another visit in a few days' time, Sophie. We'll put our heads together and come up with something that will scare my boys right out of their boots."

Chapter Eleven
A Foiled Scheme

Sophie McCord

After Amelia left, Sophie tended to little Madeline in the upstairs nursery. She set the child down on the changing table. Sophie's husband had made the table when he first learned he'd soon become a grandfather. He'd built it even before he made the child's cradle.

The baby chortled and babbled. Usually, Madeline's antics charmed Sophie. She'd often respond with words of endearment or a French lullaby, but at the moment, Sophie was out of sorts.

Her scheme had failed.

Sophie aired her grievances in French. Speaking in her native tongue helped her feel a trifle better. While the baby didn't offer any suggestions, she didn't argue with Sophie's views on matchmaking. Sophie expounded on thwarted plans, stubborn friends, and irksome menfolk. The child paid little attention, which was probably for the best.

Her husband knocked at the door before coming into the nursery. "I heard you fussing in French. Always worries me a mite."

"I'm telling Madeline how my grand intentions amounted to nothing."

Robert came to her side and smiled at the baby. "I don't know anything about any grand plans, Maddy, but I do know your grandma sounds pretty miffed."

Sophie removed the wet diaper. Robert picked it up by the corner and dropped it in a nearby pail. Sophie gave him an appreciative smile. Her husband was far more helpful with Madeline than he'd been with his children. In those days, he hardly knew what a diaper was, much less where to put a dirty diaper.

"One thing's for certain, Maddy." He leaned against the nearby windowsill and crossed his arms. "I'll bet Mimi isn't sore with *you*."

Sophie gave a show of exaggerated dismay as she fastened the baby's clean diaper. "Of course, not! Grandmothers never get angry with their precious grandchildren. *C'est impossible!*"

"The boys?"

Sophie frowned. Her and Robert's three boys weren't in Bethany Springs. They worked the McCord ranch in the next county. Far away from the peace of Bethany Springs. Thank goodness. She loved her boys but wherever the McCord boys went, mayhem followed.

"Non. They are fifty miles away."

Robert murmured thoughtfully as he continued to mull over the question of who had provoked Sophie's ire. He knit his brow and watched the baby as he tapped his chin.

When Sophie finished with the diaper, Robert gently nudged her out of the way. He spoke softly to the baby, lifting her tenderly in his arms. Madeline settled against his shoulder and looked impossibly small in Robert's loving hold.

"You're just a perfect little angel, aren't you Madeline?" he asked.

Sophie's breath caught. She loved to hear Robert talk to the baby. Her gruff, cowboy always tempered his voice when he held Madeline. The sound and the sight of him melted her heart. Madeline brought out her husband's soft side.

Unable to hold back, Sophie cupped a hand to his jaw. "*Mon amour.*"

"Oh really, now?" His eyes twinkled. "I reckon that *monamore* stuff means I'm not the one in hot water?"

"Not you."

"Can't imagine it's Marie?"

"Non. She's done as I asked and rested this morning while I watched the baby. The person in the water is your brother!"

"My brother?" Robert frowned. "You're mad at Wade?"

"Yes. And Amelia too." Sophie scoffed. "I'm mad at both."

The baby squirmed. She was ready to nurse. Robert patted her back as a look of bewilderment came over him. "I just saw Amelia leave, but Wade's not even here. How'd he manage to make you mad when he hasn't been around?"

"I told him to come for lunch today because I knew Amelia would be here to see the baby."

Robert grimaced. "Oh no. Sophie, darlin-"

"Don't Sophie-darling me. I know what I'm doing."

"Amelia Honeycutt does *not* like Wade. My brother can't figure out why. I suppose it's on account of Wade's reputation as a lady's man."

"I don't know her reasons, but Amelia cannot spend the rest of her life mourning George."

"I agree. But I'm not the one you need to convince."

Sophie dismissed his concerns with a wave of her hand. "I ordered all sorts of goods to make a fine lunch. I sent letters to both Wade and Amelia. And what happens? Amelia arrives but leaves early. Wade might come but who can know?"

"Wade'll come. He's not one to turn down your cooking."

"Poo! It hardly matters now."

The baby's fussing grew louder. Robert jostled her a little, trying to soothe her complaints. His mouth curved into a smile.

"This is terrible news," Sophie grumbled as she reached for the baby. Cradling the child in her arms she gave Robert a chastising look. "I don't know why you are smiling."

"Well, I reckon I got good reason to."

His gruff voice startled the baby causing her to fuss.

Robert soothed her with a soft word and continued in a hushed tone. "I'm smiling because I'm starting to think there's hope I might get something other than a ham sandwich for supper."

Sophie sighed as she left the nursery. Robert followed. She carried the baby to Marie's room and was about to knock but Robert set his hand on her shoulder. With a gentle motion he brushed a lock of hair from her eyes.

He spoke, his tone quiet. "I'm sorry your matchmaking plans didn't work, darlin'. Next time, I promise to do what I can to help."

Sophie laughed softly. "Thank you, Robert."

Robert brushed a kiss across her cheek. "You own my heart, Sophie. I'd do anything for you."

He flashed a charming smile, the same smile that had made her swoon when they'd first met.

"I'd do anything for you *and* your fine cooking."

Sophie shook her head as she tried to keep from smiling back. "Robert McCord, you are *impossible*."

Chapter Twelve
A Visit from the Strawberry Thief

Molly

As much as Molly looked forward to having the house to herself, she had to admit it felt a little too quiet. Her father and the boys hadn't been gone half a day, and already the silence weighed heavily on her.

While she should have been working, she found that her mind wandered. Her thoughts didn't drift to her father or brothers, although she missed them terribly. It was musings of the man she'd come to think of as Henry.

In the middle of kneading bread or sweeping the porch, she'd pause, stare off into the distance and think of her Henry. What was he doing? Did he ever think of her?

Even though she might never see him again, she'd mended his shirt and tucked it in her bag. That way, if their paths crossed, she could give it back. So often during her busy day, she'd imagine seeing him again. Maybe he'd be in the linen shirt she gave him. The notion always made her smile as she daydreamed.

When she cast aside her daydreams only to realize that she'd spent a quarter hour lost in thought, she'd promptly chide herself. She'd work extra hard with twice her usual diligence, doing her very best to keep her mind firmly fixed on her tasks.

The day after her father and brothers left, there was a knock at the door, and she found the same ragged girl she'd seen near JoJo's house.

Molly recalled the day, how she'd forgone her wages for the dress on account of Mrs. Ward's unkind words. Moments later, she spied the girl darting from the Wards' orchard, carrying a bucket of strawberries. The girl had likely stolen the strawberries, but the way Molly saw things, the Wards deserved that and more.

She winced. Kindness. Forgiveness. A charitable heart. More to add to her list of weekly improvements.

The girl was slim, reserved, probably eleven or twelve, the tender, awkward age on the outside edge of childhood. Her hair was braided in a sweet crown that wound around her head, woven with a pretty if tattered ribbon. At that age, Molly had one moment fussed over her dress, and in the next ran off to skip stones at the creek with her brothers.

"Elsie? Isn't that your name?"

"Yes, ma'am."

"Can I help you?"

The girl shifted nervously in her simple muslin frock that hung a few inches too short. She spoke in a polite, earnest tone, her eyes brimming with hope. "I wanted to ask for work." She gulped and spoke hurriedly as if trying to finish before losing her courage. "I could sweep the porch. Or clean your chicken coop. I can hoe the garden or scour pots. I'm a hard worker."

A pang of sympathy squeezed Molly's heart. She didn't need the help, or better said, couldn't pay for help, but didn't want to turn the girl away. Times were hard for most folks living on the ridge. "I'm certain you are a hard worker. I can't pay you, but I could give you a bite to eat."

The girl looked pained. Molly knew how difficult it was to accept an offer of charity. She hastened to add, "if you're willing, that is."

The girl nodded and without another word took the broom from the porch corner and began sweeping. Over the course of the morning, she worked diligently. When she finished sweeping, she stacked the firewood. Next, Molly sent her to the chicken coop with a bucket of vegetable scraps and a basket for the eggs.

"The black hen is a little ornery," Elsie explained shyly when she returned a quarter hour later. She gave Molly the basket of eggs.

"I'm sorry, Elsie, I should have warned you."

"I talked to her and told her she was pretty."

"That's what I do," Molly said with a laugh.

"I could brush your horse for you. She's got sticker burrs in her mane."

"Vixen would love the attention. She can be ornery too, but usually just with menfolk. She's fine with girls. You'll find a brush in the shed beside the coop. When you're done, it'll be time for lunch."

Molly cleared the kitchen table of her sewing supplies. With her father and the boys gone, she'd used the big table for cutting fabric and stacking her finished work. Humming softly, she thought how nice it was to have company, especially a girl.

Another knock at the door drew her attention. To Molly's surprise, it was JoJo.

"I've been thinking and thinking about the dress you made for me," JoJo said. "None of my friends have ever given me anything so special."

Molly smiled despite her memory of Mrs. Ward's words about Papa. She'd never imagined JoJo considered her a friend but wouldn't argue. "When are you leaving?"

"Not soon enough to suit me." She held out a basket. "I brought you and your family strawberry jam along with fresh strawberries Father picked this morning."

"Thank you. What a treat. The boys are away with my father, but everyone will enjoy the jam."

JoJo looked pleased. She never looked pleased, certainly not with Molly.

"Where are my manners?" Molly said, flustered. "Would you like to come in?"

"I should be on my way. Mother will wonder where I am."

Molly glanced down at the basket, wondering if Mrs. Ward knew about JoJo's gift. Perhaps not. What did it matter? She could hardly refuse such a wonderful present. The berries gave off a sweet perfume and the jam would be delicious on a slice of warm-from-the-oven bread.

Just then, Elsie returned from the garden. She skipped along the path, looking pleased with herself and eager to eat lunch. When she saw JoJo, she stopped abruptly.

"What is that little imp doing here?" JoJo demanded.

"She's doing some chores for me." Noting Elsie's trepidation, Molly called to her. "I hope you're hungry."

"You're *feeding* her?"

"I am indeed. She's a hard worker. Come on, Elsie. Don't be bashful."

Elsie walked the rest of the way to the house, eyeing JoJo warily.

"You're the McKittrick girl, aren't you?" JoJo wrinkled her nose.

"Yes, ma'am."

JoJo's expression hardened. "You'd best not let her stay long, Molly. The McKittrick family like to help themselves to the property of other people."

Elsie didn't say a word. She paled and bit her lip.

JoJo snorted. "Even worse, she likely has cooties."

"I do not," Elsie's voice trembled.

JoJo ignored her protests, speaking instead to Molly with a stern warning. "Trust me, Molly, you do *not* want to catch cooties. Let me take a look, girlie, come to the edge of the porch."

Molly felt sorry for Elsie. In the back of her mind, she knew she ought to defend the poor girl. She tried to think of an answer to JoJo's accusations. As she stood tongue-tied, JoJo made it clear she intended to prove her point. She very nearly dragged the poor girl to the porch railing.

"Do you know what they look like?" JoJo demanded.

"No, I don't." Molly gave Elsie an apologetic look. "I've never had them."

"Neither have I," Elsie said quietly.

"I have," JoJo said. "Once."

Molly drew a sharp breath of surprise. Miss Perfection had lice? It seemed impossible that bugs would have the nerve to stroll around the hair of JoJo Ward. Molly couldn't keep from recoiling as she eyed JoJo's head with alarm.

"I don't have them anymore," JoJo fussed. She rolled her eyes. "I caught them from my cousin. Mother made me promise not to ever tell anyone. She was fit to be tied and didn't speak to her sister for a whole month. Mother had to rub pine tar on my head every day for a week. The nits look like rice, by the way."

JoJo peered at Elsie's head. She told the girl to move her hair this way and that. Elsie did as she was told. The girl's hair was a lovely copper color, and somehow Molly knew Elsie was proud of her glossy tresses.

"Who braided your hair?" Molly asked kindly. "Your mama?"

"I don't have a mama." She kept her eyes averted. "I did it myself."

"That's remarkable," Molly said. "All right, JoJo. If you haven't found any by this point, I believe it's safe to say you won't find any."

JoJo harrumphed. "I'm almost done."

Elsie gave JoJo a wounded look but remained quiet. Molly couldn't help feeling badly for the girl. Clearly there was some bad blood between the Wards and the McKittrick clan that went beyond a few stolen strawberries.

Elsie should not have taken them to be sure. Still, it was unkind to suggest the girl was dirty. The girl's greatest fault was likely pilfering berries. Then again, she might not have eaten in a day or so and stole the fruit purely out of desperation.

JoJo gave up the search and was soon on her way, leaving with dire warnings of the McKittrick family. Molly set out lunch which the girl ate hungrily. Despite her appetite, the girl had the good manners to pray before eating.

"And dear Lord, please help our neighbors stay safe against the outlaws. In Jesus's name, we pray."

Both Molly and Elsie said, "Amen," in unison.

Molly frowned. "What outlaws?"

The girl looked abashed.

"Go on," Molly said. "I'd like to know if there are outlaws about."

"Seems there's been some thieves prowling around," Elsie said tentatively. She swallowed hard and looked fretful.

"I hadn't heard anything."

"I don't want to frighten you, ma'am."

Molly smiled, trying to put the girl at ease. "It frightens me more that you call me ma'am than it does to hear there are thieves about."

The girl nodded, a shy smile tugging at her lips. She began to eat. It seemed she ate with a manner that was deliberately slow as if trying to hold back. The poor child. Molly wondered when she'd had her last meal.

"They might be skulking about in search of the hidden Presidio treasure," Elsie offered.

Molly smiled. "My brothers like to talk about the Presidio treasure. They say some old prospector hid his silver in one of the mine shafts years ago."

Elsie nodded, wide-eyed. Molly could plainly see that the girl fully believed in the ridiculous story. Molly had heard the far-fetched tale more times than she could count. Will and Jack had talked of nothing else when the family first came to Bethany Springs and it appeared that young Elsie put even more stock into the myth than Will and Jack.

"He left his fortune in one of those tunnels," Elsie said.

Molly sighed. "He left it behind so he could propose to the girl he loved."

"He intended to return for the silver, but when his sweetheart refused his offer, he died of a broken heart."

"That's not the story I heard," Molly said. "I heard he never returned because he was killed in a saloon."

Elsie frowned. "That's not very romantic."

"Either way, he's passed on."

Elsie shook her head. "Unless he lurks in the mine, searching for more silver."

Molly smiled at the girl's lively imagination. She changed the subject to say how nice it was to have company. Elsie agreed, and spoke of the pleasant conversation and delicious food. She added a few comments, suggesting it had been a while since she'd enjoyed either.

Before Molly could respond, Elsie spoke of her grandmother, the woman who'd raised her up until a few months ago. Molly could hear the love in Elsie's voice.

"After Gramps passed away, Gran turned all her love and affection toward books," Elsie said. Blushing, she added, "And me as well, though I often suspected she loved books a tad more. She said they didn't ever talk back."

Elsie smiled wistfully. "I got my love of reading from Gran."

Molly chuckled, pleased that the girl was coming out of her shell.

"I'm sorry about JoJo Ward," Molly said. "I want you to know I didn't suspect you had cooties."

Elsie shrugged a shoulder. "I think JoJo is..."

"You think she's what?" Molly lowered her voice and spoke in a conspiratorial tone. "You can tell me."

"I think JoJo Ward *is* a cootie."

Molly laughed, unable to hold back her amusement. "JoJo can't help herself."

Elsie seemed to feel more and more at ease as they lingered at the table. Molly was glad. She had chores to do but welcomed the chance to visit with the vivacious girl. Elsie spoke freely, asking about Molly's various projects spread across the far end of the table.

"Did you make that handkerchief?" Elsie gestured to a pile of sewing materials atop a chair.

The small, embroidered square rested on a bolt of fabric. Molly had almost forgotten about Henry's handkerchief, surprisingly. Over the past few days, she'd held it and thought of her handsome Henry. Each time, she'd get lost in thought. After letting her mind wander, she'd catch herself and, feeling silly, would hastily set it aside and carry on with her work.

"Last week, a gentleman came to my rescue." Molly blurted the words.

Elsie parted her lips with surprise. For a moment, she said nothing, but then she laughed softly and nodded. "Really? A *gentleman?*"

Molly told the story of Vixen's antics, the ripped shirt and hidden handkerchief with the embroidered letter H. She explained how she'd decided on his name even though it was likely something other than Henry. Elsie was almost breathless with wonder, eager to know more. She was too shy to ask very many questions, but Molly could see the curiosity in her eyes.

"It sounds so romantic," Elsie said softly. "Henry sounds like a knight in shining armor."

"You have quite the imagination."

Elsie laughed, covering her mouth with her hand. Slowly she lowered her hand to reveal a sweet, playful smile. "I mean no disrespect, ma'am, but..."

The girl's words faded. She kept her attention fixed on her food, a smile playing upon her lips.

"But?" Molly asked.

"I might have an imagination. Gran used to say the same thing." Elsie lifted her gaze. "But *you're* the one who gave this kind stranger the name of Henry."

Molly had to laugh, admitting the girl made a fair point.

Elsie sighed. They sat a while longer in companionable silence until Elsie spoke of chores she ought to attend. She thanked Molly for the food and took her leave. After Molly cleared the dishes, she spied the girl in the garden chopping weeds from the rows of green beans. Later, the girl carried water to the fruit trees in the orchard. Molly marveled at her diligence and boundless energy.

In the late afternoon, Elsie returned to the house. She stood in the doorway, looking bashful. "What more can I do for you?"

"Heavens, I can't think of a single thing. You've done so much."

The girl smiled. Her cheeks colored. A quiet moment stretched between them until the girl spoke softly. "I'll take my leave then."

Molly wished she could think of another task for the girl but could not. "All right. Thank you, Elsie. I've enjoyed your company."

"Yes, ma'am. I have as well. I thank you for the food. You're a mighty fine cook."

"It was nothing." Molly winced at the girl's words. The lunch hadn't been anything remarkable. In hindsight, she wished she'd made something more than stew.

Elsie said a quiet goodbye.

Molly listened to Elsie's footsteps as they faded. She sat unmoving, half expecting her to come bounding back into the cabin with some tall tale about who knew what. The girl, however, did not return.

Molly resumed her needlework after a short spell, noting the heavy silence. Without Elsie, the house seemed especially lonesome. If only she'd thought to ask Elsie to stay for supper.

That would have been a fine idea. The thought filled her with remorse. The poor girl was painfully thin.

Perhaps Elsie would return in the days to come. Molly hoped that might come to pass for she would surely welcome the company. She'd be certain to not only feed the girl several hearty meals but would also send her home with a basket of food.

After she finished the trim on the bonnet, she set it with the others. Sewing gratified her because the work was plain to see. Hats and shirts and dresses lasted for a long time, unlike cooking or cleaning. Meals were eaten and forgotten. Cleaning, scouring, and laundry were hardly any different.

Needlework, whether sewing a new garment or adorning cloth with embroidery, was something that remained. The work made her heart happy, not just because Brigit had taught her, but for the simple, lasting evidence of her efforts.

Papa was right. She was a tad prideful.

In a day or so, she'd ride to Bethany Springs and try her luck again at the mercantile. If she could manage to get just a few dollars, she'd have enough for the rent payment.

Just before dusk, she ventured to the chicken coop to make sure the door was secure. Vixen grazed in the paddock behind the shed. Her coat shone in the last rays of sunshine. A chilly breeze ruffled her mane, showing off Elsie's hard work.

When Vixen came to the rail, Molly glimpsed more of Elsie's efforts. The girl had braided a daisy into the mare's forelock and tied it with a thread from the burlap sacks from the shed. Vixen hung her head over the rail and sniffed Molly's pockets.

"I didn't bring you anything, Vixen. I'm sure you got plenty of treats today. Don't expect me to fuss over you like our friend, Elsie."

Vixen wandered away to graze.

As twilight drifted to dusk, the sunset splashed the sky with streaks of violet, lavender and rose. An evening songbird trilled. Papa told her it was a Chuck-will's-widow, a bird that especially liked to sing just before nightfall. With the first stars twinkling in the darkening sky, Molly thought of her father and brothers. She offered a quick prayer that the mineral springs would heal her father. She added a request that He watch over her brothers too.

With a wistful sigh, she left the corral to finish her chores.

After Molly peeked in on the chickens, she made her way back to the cabin. Partway back, a curious feeling came over her. The hair on the back of her neck prickled. The tale of the phantom prospector drifted through her mind.

Feeling utterly foolish, she retraced her steps. Pausing on the narrow path, she saw what was amiss. In the shadows of Papa's work shed, Elsie slumbered. She rested in the hay, curled beneath an array of carefully arranged burlap feed sacks.

Chapter Thirteen
Daniel Finds Molly

Daniel

As Daniel rode along the ridge, he met with several families. Everyone wanted to know when the mine would reopen. They were pleased to learn the mine would be up and running as soon as it was safe. Lord willing that would be less than a few weeks' time. People were especially grateful to learn the Honeycutt family would forego the rent until the mine was reopened and folks had a chance to get back on their feet.

The cabins for the miners had been built some twenty years earlier by the Presidio Mining Company. They were not terribly sturdy houses when they were built, and now some of them were practically falling down. Daniel's mother wanted to ensure workers were properly housed. To her thinking, the miners would be more likely to remain in Bethany Springs if they had comfortable homes.

Most mining camps were filthy, with cabins not fit for livestock. When his mother took on the Presidio Mine, she vowed workers would live in clean, warm homes. To that end, she had started building new cabins with two and sometimes three bedrooms, and kitchens equipped with sturdy stoves. The cabins would boast windows, porches and room out back for a garden and fruit trees. The properties would be fenced so families could keep a few head of cattle if they chose.

Although the new cabins were going up, the prospect of fine homes hadn't been enough for some folks. With the accident, several families had given up and moved on. The old cabins stood empty. Daniel wondered if they might have been convinced to stay if the new cabins had been completed, and if they'd known the rent would be forgiven.

As Daniel visited each house, he did his best to look into the home to see if Mack was inside. He spoke a little louder than necessary as well, hoping she might hear him if she was there. No luck so far, though.

Daniel made sure to ask about vandalism and thieves as well. No one said a word about robberies or any trouble. He asked a few pointed questions but folks either didn't know or didn't want to say. Some might not want to talk for fear of retaliation. Midday, he arrived at a cabin that belonged to a young couple who offered to share a meal with him.

He was mighty hungry. He'd packed some provisions but the aroma coming from the cabin smelled more appealing. He gratefully accepted the invitation.

It was over a fine meal of chili and cornbread that he learned details of the girl he'd come to think of as Mack. The woman spoke of Molly and her fine sewing skills. She added that Molly's name was Molly Anne Collins.

Upon hearing her name, his heart warmed.

Molly Anne Collins.

Tension rolled off his shoulders. He couldn't hold back a foolish smile. Land sakes, he felt like a lovesick boy. Thankfully, his hosts paid him no mind. He felt keen to rush off, to set out for her family's home. Despite his strong need to see Molly, he held back. It wouldn't do to hurry off, after all, he needed to observe some semblance of manners.

Instead of galloping away to find Molly, he stayed put. He accepted a second helping, visited with the family, and complimented the wife on her fine cooking. After the meal, they directed him to the Collins home. He was grateful to note that he could finish speaking to the remaining mining families on the way. He visited the handful of cabins to deliver the news, saving the Collins home for last.

The Collins family lived in one of the larger cabins some distance from any other homes. As he approached, his heart quickened. His memories returned with a rush of pleasure. He couldn't imagine what he'd say but didn't much care. So long as he could finally see her again and know that she was safe and sound.

A horse stood tied to a railing. A girl brushed its coat, unaware of his approach. Daniel recognized Molly's mare, Vixen.

"Howdy, miss." Daniel spoke quietly, hoping to avoid startling the girl.

Despite his efforts, she was more than startled. She stared, stricken, turning white. Clutching the railing, she shook her head, her lips moving as she tried to speak.

The eyepatch often scared womenfolk, although rarely to this degree. He stopped his horse a few paces from the girl. Before he could introduce himself, the girl spoke.

"What do you want? We don't have any money."

Daniel winced. Most of the mining families spoke of having to watch every penny. He sympathized with all of them.

"That's all right," he said gently. "I'm not looking for payment. Fact of the matter-"

"The law will catch up to menfolk like you."

"Beg pardon?"

"Stealing from innocent folks."

"Now, hold up there, missy. I'm not stealing from anyone. The Honeycutts aren't thieves."

She blinked. Her cheeks colored. "You're Mr. Honeycutt."

"I am. I didn't mean to startled you. I ought to have introduced myself. My apologies."

"I thought you were an outlaw. There's been some trouble lately with thieves. Makes a person sort of suspicious. Just the other day, a couple of young fellas knocked on my door. They didn't look much older than me. Just the same, I ran out the back door and hid in the brush till they left."

The girl's voice trembled. Daniel winced as he imagined her hiding in fear. She was just a child, no more than twelve years old.

The girl went on, full steam, eager to tell why she thought he was a thief. "And right after, my elderly neighbor found someone had come into her home and stolen three silver spoons."

"I've heard there was some trouble on the ridge." Daniel tried to temper his tone to keep from showing his anger. "I wasn't sure how widespread."

"I'm not sure either. I'm mighty sorry for suggesting something untoward. I hadn't ever seen you before around these parts. I figured..."

"My name's Daniel Honeycutt."

"Pleased to meet you, sir. I'm mighty sorry to have suggested you were some sort of crook."

Daniel tried to make light of the mistake. "Well, shoot. I've been called a few things before but never a crook. Do you live here?"

"No, sir, I'm just staying with Molly for a spell. Since my folks are away. I've been here since yesterday."

She wrapped her arms around herself. The girl was thin. He couldn't help a wave of pity. The poor kid didn't have an ounce to spare.

"What's your name?" he asked kindly.

"Elsie. Elsie McKittrick."

Daniel recognized the name. His heart sank. According to his mother's ledger, the McKittricks lived in one of the cabins that now stood empty. Whatever kin she had were gone. Every stick of furniture had been removed from the cabin. It looked to him that the McKittrick family had hightailed it from Bethany Springs, with no aim to return.

"Well, Elsie McKittrick, I need to have a word with Molly Collins. Can you show me to the house? I don't want to scare anyone else today."

Elsie flushed and nodded. "Surely."

He dismounted and hitched his gelding to the railing. Elsie walked up the path. He followed. A time or two, she glanced over her shoulder as if trying to piece together a few things about him. Her eyes sparkled with curiosity. He took off his hat and raked his fingers through his hair as if that would help his appearance after spending the whole day in the saddle. Not likely.

"You've probably heard the other rumor going around, Mr. Honeycutt."

"Is it about me or my family?" he asked, his tone a little gruffer than he'd intended.

"No, sir. Folks have been talking about bags of silver hidden in the mine."

Daniel scoffed. As they walked the narrow path, the Collins home came into view. A tidy, cabin with brightly colored curtains adorning the windows. Flower boxes brimmed with bright blossoms. His heartbeat quickened.

Meanwhile, Elsie prattled on about the mysterious prospector who left heaps of silver in one of the mine shafts. "Some folks say he left a fortune up there."

"Sounds like a tall tale."

"Those are the best kind of tales," she said with shy laugh. "Anything less is hardly worth telling."

She seemed taken with the idea of the hidden cache and went on breathlessly about notions of bandits and treasure maps and other nonsense.

"Folks better not be poking around that mine," Daniel said. "It might be dangerous."

Daniel heard a woman's voice coming from the house and in an instant knew it was Molly. His heart skipped a beat. *There's my girl.*

His girl? Where had that idea come from?

Molly called again, asking Elsie to help with a task inside. He turned to find Elsie regarding him with even more interest than a moment before. Too late, he realized that he'd spoken the words aloud, the words that announced Molly was his girl. He knit his brows and tried to ignore the girl's curious, almost teasing smile.

"Molly Anne," Elsie called with a playful tone as they reached the porch. "You have a gentleman caller."

"A gentleman caller," Daniel muttered.

"Well, you are just that, Mr. Honeycutt. A gentleman. And a caller."

She gave him a look of wide-eyed innocence. Sparks of amusement lit her eyes, belying her attempt to look well-meaning. The little scamp wasn't helping matters one bit.

When he'd first ridden up to the Collins home, he'd scared the poor girl half out of her wits. Now Elsie could scarcely hold back a burst of girlish laughter. She'd heard his words about Molly being *his girl*. It was clear. What else was clear? The words seemed to make her mighty happy.

He shook his head with a silent warning not to say anything. The gesture didn't have its intended effect. If anything, Elsie seemed more amused. She giggled, quickly covering her joyful smile with her hand. Daniel removed his hat and grimaced with an uncomfortable mix of awkwardness and anticipation.

Molly came to the door, stopping abruptly.

"Henry," she exclaimed. "I can't believe you're here."

"Mack." He said the name without thinking. He understood her name was Molly, of course, but part of him still thought of her as Mack.

She frowned.

Daniel's breath stilled within his chest. Time seemed to stand still. Silence stretched between them. His gaze drifted from her eyes along her slim, feminine form, taking in her narrow waist and a hundred other lovely aspects.

It was a lingering, overly forward gaze but he couldn't stop himself. The yearning overpowered his usual good manners. He'd apologize for his behavior one day if he ever managed to get his wits about him.

She'd mentioned a man named Henry. Who in tarnation was Henry? Did she have an admirer? A low growl rumbled deep in his chest. Not a moment ago, he'd fretted about his manners. Now he fretted about a rival.

She startled at the sound of his rumbling growl. Almost as quickly, she recovered her senses and lifted her chin. "I mended your shirt. And pressed your handkerchief."

"His name's not Henry," Elsie said with a soft laugh. "It's Daniel Honeycutt, which is a bit of a surprise, don't you think?"

"Hm?" Molly shook her head, still bewildered. "Surprise?"

Elsie gave another playful laugh. "Henry, your knight in shining armor, turns out to be a Honeycutt. Don't you recall what you said?"

Molly darted across the porch to hastily cover Elsie's mouth. "Elsie. Hush, now."

Elsie did not, or rather could not, utter one more word, but Daniel could plainly see the laughter in her eyes. He was still fuming about Henry. Who was this rascal? Had Molly made him a shirt as well?

He lifted his brows with a silent inquiry, but Molly ignored the unspoken question and shooed Elsie away with instructions to check the bread in the oven and peel the potatoes and carrots.

"Go on, Elsie," Molly said nervously. "And set the rest of the strawberry jam on the table."

The girl agreed readily, skipping inside with a light step.

Daniel and Molly were left alone on the porch. The quiet evening added to the strained silence, pressing in from all sides. For all the awkwardness, Daniel couldn't help a surge of happiness. Molly. Finally. He'd thought about her for a long time and wondered if he'd ever see her again. Now, after what seemed like years, he was face to face with his Molly.

Molly swallowed hard before beginning her explanation. "I should explain about the name Henry. I decided you were called Henry on account of the handkerchief."

"What handkerchief?"

"The one I found in your shirt pocket."

Daniel recalled the handkerchief, one of several dozen his mother had made for him and his brothers over the years. Some were embroidered with an H. Others had the family's name stitched in a corner. Molly must have found one with the single letter.

She went on. "We never introduced ourselves, but I thought about you a time or two since then and, well, it's just silly, of course, but I made up a name for you."

"You made up a name?" He smiled as he let out a sigh of relief.

"Yes," she said primly. "It seemed perfectly reasonable at the time. I decided your name was Henry."

He managed, barely, to keep from chuckling at her account. She was mortified. Clearly. As the son of Amelia Honeycutt, he'd been raised to treat women politely. He ought to confess he'd also come up with a name for her, although it hadn't been something he'd invented. The name came from the tag she'd sewn in the shirt.

Another mischievous part of him wanted to ask about her views of the Honeycutts. But he wouldn't do that. He didn't want to know. After riding the length of the ridge and seeing how much some of the families were struggling, he could understand her views. Her low opinion came from the mine closing with no idea when it might reopen. Folks needed work or else risked losing their pride.

He could understand that bit about pride.

Molly spoke. "I made up a name for the simple reason that I'd forgotten to ask who you were. I regret that now."

"It's no trouble."

"Thank you," she said pointedly. "Mr. Honeycutt."

A soft wind rustled across the trees and wafted the length of the porch, making the swing sway and creak. Off in the distance, a lone coyote yipped. The breeze carried a sweet, honeyed scent that reminded him of Molly. The scent left him a tad lightheaded, yet he yearned to draw nearer.

He shook his head to clear his thoughts. "You shouldn't call me Mr. Honeycutt. I'm not that much older than you. What? Maybe eight or ten years?" Asking her age was indelicate but he pressed on, stretching his hand out in greeting. "I reckon you ought to call me by my given name, Daniel."

"I'm Molly. My family sometimes calls me Molly Anne."

She smiled and set her delicate hand in his. He took her hand, catching his breath as her silken skin brushed his work-roughened palm. His heart shook. How was it possible? After resolving himself to a life alone, he'd come face to face with a girl who stole his breath. Molly was everything he swore he never wanted.

Sweet. Gentle. Gracious.

Despite all his doubts and all his trepidation, he clasped her hand and held it tenderly. He was at least a head taller he noted. He inhaled her flowery scent, aware of every lovely aspect of Molly Anne Collins. Mack. Inwardly, he winced at the silly made-up name.

A trickle of sweat rolled down the back of his neck. Her hand felt impossibly delicate. Her amber eyes sparkled with curiosity. She appeared pleased to see him, or so he hoped. Despite his hopes, his wounded pride mocked him for riding up the ridge to search for his girl.

Chapter Fourteen
The Invitation

Molly

The sight of Daniel Honeycutt standing on her porch astonished Molly. The touch of his hand only made matters worse. He wore the linen shirt. And that simple fact thrilled her foolish heart. She probably wore the same dopey smile that Jack liked to point out. She schooled her features and tugged her hand from Mr. Honeycutt's and invited him inside.

He obliged.

After a moment of awkward silence, Daniel told her the family intended to forgive the rent. His words both shocked and offended. She'd lived in a half-dozen mining towns. Papa tended to argue with mine owners or foremen about how to manage things.

Because of their frequent moves, Molly knew a thing or two about the sort of men who owned or managed mines. None gave a fig about their workers. In all the mining towns she'd known, not once had any of the rich owners offered a helping hand. If anything, they raised rent or made the men work longer hours in times of need.

Bethany Springs was pretty much like the other mining towns she'd seen, but it was clear, the new cabins being built would make it far nicer. Molly wouldn't allow herself to trust their motives. "Why would you extend such an offer?"

"My family wants to make certain that folks don't decide to up and leave. We intend to open the mine in a few weeks. Can't do that if miners are leaving town."

Molly knew some families had left, seeking work elsewhere. Some set off for Colorado, others intended to travel as far as California. Everyone talked of richer mines, fine places where the streets were paved with gold. Or silver.

"I don't intend to accept your offer of charity, Mr. Honeycutt," she said.

"Call me Daniel. And this isn't charity."

Molly squared her shoulders. "The Collins family pays their way, Mr. Honeycutt."

Elsie wandered into the parlor, stopping beside a chair heaped with fabric, her lips curved with an impish grin. "You mean to say, Daniel."

Molly groaned inwardly. She'd never imagined the man she called Henry was, in fact, a Honeycutt. Or that he'd one day appear at her door. Molly had admitted to Elsie that she admired her rescuer. It was clear that Elsie's imagination sparked with all sorts of mischief.

Molly tried her best to ignore the girl.

"I don't need your charity." Molly gestured to the bonnets. "I plan to go to town, to the mercantile. Once I've settled things with Mrs. Pittman, I'll have enough to pay."

Daniel spoke. "I'm trying to tell you, there's no payment required this month, Miss Collins."

"Molly," Elsie corrected, her smile widening. "You mean to say Molly."

Molly narrowed her eyes at Elsie. At least one person was enjoying this uncomfortable exchange.

Ever since the day Molly met Daniel Honeycutt, she'd imagined what it would be like to see him once more. Only, in her imaginings, she pictured meeting him in a field full of wildflowers where he'd gaze into her eyes and whisper sweet things, not offers of charity.

But that was neither here nor there.

Daniel scowled, looking especially fearsome with his eyepatch and unshaved jaw. He glanced around the room as if seeking something or someone. He grumbled softly, the same growl reverberating from his chest as earlier on the porch.

"I heard you live with your father and two brothers."

"She does," Elsie offered before Molly could reply. "They went to Bethany Hot Springs with Mr. Armstrong in hopes Mr. Collins could find some relief for his injured leg."

Daniel nodded. Judging from his darkening expression, he was not happy with Elsie's reply. Molly had to marvel at the girl who'd been so reticent just a day ago. Now she was more than happy to share all sorts of news.

"Bethany Hot Springs?" Daniel muttered. "So, she's here alone?"

Elsie looked affronted. "No, sir. She's here with me."

Daniel scoffed. "Glad to hear. Molly has a sixty-pound girl to keep her safe from the outlaws."

Elsie didn't appear to know quite how to respond, judging from her bewilderment. The girl seemed to take offense because Daniel suggested she wasn't up to the task. Instead of arguing, she remained quiet, silently pouting at his insulting remark. Without a word, she picked up the needlework Molly had given her, sank into a chair and began to practice her chain stitches.

"I'll be perfectly fine," Molly explained. "And I'll pay our debt when it's due, if you don't mind coming back."

Daniel wandered to the fireplace. The night before had been chilly, and Molly tried to start a fire to warm the cabin. It was a task her brothers usually managed, or Papa when he was home. Molly struggled to get more than a few sparks. Perhaps the wood was damp. Elsie hadn't been much help either. They'd given up after a few attempts that only resulted in puffs of smoke wafting across the parlor.

"My brothers can bring you the payment, if you prefer," Molly offered, trying to draw his attention from the remains of singed wood scattered across the fireside.

"What happened here?"

Elsie looked up from her needlework. "That was the fire we made last night, or tried to make," she said cheerfully, her wounded feelings forgotten.

Daniel chuckled. "How'd that turn out?"

Molly wanted to point out that he could see for himself.

Elsie spoke first. "Just a whole bunch of smoke, sir. The two of us 'bout busted our sides laughing and had to run to the porch because the smoke got us laughing *and* coughing at the same time, so we sat together on the porch bench wrapped in a blanket, talking and listening to the owls while the room aired out a bit."

Daniel listened with amusement. Molly folded her arms.

Elsie glanced at Molly. "That's how it turned out. Am I missing something?"

"I don't believe so," Molly replied. "I'm certain you described the entire catastrophe and then some."

Elsie blushed, lowered her head, and resumed her needlework. "My grandma used to tell folks that I'm a chatterbox. That every single one of my stories starts with Adam and Eve."

Molly had to smile at that. Daniel did too. His smile made him even more handsome. Flustered, she turned away.

"I just recalled that I've mended your shirt, Mr. Honeycutt." She hurried away, grateful for the excuse to put some distance between her and Daniel Honeycutt. The shirt sat upon a stack of fabric. She let out a trembling sigh. "Dear Lord, help me keep my wits about me."

She listened to Elsie and Daniel talking, noting the deep timbre of his voice in comparison with Elsie's sweet tone. The girl spoke of a man she'd met who wore an eyepatch. All the children were scared, but she thought he looked like a pirate in the stories she liked to read.

Molly drew a sharp breath. Heavens! Elsie had certainly overcome her shyness. Molly was about to add another prayerful request, that Elsie remember to hold her tongue. To Molly's great relief, Daniel laughed about the pirate comment.

"I'm a cowboy, not a pirate."

"That's a good thing," Elsie said. "No sea or ships anywhere around here."

Molly returned to the parlor to find Elsie inviting Daniel to sit at the table. He agreed and took the chair across from the girl. When Molly stopped in the doorway, he offered her what looked like a smug smile.

"Hope you don't mind," he drawled. "I'd like to visit a little and find out just how soon your brothers will be home."

"They won't be home for at least a week, sir." Elsie said. "Accordin' to the note they sent Molly this morning."

Molly closed her eyes, wondering if the good Lord had time for another appeal.

"Which is fine by me," Elsie added. "Me and Molly get along, sir. We're like two beans in a pod."

Daniel rested his elbow on the neighboring chair. "I think you mean peas in a pod."

"That's right," Molly blurted, trying to gain a foothold before the girl set off on another tangent. "Peas in a pod. That's just what we are, Elsie and I."

"That's true," Elsie said.

"Mr. Honeycutt, I can assure you, we'll be fine. No need to worry. Here's your shirt. I mended the sleeve. The stitches hardly show. I don't mean to boast but I'm known for my expert stitches."

Daniel looked dismayed. "Hope I don't have to give this shirt back. I'm rather fond of anything crafted by MAC."

Molly's face warmed. Was Daniel trying to charm her? Was he *flirting*?

"That's very nice of you to say," Elsie said. "Molly likes nothing better than to hear how much folks like her sewing."

"Well, I..." Molly's words trailed off as Daniel regarded her with another one of his handsome smiles.

Elsie set her needlework down. "What about the handkerchief? Don't you want to give it back? Or are you going to keep on sleeping with it under your pillow?"

Daniel lifted his brows.

Elsie prattled on. "You ought to just give it to her, sir, she's real fond of that handkerchief." She turned to Molly. "Could we ask Mr. Honeycutt to stay for supper?"

"Supper?" Molly asked.

Elsie turned back. "We're making Brunswick Stew, sir. My gran used to make it all the time, back in Nacogdoches. And Molly promised to make a strawberry pie."

In the following silence, Molly felt the weight of expectation. Both Daniel and Elsie waited for her to offer a proper invitation. With no polite alternative, Molly proceeded to the best of her ability. "What a lovely stew, goodness. I meant to say lovely idea. Would you care to join us, Mr. Honeycutt?"

He smiled. Her heart warmed, a soft melting feeling.

"You mean Daniel," Elsie said.

Chapter Fifteen
Amelia visits her Husband's Grave

Amelia

Once a month, Amelia made the trip to the Honeycutt family burial plot to tend to her husband's grave. The site lay beneath a grove of majestic oaks on a hillside that overlooked the Bethany River, a portion of the original ranch that had been in the Honeycutt family for nearly one hundred years. The rolling hills beyond stretched as far as the eye could see.

Amelia tied her horse to the wrought iron enclosure. Carrying her bucket of tools in one hand, she opened the gate with the other. George's parents were buried here when he was scarcely out of his teens. Amelia had never met them. The climate and the passing of years had weathered the headstones, leaving the inscription too faint to read. The aging stones were fragile. Each spring and fall, she planted flowers by their headstones, but never dared clean the delicate marble.

That was the trouble with marble or sandstone. Softer stones couldn't withstand the elements. Not like granite. Which was the reason Amelia had made sure George had a fine stone of dark, everlasting granite.

When he first passed, Amelia didn't have the money to buy a granite headstone. No, that had taken time, years in fact, for her to save what she needed.

But it had been worth the expense.

She took her tools out of the bucket, filled it with water from the jug she'd brought and set about washing the granite with a soft brush. As was her custom, she shared her thoughts on important matters that she didn't like discussing with the small picture on her vanity.

"Good morning, George. Ever since I visited Sophie, I've been meaning to talk to you about the boys. Turns out, Sophie McCord had more than a new hat. She has a granddaughter. A precious girl. I'm sorry to say that I'm quite envious."

She imagined George listening with a lopsided smile, his gray eyes glinting with humor. George Honeycutt had been a handsome rascal who'd owned her heart from the first time she set eyes on him at a debutante ball in New Orleans.

George had come to Louisiana to deliver a herd of longhorns and stayed on in hopes of drumming up more business. He'd never planned on getting roped into a fancy shindig, much less to find the one girl who made him want to settle down.

Not everyone was keen on the match. Her parents had been furious. When they met George a few days after the cotillion, they were certain he was all wrong. *Too old. Too rough. A Texan!*

She didn't care if George was fifteen years older, or that he occasionally smoked a cigar and drank spirits with Robert McCord. She'd fallen in love and told her parents if she couldn't have George Honeycutt, she simply wouldn't have any man.

Her parents never could say no, not for long. By and by, Amelia got her way and married George on her nineteenth birthday.

Five years later, in the twilight of the War Between the States, she was a mother to two small boys with a third child on the way. And she was a widow. With her parents gone as well, she found herself utterly alone. For the last twenty-four years, she'd come every month to "talk" with her late, beloved husband.

It was probably silly, and Amelia didn't abide by silliness, but she found comfort in the visits.

She worked carefully, scrubbing the top and sides with a horsehair brush. Water rivulets dripped down the smooth, polished face, washing away the dust.

"Ever since I held that darling little girl in my arms, I've tried to think of a scheme to get the boys married." She stood back to look at her work.

"I've tried to be polite but persistent, of course."

She dried the stone with a rag and polished the smooth surface with a soft cloth. "But now I'm wondering about something else that has me worried. I'm beginning to think Daniel's terrible injuries weren't an accident. I believe the three boys are part of a secret group that takes the law into their own hands. And the last thing I need," her voice shook, "is another headstone to visit every month."

She took a moment to compose herself before going on.

"So, I got to thinking. If they settle down, they'll be content to stay home with their wives and, Lord willing, a great number of little Honeycutts. I'm praying for a granddaughter. It might be putting the cart before the horse, but there it is."

She filled the bucket again and watered the rosebushes. Crouching down, she yanked a few weeds, then picked up her tools and put them in the bucket. It was too early to plant the daisies she'd started from seed. The end of April could still bring cold, stormy nights. The daisies would have to wait till next month.

"That's my plan, George darling. I'll write the governor and explain Bethany Springs needs a proper sheriff of our own. Then I'll have a little chat with the boys. I'll give them six months to court a girl and settle down."

She paced back and forth, trying to imagine each boy's response. What if they refused? What then? Stopping abruptly, she addressed the headstone. "If they don't go along with my perfectly reasonable request, I'll cut off their monthly family income. Our sons will have to work hard for cowboy wages. Let's see what those scamps say about that."

She sighed wistfully. "Sometimes I think I've become a cantankerous, disagreeable woman. It's a man's world. I feel plum worn out."

A pang of sadness struck her heart. She'd been not much more than a girl when she married George. At all of nineteen, she'd been so sure of things and still presented herself as a delicate Southern belle. What would George think of her now? He'd probably think she was tough and bossy, not qualities he admired in a woman.

She drove herself hard. Some days, she didn't think of George till she said her prayers at night. In those moments, she'd catch herself and feel a rush of sorrow, not to mention guilt. Her memories faded a little more each day, it seemed, and yet, the loss often felt new and raw.

Time had flown. She hadn't had time to enjoy her boys when they were small. And while she'd made her way in the world, and earned a small fortune, she yearned for something more. It was time, she'd concluded, time to make new memories with sweet-smelling, dear little grandbabies. This time she'd be certain to appreciate every fleeting moment.

"I'm so used to doing things on my own, sometimes I forget about asking for help," she said quietly. She let her gaze wander to the stretch of pastureland down the hillside. Longhorns grazed, belly-deep in the grass. "But I'm praying, George. I'm asking for the good Lord's help to turn our three ornery boys into family men."

Chapter Sixteen
Daniel Beds Down in the Shed

Daniel

Daniel happily accepted the dinner invitation. Molly explained it would be ready in an hour or so. He left her to do her work and took the opportunity to survey the property. The Collins family kept things tidy. A garden plot took a large portion of the land. Seedlings sprouted from the dark, fertile soil.

He made himself useful while waiting for dinner. First, he mended a latch on a gate. Next, he hauled the wood from where a tree had fallen. After he sharpened an ax he found in the shed, he cut and split the wood. He selected a few pieces and brought them inside to stack by the fireplace.

When Daniel saw a young man on the road, he hired him to take a note to the Honeycutt Ranch in the morning. He hastily wrote a note to his mother to explain he'd be gone longer than he expected. When he was done, he gave the young man a coin and explained the note was for Mrs. Honeycutt.

It wasn't too much longer when Elsie called him to eat. They sat down at the table. Daniel offered to say a blessing before the meal. Molly accepted his offer. He knew she'd been reluctant to invite him for supper. Her willingness to let him say a prayer felt like a small blessing in itself.

Molly Anne Collins was a good cook. Daniel knew that even before he took his first bite of the savory stew, and, lest he had any doubt about the matter, Elsie spent much of the meal boasting about Molly's skills.

"She'll make a fine wife one day," Elsie assured him for the third time.

At first Molly had blushed with mortification at the girl's obvious attempts to point out her qualities. By the time she served the strawberry pie, she'd overcome her embarrassment. "Quit trying to marry me off. I have no intention of being a fine wife one day. My father needs my help."

Daniel accepted a slice of the pie, still warm from the oven. "I do agree, you're a good cook."

"Thank you," Molly replied. "I can't send you off with an empty stomach this evening."

Elsie nodded. "Especially after Mr. Honeycutt did all that work. Isn't that right, Molly? Splitting those logs for firewood. Mr. Honeycutt will make a fine-"

"Hush, Elsie," Molly gently chided. "Quit your matchmaking and eat your pie."

"I'm not leaving," Daniel said.

He noted the stunned silence as he took a bite of the pie. Both Molly and Elsie stared at him in disbelief.

"This is mighty fine strawberry pie." He took a swallow of coffee and another bite of the dessert.

Elsie's lips curved into a smile, but to his great surprise, she remained quiet. Not a peep came from the girl as she took a dainty taste of the pie, her eyes sparkling with amusement.

Molly sat rigidly with her fork poised over her untouched dessert.

"I intend to stay to make sure no one troubles you two girls."

"That's nice," Elsie said. "Molly told me how lonesome the house felt without her menfolk."

"Exactly," Daniel said. "Not to mention dangerous. I can't in good conscience leave two girls alone while there are criminal types roaming around."

"No, sir," Elsie replied.

"I'll bed down in the shed by the corral. That way I'll be a respectable distance from the house, but close enough to help in case there's any trouble."

"In the shed?" Molly asked. "Do you mean my family's shed?"

"That's what he said," Elsie replied. "That way he'll be a respectable distance from the house but close enough if there's any trouble."

"Won't your family be expecting you?" Molly asked slowly.

"She's trying to ask if you're married," Elsie added.

Molly narrowed her eyes. Elsie directed her attention back to the pie.

"I'm not married," Daniel said, trying to hide his smile.

Molly set her fork down and folded her hands. He saw the storm clouds gathering and felt the chill in the air, but it didn't matter one bit. He'd made up his mind.

"You can't stay in our shed," Molly said, firmly. "It's untoward."

"I suppose the shed doesn't really belong to your family," Elsie mused.

"What do you mean by that?" Molly demanded.

"On account of the land belonging to the Honeycutt family."

Molly turned her stormy gaze to the girl who didn't seem to notice the dark look.

"I suppose you could say that Mr. Honeycutt's staying in *his* shed." Elsie eyed the strawberry pie in the middle of the table. "May I have seconds?"

"Of course," Molly said, her tone softening. "No need to ask, Elsie."

Molly regarded the girl with a kind expression. It seemed to Daniel that much of the time the two girls had a sisterly sort of friendship. Other times, Molly fussed over the girl in a maternal sort of way. He found it heartwarming for it looked as if Elsie could stand a little tender loving care.

On the other hand, Molly mostly ignored him for the rest of the evening, choosing instead to keep her distance, every so often casting him a disapproving look as she tidied the dinner dishes. Before he took his leave, he built a fire for them in the fireplace.

Elsie marveled at the warmth and held her hands out to the crackling flames. "Golly, that feels mighty fine. But what about you, Mr. Honeycutt? Are you going to be warm enough down in your shed?"

Daniel noted with amusement the way Molly's shoulder stiffened when she heard the words, "your shed."

"I'll be fine. It won't be too cold tonight. Not for me. I spend many a night in a bedroll out on the range."

He bid them goodnight, went down to the shed, found his bedroll in his saddlebag, and spread it out on the hay. After, he checked on the gelding and gave him a helping of grain he'd tucked into his saddlebag. Just for good measure, he gave some to Vixen, too.

"Maybe we can wipe the slate clean. What do you say to that, Vixen?"

A short while later, just when he was about to turn in, Molly appeared in the doorway. Silhouetted against the moonshine, she looked slight and fragile, and he was pleased that he'd made the decision to remain. The notion of someone causing Molly Collins any trouble sent a wave of white-hot fury through his heart.

"Are you coming to check on me?" he drawled.

"I fretted about the cold night air." In the darkness he was able to make out the shape of a blanket in her hands. When she held it out, he took it from her with a word of thanks.

She stood there for a long moment as if unsure what to say or do. He knew she didn't want him there. It pleased him that she'd come to the shed and fretted about his comfort.

"Thank you for building the fire," she said.

"Happy to help."

"You must be tired," she said, her tone timid.

"A little, I suppose. I was about to," he paused and then laughed. "I was about to hit the hay."

He winced at his clumsy joke. To his relief, her shoulders moved with a sign of amusement. She shook her head and grew still. Silence stretched between them.

After a long moment, she spoke. "What would people say if they knew I had a gentleman staying while my family was away?"

He grimaced, disliking the implications. Naturally, he didn't want her to risk her good name. She had to consider not only her own reputation but that of her family. Just the same, he couldn't allow her to send him away. Not with the threat of thieves lurking around the mine.

He spoke in a quiet but firm tone. "They'd say the man wanted to protect a vulnerable woman."

In the quiet, he heard a sharp intake of breath. Had his words surprised her? Was that so odd that he would want to shield her from any harm? Especially with a young girl staying in her home, a delicate peculiar girl who talked just a little too much.

A moment passed before he heard her say quietly, "Thank you. You're very kind. This will be the second time you've helped me."

He smiled. "I'm happy to help. Shoot, I'm even making friends with Vixen. I petted her twice today, and she only nipped me once. I gave her a little of the gelding's grain, just now. I'm pretty sure we're going to get along. Eventually."

Molly laughed again. His heart thumped and a smile tugged at his lips. The sound of her laugh made him wish for a little more moonlight. He liked the sound of her laugh and yearned to see her pretty, smiling face as well.

She was nothing like other girls.

There'd been a time when women liked his pleasing looks even more than his family's name and wealth. Things changed after the incident with the cattle rustler. After that, ladies recoiled from his looks. They didn't much care for a beau with an eyepatch.

With Molly, everything seemed different, easier somehow.

He wondered why she didn't want to marry. Was there some other reason, or was it solely because she wanted to care for her father? One thing he knew for certain, Molly Collins was a strong, stubborn, spirited female. She'd make a fine mother and wife. Seemed a shame that she would never marry. Never raise up a family.

"How long do you intend to stay?" she asked.

"For as long as I need to. I don't mind bedding down here in the shed."

"Well, I suppose I can't stop you. Seeing as it's your shed."

There seemed to be a slight smile in her voice. No, she couldn't stop him. Not because he owned the shed, but because he wouldn't leave her defenseless. He kept his lips buttoned, however, resisting the urge to agree that no, she could not stop him. Hardly. He'd sleep out on the road if it meant she was safe.

She went on. "But I won't accept your offer to forgive the month's rent. Firstly, the Collins family doesn't accept charity."

"Hold up," he growled, trying to stop her.

Molly did nothing of the sort. Instead, she forged ahead. No surprise there.

"Secondly," she went on, "I don't want my father to be obliged to work in the mines. If we accept your offer, it will imply that he will return to the Presidio Mine. Which will not happen. Not if I have anything to say about it."

He gritted his teeth. She was impossible. Stubborn. He forced himself to agree. "Suit yourself."

She seemed surprised. It took her a moment to reply. "And I intend to go into town tomorrow. So, there won't be any need for you to remain."

"I'll take you to town. You're not going by yourself, not with outlaws wandering around these parts. They'd make short work of you and the chatterbox."

She gasped with indignation.

He forged ahead. "They'd lighten your wallet in the blink of an eye. That's what outlaws do."

They often did more, but he didn't care to speak of such things. He didn't want to upset her sensibilities. She was a gently raised female, likely unused to stories of crime or mayhem.

She lifted her chin. "All right, I suppose I can't stop you."

"Exactly right."

He heard a thud, the sound of her boot hitting the ground with indignation. He didn't take her for the type that stomped her foot. No. Molly Collins was far too practical to give into such things and, for that reason, he felt a mischievous sense of amusement.

She went on. "If you insist on going with us, we'll be leaving mid-morning. After breakfast."

Without waiting for him to reply, she turned on her heel and strode back up the path to the cabin. He leaned against the post and watched her until she got to the cabin and vanished inside.

A smile played on his lips. He'd be sure to stay till her family returned. Which would gall her. No matter. Molly would be kept safe.

Chapter Seventeen
Dreams of Treasure

Elsie McKittrick

The nights she dreamt of Gran, Elsie usually woke in tears, the sound of her sniffles and sobs drawing her from sleep. Often, she'd speak to the fading image in her mind. She'd tell her Gran how much she loved and missed her, that she was mighty sorry for all the times she'd jabbered on, wearing the poor woman out. Saying the words aloud comforted Elsie. Sometimes she even thought that she heard Gran answer.

Don't you fret, sweet pea. You were the best thing to come along. A balm to my lonely soul.

Nestled in her bed, she talked to Gran. Nothing special. Why, she didn't even mention how long Uncle Dwight had been gone. No need to make Gran worry. She frowned, wondering if Gran would know anyway.

The wind blew softly about the cabin, whispering through the tree limbs.

Elsie's thoughts drifted to something she'd spied that evening after Mr. Honeycutt retired. Standing by the warm fire, she noticed a collection of journals on the bookshelf. One of the journals had the words "Presidio Mine" written down the spine.

Molly talked about her father's love of mining and geology. Everyone knew Mr. Collins was very smart, not to mention brave. Folks said he ought to have been the foreman all along. Everybody she knew agreed. All except Uncle Dwight, who didn't count.

The Presidio book sparked a deep curiosity. Elsie wondered if Mr. Collins had written about the hidden silver. Molly said he enjoyed sketching and making maps. Elsie yearned to ask for permission to see the book, perhaps even read a few pages.

She didn't dare ask for fear of appearing nosy. She'd already caused a stir when she finagled a dinner invitation for Mr. Honeycutt. The last thing she wanted to do was to overstep *twice*. Molly had already been so very kind to her. It wouldn't do to ask too many impertinent questions.

Despite her good intentions, Elsie's imagination took a firm hold. If she could only take a peek at Mr. Collins' journal, she might learn the whereabouts of the storied Presidio treasure. Excitement stirred in her heart. She pictured all the wonderful things she could pay for with such a fortune. The silver could help so many folks. Maybe even Molly. *Especially* Molly.

Tossing the blankets aside, Elsie slipped from bed and tiptoed down the hallway. As she passed Molly's door, she glimpsed a startling sight. To her utter shock, it looked like two people stood side by side in the shadows. She almost let out a panicked cry, for it appeared that the stiff figures were *headless*. Slowly, it dawned on her. The ominous shapes were the dress forms Molly kept in her sewing corner.

Feeling foolish, she crept the rest of the way down the corridor.

A warm fire glowed in the fireplace, remnants from Mr. Honeycutt's blaze. Warmth emanated from the hearth.

Carefully, and with a pang of guilt, Elsie took the book from the top shelf. She hastened to the fireplace and sat on a nearby chair. Over the next hour, she leafed through the book.

Detailed drawings and notes filled page after page. Molly had said her father was fascinated by mines and she surely wasn't kidding. Mr. Collins admired rocks as much as Molly liked sewing. Both topics seemed a tad dull to Elsie's thinking.

To her disappointment, she found not one mention of hidden fortunes. Slowly it dawned on her; if Mr. Collins had found anything, he'd hardly sketch out the precise location. Why, if he'd found the treasure, Molly wouldn't be frantically sewing bonnets because they'd have more money than they could count. No. Of course he hadn't found the missing silver.

"You're a nitwit, Elsie McKittrick," she said softly.

Still, she clung to the hope of hidden treasure. The secret silver might be tucked in some dark corner. Her heart thrilled to imagine that the stories were true. She imagined herself striding into the Presidio Mine, lantern held high. Entering the mine might be scary, but she would not allow herself to be daunted.

Before closing the book, she found a small sketch of a passageway. It was short in comparison to the other passages in the mine. Mr. Collins had jotted a note beside the drawing, labeling the passage a vestry.

Elsie had heard the word before. It had something to do with a church. The word made no sense but still captured her imagination. The small passage held some meaning for Mr. Collins. She was certain. A glimmer of hope sparked inside her. Perhaps the vestry held some clue to all the stories she'd heard from her uncle and other folks along the ridge. One day, she vowed, she'd find out for herself. With a smile, she set the book on the shelf and crept back to bed.

Chapter Eighteen
Another Trip to the Mercantile

Molly

Molly spent a restless night, tossing and turning, trying not to think about the man, a near-stranger, sleeping in the shed. The notion seemed deeply scandalous. On the other hand, she couldn't help feeling some small bit of giddy happiness. It pleased her to know that Daniel wished to remain nearby to keep her and Elsie safe.

For so long, she'd thought of *herself* as a caretaker. It seemed strange to allow a man to care for her, especially a man she hardly knew.

She awoke before dawn, said her prayers, dressed and made coffee. As the first rays of sunshine peeked over the horizon, she made her way to the chicken coop to gather eggs. All the way down the path, she thought of Daniel Honeycutt, wondering if he'd really stayed the night. When she reached the door of the shed, she looked inside and found him fast asleep.

She smiled to see him sprawled across the hay. His large frame took up most of the hay pile. He lay beneath the blanket she'd given him the night before. An unshaved scruff darkened his jaw. Even while sleeping the man frowned. She found herself wondering why he looked so fearsome in the depths of slumber.

Did he not sleep peacefully? A pang of sympathy squeezed her heart. She wondered how he got injured. Chiding herself, she turned away.

After she returned to the house, she busied herself with laundry. She scrubbed a few of Elsie's garments and hung them on the line. Little Elsie had managed to dirty the only dress she owned. Thankfully, Molly had almost finished the girl's new dress. She hurriedly completed the hem, and the frock was pressed and ready to wear by the time Elsie woke.

Molly prepared a breakfast of bacon and eggs.

Daniel knocked before entering the cabin, a smile wreathing his face.

"Smells mighty good," he murmured appreciatively.

Elsie served him a cup of coffee and showed off her new dress. "What do you think? Isn't Molly clever?"

"She is indeed," Daniel said.

Molly sighed, refusing to comment on Elsie's schemes. She tried to avoid stealing glimpses of Daniel as he sat at the table. He looked handsome as ever in the same shirt he'd worn yesterday, the shirt she'd sewn.

Over breakfast, Daniel explained that he would take them into town. The two girls could ride Vixen. He hoped the mare would accommodate both girls without too much fuss.

"What do you mean by that?" Molly asked, trying to suppress a smile. "Are you suggesting she's persnickety?"

Elsie chuckled. "Yes, what could you mean, Mr. Honeycutt? Are you trying to say Vixen is troublesome?"

Somehow Daniel managed to sidestep the entire conversation. Instead of answering, he asked Elsie to pass the strawberry preserves that JoJo had brought. He turned the topic back to the fine strawberry pie Molly had made the night before while spreading jam on his bread.

Later, when Daniel had saddled both his horse and the mare, Molly noted that he offered Vixen some sugar cubes that he must have taken from the breakfast table. The mare accepted them eagerly and without rancor. Daniel offered Molly a satisfied grin and offered to help the two girls to the saddle.

"I can manage," Molly protested.

"So can I," Daniel countered.

In the next instant, he clasped her waist and lifted her effortlessly. Molly felt her heart flutter. She fixed her gaze on some distant point on the horizon to avoid meeting his eye. Next, he settled Elsie on the saddle behind Molly. The girl wrapped her arms around Molly and laughed with girlish excitement.

"I've only been to Bethany Springs a couple of times," Elsie said. "When my gran brought me to stay with my uncle."

Daniel and Molly exchanged a lingering look as they set off down the road.

"Why did your grandmother bring you here?" he asked gently.

"Gran was in a bad way. The doc said it was her heart. Said that Gran didn't have long for this world. She gave my Uncle Dwight some money to take care of me. A month later, she passed on."

Molly knew the story. Elsie had told her the night Molly found her sleeping in the shed. Elsie's grandmother had cared for the girl since she was a baby. What had happened to Elsie's parents was uncertain. The elderly woman had paid her son to watch over the girl a short time before the mine's collapse.

"Where's your uncle now?" Daniel asked.

"Not quite sure," Elsie said with her usual cheer. "They lit off after the accident to look for work. He said they'd be back to collect me once he was settled. They're taking longer than I expected, probably because his new wife doesn't much care for me."

Daniel's gaze darkened. Molly could tell he was as appalled as she'd been when she first heard the story. Elsie talked of her uncle's return with the utmost certainty. Her childish innocence and faith hurt Molly's heart.

"Lucky for me," Molly said lightly, "Elsie is a delight and has been good company while my family is away. A perfect treasure."

Elsie chuckled and tightened her arms around Molly's middle to give her a gentle hug.

They made their way along the mountain trail just as the morning mist lifted. The trail led past the mine and Molly couldn't help feeling a wave of apprehension as they drew close to the mine opening. The shaft was quiet now. Nothing but boulders and debris, the remnants of the explosion that had caused so much chaos and havoc.

Elsie, as usual, was a chatterbox, carrying on about what had happened that terrible day. How everyone knew that it was Molly's father who had saved the injured men.

Molly said nothing. She didn't want to think of her father descending into the shaft, risking life and limb. The men he'd carried out of the mine had since recovered. Her father, however, still suffered from his injuries. She prayed the mineral waters would restore his health.

They made their way down to the town of Bethany Springs. Daniel said little other than to comment on the changing seasons. While they still had some cold nights, the spring edged closer to summer. Warm breezes carried the scent of flowers. Even the cactus bloomed. Bees buzzed around the bright yellow blossoms.

When they got to town, Molly and Elsie went directly to the mercantile. Daniel tended to the horses. He rode his gelding and led Vixen to Mr. Armstrong's livery.

The mercantile was busy. Molly and Elsie had to wait for several shoppers to pass through the door before they could enter. Molly glanced over her shoulder and spied Daniel talking to an older lady.

Daniel took off his hat and kissed the woman on the cheek.

Elsie explained that the woman was Daniel's mother, Amelia Honeycutt.

Molly couldn't help staring. Amelia Honeycutt. She'd heard the name often but had never seen her in the flesh. And here she was, the woman who owned so much of Bethany Springs along with the Presidio Mine. To Molly's surprise, the woman turned to fix her gaze on Molly and Elsie. Molly felt her face warm under the woman's scrutiny.

Another woman stepped out of the livery door. She was every bit as elegant and refined. Molly shrank back, wishing she could hide from the women's curious gaze.

Surely Daniel wouldn't tell his mother or anyone else that he'd stayed the night in the Collins' shed. A shiver of dismay rippled down Molly's spine. She turned away, stepped into the mercantile and retreated inside to escape the attention of Amelia Honeycutt.

Chapter Nineteen
Miss Sophie's Curiosity

Daniel

Daniel rode to the livery. He heard someone call his name and almost didn't recognize the person calling him was his mother. He had two good reasons for the small mistake. For one, he was lost in thought, mulling over the topic of Molly Collins.

Second, Mama rarely wore a dress. Almost never, much to the dismay of her dear, childhood friend, Miss Sophie. No, Mama preferred trousers. Ranchers, even lady-ranchers, didn't have time for the fuss and bother of fancy frocks. Anytime Daniel spied Mama in a dress, she was either on her way to the bank or to spend the day with her childhood friend, Sophie McCord.

Today, Mama wore a light blue dress that she'd owned since Daniel could remember. She also wore a bonnet that matched the trim of her dress and was just as old. Miss Sophie was dressed in an elegant frock, one that was likely new. She liked her fancy clothes. The fancier, the better.

Both ladies eyed him with a curious gaze.

Daniel doffed his cowboy hat and bid Mrs. McCord a polite hello. "Nice to see you, Miss Sophie."

She snickered. "It's been an age since I've seen you, Daniel Honeycutt. Where have you been keeping yourself?"

Before Daniel could answer, a barn hand took the gelding and mare from him and led them away. Daniel told another youth that he'd be back for the horses in an hour or two. He wanted them untacked, stabled with hay and buckets of fresh water.

The sidewalk was crowded with cowboys and town folk. Daniel ushered the ladies out of the flow of passersby.

"I had been staying at the ranch. The last week or so, I've been working on Presidio affairs." He turned his hat in his hands, noting the frayed rim. Had Molly noted the worn Stetson? Shaking off the notion, he returned his attention to Miss Sophie, who eyed him with curious interest.

He laughed nervously. "Mostly I've been trying to stay out of trouble and keep my mama happy."

Sophie smiled at him. "I wish my three sons tried half as hard as you Honeycutt boys. You know, the other day I had to go to Uvalde to bail out one of those rascals?"

Daniel wondered which one of the boys got into trouble. He'd grown up with the McCord boys and gotten into a fair number of scrapes with the wild bunch. Before he could ask, Miss Sophie went on.

"Why don't you come and visit your Aunt Sophie every so often? I miss seeing my boys. And by that I don't mean my *own* boys."

She sighed dramatically. "They're more trouble than I can manage. I'm not sure where I went wrong. I'd rather spend a little time with some nicely behaved young men like the Honeycutt brood. Next time your mama wants to come for a visit, why not come along and bring your rascally brothers?

I'll make those tea cookies you're fond of. Robert can smoke a brisket or two. I'd sure like to catch up."

Catch up? Daniel doubted that very much. More likely, Miss Sophie wanted to give him a talk about settling down once and for all. She'd pester him about marriage, then she'd grumble about her own dastardly sons. The last thing he wanted was to catch up with Miss Sophie, especially if his mother joined in on the conversation. Together, the two ladies were formidable. He'd rather venture unawares into a hive of honeybees, a nest of water moccasins, or a thicket of mesquite.

He coaxed his lips to a polite smile. "Yes, ma'am."

Mama narrowed her eyes. "What are you doing in town? I just got your note that you were staying up near the mine for a few days." She peered into the Armstrong livery to study the two horses the barn hand untacked in the aisle. "That's a mighty pretty little mare. Where did you find her?"

"She belongs to the Collins girl. Molly Collins. I brought Molly into town so that she could do some business at the mercantile."

Neither woman spoke. His heart dropped. Why had he mentioned the Collins girl? Why? Mama and Miss Sophie's eyes grew round as plums. Miss Sophie murmured a few indistinct words that sounded like she was on the verge of a slew of pesky, meddling questions. And Mama got the same astonished look in her eyes, like she was preparing a few dozen of her own.

Miss Sophie set her hand on her hip. "Daniel, are you saying that you came to town with a girl?"

"Yes, ma'am."

Her lips curved into a delighted smile. "Well, I'll be."

"Actually, I came to town with two girls."

This bit of new intelligence made Miss Sophie's smile fade. Mama pressed her lips together into a thin line of disapproval. Miss Sophie said nothing. Daniel could only imagine how much effort this cost her. Clearly, a hundred questions swirled in her mind. Still, she remained quiet and let Mama lead the charge. Which, naturally, she did.

"What's that supposed to mean?" Mama blustered. "*Two* girls? You hardly bother giving the time of day to any single female, despite my best efforts, and now you've come to town with two of them?"

Passersby stared. A couple of youths, leaning against the barbershop doorway, laughed aloud. A cowboy Daniel recognized from the feedstore grinned at him and tipped his hat at the two ladies as he sauntered past.

Daniel spoke. "Yes, ma'am, one of them is just a little gal maybe eleven or twelve, a neighbor of the Collins girl. While Molly Collins is about nineteen or twenty, I'd say. Not exactly sure."

Both ladies watched him with accusatory expressions as if trying to detect some inconsistency in his story.

He started to feel a mite uncomfortable. He tugged at his collar which for some danged reason suddenly itched something fierce.

"What's the girl going to do at the mercantile?" Mama asked.

"She's trying to sell some of her sewing to make ends meet."

Mama look dismayed. "I can hardly stand to hear people having a hard time making ends meet. That danged mine is more trouble than it's worth. I feel just terrible how it's led to hardship. I think I'm getting soft in my old age."

Daniel went on. "I told her that she didn't need to pay rent this month, that I wouldn't collect payments until the mine reopened, but she's a stubborn one. I'm trying to help her out."

Sophie's brows lifted. Her smile returned. "Help her out?"

Daniel felt increasingly uneasy. It was bad enough that his mama was staring at him like he was guilty of some untoward behavior. But add in Miss Sophie and he was facing a whole other level of prickly discomfort.

He didn't want to mislead his mother about staying on the Collins property, of course. On the other hand, he didn't want to risk that someone might overhear the peculiar arrangement. How could he explain politely that the girl needed to be protected without sounding like he had some sly purpose of his own.

Nor did he want to talk about the purported danger that prowled the canyons and trails by the mine, for that would only make Mama worry even more. He was thankful there hadn't been any more trouble. There was a good chance the thieves had moved on to better pickings since most folk around the mine were going through lean times. That didn't mean he planned on leaving his girls to fend for themselves.

Just then, Miss Sophie's eyes got a certain gleam in them that made Daniel even more nervous. Miss Sophie and Mama were friends before the two of them got married, which meant there was never a time that he *didn't* know Miss Sophie. He knew her gestures. He knew her expressions. He understood her pointed looks almost as well as those of his own mother. The two women were as close as sisters.

Miss Sophie smiled, but it was the smile she'd given him when he was a boy of eleven the day that he and his brothers, along with the McCord boys, had shot out the windows of the haybarn and started a small fire in the loft.

There'd been lots of screaming and shouting. Mama had cussed a blue streak, though she'd denied it later. Since Mr. McCord was taking a nap in the back yard, dozing in the hammock, Mama and Miss Sophie took it upon themselves to put out the fire. They'd doused the flames with water, stomped the embers and given the boys a blistering talking-to.

He and his brothers, along with the McCord boys, had a long month of dreary chores Miss Sophie had come up with just to teach all of them a lesson. He saw the same female fury flickering in her eyes. Slowly it faded.

Sophie elbowed his mama in the side. "Why, Daniel, I think it would be nice if you introduced us."

Mama frowned. "What do you mean?"

"Amelia," Miss Sophie said. "Stop being dense. I mean, Daniel ought to introduce us to the girl at the mercantile. I would like to see what her sewing looks like."

Daniel flustered. Miss Sophie was not very forgiving when it came to ladies' garments and whatnot. "I'm not entirely sure if that's a good idea."

Sophie frowned. "I don't know what you mean, it's not a good idea. I always like to see the local handiwork. If I could find a good seamstress, it would save me the trouble of going to Galveston or Houston. Isn't that right, Amelia?"

Mama didn't respond at once, which prompted another elbow nudge from Sophie. "Isn't that right, Amelia?"

Mama still seemed a little incredulous. "Yes, it does sound right," she replied slowly. "Why don't you introduce us, Daniel?"

Daniel tried to suppress a groan. His mother's voice held a certain note of steel, the same type of tone that always meant any sort of argument would meet with a grim end. Still, he knew that Molly would be mortified under the circumstances. He couldn't tolerate the idea of her humiliation.

"How 'bout I bring her to the ranch, Miss Sophie? Along with Mama. We'll have some of your famous tea cookies. She can show off some of her handiwork privately."

Sophie narrowed her eyes, suspecting a trick.

He set his palm over his heart. "It would give me an excuse to call on her."

Inwardly, he grimaced, unsure of his own motives. Mostly, he wanted to shield Molly from a public interrogation. While Molly was made of strong stuff, she had a fragile side too, and he couldn't bear to see her suffer a moment of awkwardness or, Lord forbid, embarrassment.

Miss Sophie nodded and glanced at Mama. It took his mother a moment longer. Finally, she offered a hint of a smile. "All right," she said tentatively. "Perhaps we can take the Collins girl to Sophie's. That way both Sophie and I can visit with her."

Daniel couldn't help feeling a little sorry for Molly, and yet he'd gotten a bit of a reprieve not only for himself but for her as well. He bid the ladies good day, promised to send word of his plans concerning the rental properties by the mine, and set off for the mercantile.

On the way to the shop, he found himself searching the crowds for Molly. Even though he knew she was inside the mercantile, he couldn't help the urge to seek her out. When he reached the mercantile door, he heard her voice, soft and gentle, and he felt tension ease from his shoulders.

There's my girl.

Chapter Twenty
Will You Take this Man in Holy Charity?

Molly

Mrs. Pittman remembered her, of course, and judging from the expression on the woman's face, she wasn't at all pleased to see Molly return with more sewing samples. With hardly a word of greeting or acknowledgment, she checked the bonnets and shirts, probably looking for Molly's tags. When she didn't find any, she gave a discontented harrumph.

Molly winced. She was grateful that Daniel was at the livery and not right there to see Mrs. Pittman turn her nose up at Molly's work. The woman peered at the stitches, muttering about handiwork. Molly's hope faded.

The shopkeeper couldn't decide what she liked less, Molly's sewing or Elsie's flitting about the shop. The girl chatted with other shoppers, offered suggestions on their purchases, and comforted a fussy baby belonging to a harried young mother. While Elsie went about things in her usual cheerful manner, Mrs. Pittman's dour manner offered a stark contrast.

"I just don't know if we need any bonnets," Mrs. Pittman grumbled. "They seem a little fancy for my customers."

Molly could hardly summon the words to argue about the value of her pieces. She stood stiffly, praying the woman would change her mind. Instead, the shopkeeper studied the bonnets with a look that bordered on contempt.

"Besides, I don't know if I want to do business with someone from a mining family."

This wasn't the first time Molly had met with prejudice. When a mining community sprang up around a successful operation, the newcomers were often viewed with disdain by the folks who'd always lived there. Molly had heard various insults over the years. Grubby miners. Dirty prospectors. Filthy scavengers.

It was clear that her efforts would amount to nothing. Yet again. Wordlessly, she began to gather her samples. Mrs. Pittman folded her arms and regarded her with cool disdain.

Suddenly, Mrs. Pittman's demeanor changed, and it changed quickly. It happened when Daniel Honeycutt stepped into the mercantile. Molly heard his entry. The doorbell jangled. His deep voice echoed across the mercantile as he greeted a neighbor. A moment later, he strode down the aisle, stopping beside Molly. He locked eyes with her, offered a gentle smile, and gave the shopkeeper a quick nod.

"Howdy," he said, removing his worn Stetson. "Nice to see you again, Mrs...."

"Pittman."

"Right. Beg your pardon, ma'am. I don't get to town too often."

"Is she with you?" Mrs. Pittman asked in disbelief.

"She is," Daniel replied a tad gruffly.

Mrs. Pittman's brows lifted. "Well, then. That certainly changes matters. I'd be more than happy to sell your lovely samples if you'd be so kind as to leave them."

The shopkeeper promptly offered almost twice what Molly had asked to begin with. Part of that troubled Molly. Was the woman offering charity? She never liked to accept money that wasn't earned. Despite her misgivings, she accepted the payment with a silent prayer of gratitude. She tucked the earnings into her purse and left the shop at Daniel's side with Elsie skipping close behind.

Molly's heart fairly sang at the money she'd gotten. If the bonnets sold well, she might earn a little more next month which might convince Papa that she could make enough money to support them both.

Soon the boys would be on their way to the military academy, lessening her expenses. The thought brought a pang of longing. As much as her brothers tormented her, she'd missed them terribly since they'd left for the hot springs.

Elsie sensed her relief. She smiled brightly and took Molly's hand in hers.

Which prompted Molly's worries to begin all over again. What would become of the sweet, curious, and talkative girl? Molly was certain her family wouldn't return but couldn't bear to say the words. Elsie was sure they'd come back. Why wouldn't they?

From the mercantile, the trio walked from shop to shop, eyeing the goods in the windows, stopping here and there to say hello to folks. Molly knew few people in the town of Bethany Springs. Many of the town folk knew Daniel. What was even more surprising, even more people seemed to know Elsie.

"I'd like to spend a little of my earnings. What do you two say I buy some lunch for the three of us?" Molly asked.

Elsie spoke. "Can we take our lunch with us, and stop along the way to have a picnic?"

Before Molly could reply, Daniel shared his thoughts. "Sounds like a mighty fine idea. All except for the part of you paying for lunch, Molly. I've never had a young lady pay for my meal, not once in my whole life, and I don't intend to start now."

His tone, quiet but unyielding, showed he would tolerate no arguments. The matter was closed. Molly didn't disagree. Instead, she quietly went along with his bossy and altogether ornery declarations. They stopped to buy sandwiches, some cookies, and a jar of sweet tea at a lunch counter near the mercantile.

They took the road out of town, riding side by side. Daniel told Elsie about the day he'd first met Molly and how Vixen had torn his shirt. Elsie laughed at his retelling, adding in details that Molly had shared.

Just outside of Bethany Springs, they stopped at a sunny spot by the Bethany River. Without a blanket to sit on, Daniel directed them to a few large flat rocks on the riverbank where they ate their lunch. Molly took in the sight of the sparkling waters and thought of her father and brothers. According to the letter, they'd return in a few days' time. She prayed that the spring waters would heal her father's injuries.

She dearly wished that Papa would return without pain. And yet, she hoped his healing wouldn't lead to him working at the Presidio Mine. She considered her dilemma, trying to fathom an answer to her troubles. Did she want her father well, even at the risk of him returning to the mines? If only she could find a way to make enough money so he wouldn't have to work.

After they finished eating, Daniel showed Elsie how to skip rocks across a quiet stretch of the gentle stream. To his plain surprise, Elsie was an expert. The slight girl easily skipped stones across the smooth expanse of water, a good four or five skips each try.

Daniel looked abashed but grinned as Elsie outdid his best efforts.

"Glad my brothers aren't here to see me get shown up by a puny girl," he muttered.

"Skipping rocks is the only thing Uncle Dwight ever taught me," Elsie said wistfully. "He always said that girls just needed to cook and hold their tongue, and how come I couldn't do either?"

Molly hadn't ever met Elsie's uncle, but she didn't think much of the man. Or his wife. Thankfully, the girl didn't seem very troubled by his words. Elsie sat on a rock and took off her shoes and socks and waded into the water, yelping at the cold.

"I'm just going in till the water reaches my ankles," she called over her shoulder.

Daniel chuckled. "Mind you don't step on a crawdad."

She giggled but kept her attention fixed on the sandy river bottom.

Daniel and Molly strolled along the bank, both keeping a wary eye on Elsie. Large trees grew at the water's edge, their branches reaching almost to the middle of the stream. Their roots grew toward the water but buckled and twisted along the way.

Daniel took her elbow as she stepped over a span of gnarled roots. "Watch the knees," he said softly.

Molly was so surprised by his comment, she almost lost her footing. He tightened his hold and set his other hand on the small of her back. When he'd safely squired her past the massive tree, he released her.

Warmth washed over her cheeks. "What did you mean by watch my knees?"

He smiled and clasped his hands behind his back. "I did not say a word about your knees."

She blushed and laughed nervously. Glancing back at Elsie, she wished the girl had walked with them. If she were nearby, Daniel would likely not talk about anything scandalous.

Daniel stopped beside a tree and patted the trunk. "This is a Montezuma cypress. They grow near rivers for the most part. Their roots like to twist and knot."

Molly, feeling foolish, didn't reply but nodded. The roots were indeed twisted.

"Folks call their roots 'knees'."

She shook her head and gave him an apologetic look.

He sobered as he crossed his arms and leaned against the tree. "I wanted to ask you about something different."

"All right." Molly was grateful for the change in topic. "Ask what you will."

He directed his gaze toward Elsie and grew thoughtful. Molly took the opportunity to admire his handsome profile and strong, steadfast presence. Her heart skipped a beat. Her breath caught for an instant as she waited and wondered what he wanted to talk about. Her silly hopes soared with the notion he'd want to say something about *her*.

He didn't.

"I don't believe," he said, "that Elsie's uncle is coming back."

"I don't either."

"We could take her in. You and me."

Molly felt the air leave her with a huff. She swayed a bit before gathering her wits and shaking off her surprise. "What now?"

"I've been dead set against marriage but I'm starting to think it might not be all bad."

Molly bristled. "Not all bad?"

"Don't you want to get married?"

"Not at all. I intend to care for my father, and most husbands would resent their wife doting on a father instead of them."

"Not me. I'd like the idea of doing a good deed."

Molly stared, hardly daring to say a word. A good deed? Marriage?

Daniel pushed off the tree. "If I married you, I could care for you and your father and Elsie."

"You want to marry?" Molly murmured. "Me?"

"I wasn't looking to get married, but my ideas have changed."

She wondered briefly if he might be toying with her but discarded the idea just as quickly. Daniel was reserved and reticent, not the kind of man who made such offers easily. She wondered how on earth the two of them had gotten to this astonishing conversation.

A whoop of joy came from Elsie. The girl waded upstream amidst the shimmering waves, looking very much like she was in deeper than her ankles. The hem of her dress skimmed the top of the water.

"Minnows!" she shouted. "Sure do wish I had a bucket."

Molly was struck by the sight of the girl so filled with joy, so innocent, so utterly unaware of her precarious predicament. If Molly could help her, she would, but what if helping Elsie came at the expense of helping her father? And how could she consider marriage? Much less to a man she scarcely knew.

Her heart raced as she tried to summon a proper reply. Daniel smiled as he pushed off the tree and closed the distance between them. She wanted to retreat, to turn away and gain some distance, but she stayed still.

Taking her hand in his, he held it while covering it with his other palm. "You ought to marry me, Molly. It would be a good thing for both of us, Elsie, your father and maybe your brothers too."

Molly wondered if she might swoon, right there on the riverbank, probably tumbling onto the tree's elbows or knees or whatever the case.

He brushed a kiss across her hand. "I like the idea of a good deed. Sort of like doing a little charity."

Charity. Had Daniel just proposed to her and mentioned the word *charity*? She tugged her hand from his. His brows lifted. His lips thinned. She retreated several steps, turned, and strode up the riverbank to where Elsie splashed in the shallows.

Chapter Twenty-One
The Warmth of a Good Fire

Daniel

The three of them left the riverbank and rode home in silence. Even Elsie was quiet, glancing this way and that as if trying to understand why Molly and he might be out of sorts. She rode behind Molly, her arms wrapped around Molly's waist.

She directed a few questioning looks his way, but Daniel didn't offer any explanation. He was too busy reproaching himself for his rash proposal. He'd offended Molly. Of course he had.

This wasn't the first time Daniel had proposed to a young lady. A few years before, he asked for Cordelia's hand. Back then, he recalled how much he dreaded the moment. In retrospect, he had to admit he'd proposed just to make his mother happy. She'd been so sure of the match. Cordelia hadn't been surprised in the least by his proposal. If anything, she was a tad disgruntled that he had taken so long.

Daniel had been certain to do things the proper way. He'd bought a ring. He'd asked permission from Cordelia's father. He'd gone down on one knee.

He'd done none of that with Molly. Not one thing. He'd proposed without a single shred of preparation or thought of what was fitting.

Why that was, he couldn't say. He rushed in like a fool without going about things in a way that might please the romantic notions of a young lady. What he should have done, for starters, was ask Mr. Collins for permission.

He knew that now. Perhaps that was why Molly was so exasperated and scarcely speaking to him. They rode home from the river with hardly a word. Molly looked terribly upset and on the verge of tearing up.

As if sensing some sort of disharmony, Elsie sprang to the rescue and spoke in glowing terms about Molly's father and how he had saved eight or nine injured miners the night of the accident, only stopping when he himself was hurt.

The topic seemed to make Molly more distraught.

Elsie forged on. "Everybody says that Mr. Collins should manage the mine. That he knows more about safety and building supports for shafts than any other man up here on the mountain."

That seemed to get Molly's attention. She shook her head. "No. I don't want my father to work in the mines. He's had good ideas for a long time now, but the mine owners never want to spend the money to do things properly. That's the reason we wind up moving every year or two. Because mine owners won't do the right thing."

Daniel heard the accusation in her tone and couldn't help defending his family. "My mother wants to do everything in a safe way, or not do them at all. I understand that you might not believe me. You have your own ideas. And who could blame you? After all, your father suffered grave injuries in the mine that belonged to my family."

"It's not my business to run the Presidio Mine," Molly said quietly. "But my father's well-being is very much my business."

He nodded, offering a conciliatory smile. "Of course. I'd feel the same about my mother. Family is everything."

"I don't want Papa to work at all if I can help it. Certainly not down an unsafe mining shaft. I couldn't bear to lose my father or one of my brothers."

Daniel heard the tremble in Molly's voice.

"Even though Papa loves the work. Papa loves any work, really. He's never content to stay still for too long, but he especially loves mining. Nothing excites him more than the prospect of finding a new silver deposit. Even if he won't see any of the profit, he still thrills at the wonder of discovery."

Elsie grew thoughtful. "You want him to quit work, but it seems he ought to work, especially if he can make the mine safer for other miners."

"I can't tolerate the risk," Molly said. "Or the danger. Or the worry."

Elsie murmured, voicing a small sound of disagreement.

"What is it?" Molly asked, turning to look over her shoulder. "Just say what's on your mind, Elsie McKittrick."

Elsie looked sheepish. "My gran liked to say worry was an invitation to prayer. With prayer, we could let God manage our fears. That's probably why Gran wasn't afraid of much of anything. Not even the idea of dying. When she got sick, she didn't fret. She only wanted to make sure I was cared for. Outside of that, she didn't worry at all. Gran declared she was ready to meet her Lord and Savior."

Daniel smiled. "Your grandmother sounds like a wise woman."

Elsie said nothing but her eyes shone with unspent tears.

By the time they returned to the cabin it was dusk, and Elsie had fallen asleep. She'd worn herself out playing in the stream, or so it seemed, and a short distance from the house, she'd dozed off, slumping against Molly's shoulder. Molly clasped the girl's hands to keep her from shifting and possibly tumbling off the saddle.

In the quiet of the evening, she and Daniel shared a few tender smiles about nothing at all. Molly wondered if he might revisit the topic of marriage. She wondered, too, if she might be swayed by his words. Each time he looked at her with that soft light in his eyes, her heart skipped a beat.

When they got home, he took the mare, tied her to the railing and lifted Elsie gently from the saddle. They left the horses by the shed and Daniel carried Elsie up to the cabin, where Molly showed him the girl's room. Really, the room belonged to her brothers, but Elsie had made it her own in just a few short days. Molly wasn't sure what would happen when her family returned but resolved to deal with matters then.

She tucked a blanket around the sleeping girl. A rumble of thunder drew a murmur of surprise from her lips. Daniel lifted his brow with surprise.

"A storm," she said softly. "I didn't see dark clouds on the horizon."

"I hadn't noticed either," he replied.

They stood at the foot of Elsie's bed, regarding each other with amazement. Molly had been lost in thought on the way home and hadn't noticed the signs of an impending storm. The bad weather snuck up because they were preoccupied. They stood on opposite sides of the bed, the sleeping girl between them.

Daniel spoke first. "I'll tend to the horses and start a fire."

Molly nodded. "I should gather my washing from the line before it rains."

They parted ways. Molly found a basket and hurried out the back door of the cabin, where, in the semi-darkness, she began to gather the wash. First was Elsie's dress followed by her own clothes and underthings. Thunder drew near. Lightning split the darkened sky. The air grew chilled as a north wind gusted, making the laundered clothes snap in the breeze.

Molly worked quickly trying to gather the washing. Despite her best efforts, she could not escape when a drenching, frigid rain began to fall. Rain pelted her, soaking her dress, and dousing her hair. The rain fell with such force against her face and neck that she winced as she finished her task. By the time she managed to return to the back door, her dress was soaked.

Daniel met her at the door with a fierce scowl. "I called but couldn't find you."

Molly ducked inside the door, hurrying past him. "I didn't think it would begin to rain. I could not bear to leave the clothes out on the line, not after I worked so hard to wash them this morning. Besides Elsie needs a fresh dress to wear, especially after playing along the muddy riverbank."

"I could have collected it for you."

"Hardly," she exclaimed. "I couldn't allow you to take my clothing from the line. What do you take me for?"

She hurried away, eager to escape his dark glare.

Daniel followed a few steps behind. He offered to take the basket from her, but she refused his help, setting the basket instead on a nearby table. He stalked past, went to the fireplace, and crouched by the blaze, grumbling about her obstinate ways.

Molly went to check on Elsie. She found the girl deep in a restful slumber, clearly asleep for the night. Molly managed to help her out of her sodden dress and into one of her own flannel winter nightgowns, a gown that was miles too big for the girl but would serve the purpose of keeping her warm.

By the time she returned to the parlor, her own damp dress had chilled her to the bone, making her teeth chatter. Daniel looked even more incensed by her chattering teeth and violent shivering than he had a few moments ago when he couldn't find her. He took a blanket from a nearby chair, wrapped it around her shoulders and demanded she sit in front of the fireplace to warm herself. Molly was too cold to argue.

When he had the fire built to a roaring blaze, he took a chair across from her. By this time, his furious expression had softened somewhat, probably because she was no longer trembling from the cold.

"I'm sorry," he said.

His words startled her. She waited for him to say more, but he turned his attention to the flames and grew silent. Was he sorry that he'd fussed at her just now, or sorry that he'd proposed to her earlier that afternoon?

Although she had been mortified earlier and deeply wounded by his comments about charity, the idea that he regretted the proposal troubled her even more. Neither spoke. Molly thought of Elsie sleeping in her brothers' room. If only the girl were here to keep them company, warming herself by the cheerful fireplace, then Daniel and Molly wouldn't have to suffer through this agonizing silence.

The storm, a spring squall, drummed rain down on the roof, but didn't last more than a half-hour at most. As the rain lessened, and the thunder faded, Molly wondered if Daniel wouldn't leave her soon and bed down in the shed.

Reproaching herself, she realized that of course he would soon leave. He was a decent and upstanding gentleman and would not overstay his welcome in the cabin. If anything, he might be eager to retreat to the quiet shed to escape any uncomfortable conversation.

Her heart sank. She quite enjoyed sitting near the growling bear of a man, soaking up the heat of the fire he'd built for her and Elsie. Time spent with Daniel felt like a sort of reprieve. He cared for her in his own, bossy way and she found comfort from his attention. She shouldn't want him to stay longer but couldn't help the surge of some unnamed yearning.

He spoke finally, lifting the burden of strained silence.

"I was worried," Daniel said, somewhat abashed. "There's a large tree felled on the other side of the shed."

Molly wondered what that had to do with her.

Daniel went on. "When I called for you and you didn't answer, I was troubled. I worried the storm had caused more damage, that you might need me." He stared into the fire. The flames cast a golden light across his features.

He went on. "I've never felt that way about anyone before except for my own flesh and blood, of course."

"You've never felt that way before? I just assumed you had many lady friends," Molly said awkwardly. Instantly, she regretted her words. Could she have said anything more foolish, more desperate?

"No, ma'am." A smile tugged at his lips, much to her relief. "Times I reckon that I scare them off," he added.

"Perhaps because you growl like a bear."

"I don't growl." His smile widened. "Unless I'm faced with an ornery young lady."

She gave him an answering smile, grateful to be back on familiar territory. The back and forth, the playful banter, she found easy and even a little entertaining, truth be told.

Daniel went on. "I always believed I scare them off because of my scars and my eye patch."

She wanted to offer a vigorous objection but didn't want to interrupt.

"I was engaged once before, but the girl said she couldn't abide marrying a man who looked like me. I got injured, you see, after I proposed. And the young lady didn't approve of my rough looks."

Molly listened with a heavy heart. To think a woman would discard a man because of his injuries. Dear heavens, did he suspect that was why she had rejected his offer of marriage?

"How long ago did that happen?" she asked.

He shrugged. "It doesn't really matter."

"It matters if she broke your heart."

Molly held her breath, unsure what to hope for. Of course, she didn't want Daniel to have suffered heartache. Nor did she want to think of him pining for another girl. What if he still carried some warm feelings for the girl who had so cruelly rejected him?

"Daniel, the first time I laid eyes on you, I thought you were terribly handsome, and not just because you had rescued me from a runaway horse." She was astounded by her own forthrightness. Her heart raced. Never had she spoken so freely with a man.

He directed his gaze her way. "I intend to marry you."

Molly drew a sharp breath.

Daniel went on. "You may deny me, but I will only work harder to show you that I am a worthy man. And that you and

I could make a good life together." He got to his feet. "I ought to take my leave. I can't bear to think of you sitting in that damp dress. I'll see myself out. You let me know if you need anything. Anything at all."

Molly got to her feet to face him. "Thank you, Daniel. I'm grateful that you're here. Please understand that my circumstances are uncertain. I have a duty to my family. Especially my father who might spend the rest of his days as an invalid."

"Oh, I understand, Molly Collins. There are always plenty of circumstances that will try to thwart our romance, but I won't relent."

Molly stared at him with disbelief. Elsie's words about romance rang in her mind. How many times had the girl spoken of Daniel as being *terribly* romantic?

Daniel took his hand in hers and lifted it to his lips. He brushed a gentle kiss across her wrist. The sensation sent shimmers down her frame. Her thoughts spun. Her heart raced.

For a long moment, she and Daniel stood less than half a pace away from each other. She shivered, causing a look of concern to light the depths of his eyes.

He wrapped his arms around her. "You're cold, sweetheart. I can hardly stand to see you shivering so. You ought to change into dry clothes. Can't stand to think of you catching a chill."

Despite his words, he made no move to leave the Collins' cabin. The look in his eyes suggested some new fervor. She held her breath as he lifted his hand to cup her jaw. Her breath stalled deep in her chest as he lowered as if to offer a kiss. Surely not. And yet, there it was. A kiss. Sweet and chaste, but a kiss that lingered. The touch of his lips sent a burst of warmth across her shivering, chilled frame.

One moment, there had been a glance, and the next, a kiss, and the kiss sent a cascade of wild abandon across her senses. She sank into his arms, clasped his shoulders. Her resistance crumbled. From one moment to the next, she gave herself over, submitting entirely to his strong embrace.

Sinking into his arms, she murmured a soft reply to his unspoken question. "Goodness. I never imagined."

"I never imagined any such thing either," he replied, his breath warming the curve of her neck. "I never dared to hope for anyone like you."

Chapter Twenty-Two
Amelia and JoJo Chat about Molly Collins

Amelia

Amelia Honeycutt made her way up the narrow mountain trail. In her saddlebag, she carried a new report from the Pinkerton Agency. The report revealed that John Collins was the man responsible for rescuing nine men from the collapsed mine. In the process, he had sustained his own injuries and it was for that reason she rode up the mountain trail.

She intended to speak to the man, offer him the top job at the mine and prayed the Collins family didn't plan to pack up and leave Bethany Springs.

While she went up the trail, she was determined to find out more of Daniel's goings-on. Was it too much to hope that the Collins family had remained, and Daniel had grown fond of the Collins girl? She dared not press her luck on that matter.

Still, it was worth the hope. If Daniel took it upon himself to marry, she'd have one less problem, one less boy to threaten with a reduction in wages. Not only that, but it would be easier to convince Zach and Simon to fall into line. Why, Daniel might even offer his support to her cause.

The trail widened, offering her a view of the horizon. She drew a deep breath of the crisp spring air. Sheldon wanted to tag along once again, fretting about all manner of trouble she might meet, but she was grateful for the solitude. The only sounds she heard were her gelding's hooves on the trail and various birds flitting amongst the groves of oaks and elm.

Riding past a trio of cabins, she noted with dismay that all three appeared vacant. She shook her head with irritation. No matter. She'd find new workers. As soon as word spread about the mine reopening and the new, higher wages she intended to pay, she'd have plenty of miners. She'd pay them well and supply homes for all of them.

The workers and their families would be content to live and work in Bethany Springs for years to come.

As she came around the turn, she spotted a young girl walking with a basket. It appeared to be the Ward girl. The girl's name didn't come to mind. The family had moved to Bethany Springs two or three years ago. They owned their own home, so she rarely had the opportunity to visit with them, but she recalled that the girl was a gifted musician.

Amelia called out a greeting. "Hello, there. Aren't you Trina Ward's daughter?"

The girl spun around with a cry of surprise. "Yes, ma'am."

"I thought so. Forgive me but I've forgotten your name."

"My name is Josephine, but everyone calls me JoJo."

Amelia smiled at the pretty girl and admired her dark glossy hair tied with a bright ribbon. She recalled that JoJo was the Wards' only child. Everything about the girl spoke of parents who doted on her.

Amelia had been an only child too. Her parents had her late and liked to say she'd been the little angel they never imagined. They'd indulged her, spoiled her, wanting only the best for their little unexpected blessing.

Mother and Father would certainly be surprised to see how things turned out. She was hardly the little darling they'd done everything to protect. The piano lessons, the dance instruction and trips abroad hadn't served her in the way her parents had hoped. Instead, she'd gone and married a Texas cowboy. Then the war came, took almost everything from her and left her with a broken heart.

After George passed, Mother and Father quickly followed.

Now she was a widow who never touched her piano and could hardly remember how to dance. Most days she spent in trousers, riding across her property to check the fence or a distant herd. Instead of serving tea to society ladies that morning, she rode up a mountain path, fixing to hire a man to run her silver mine. What would her dear, kindly parents think of her now?

The memories sent a pang through her heart.

She turned her attention to the Ward girl. "Where are you off to on this fine day?"

"I'm going to see my best friend."

"And who would that be?"

"Her name is Molly Collins."

"Well, I declare! That's exactly where I'm headed. I need to speak to her father, about a matter concerning the Presidio Mine."

The girl's eyes lit with interest, and Amelia could tell she yearned to ask more. The effort to remain quiet was clear in the way she pressed her lips together.

"I'm sure you're wondering, just like everyone else, when we intend to open the mine," Amelia said as she caught up with the girl.

"Yes, ma'am."

They walked along the widening, sun dappled path.

Amelia, pleased for the company, spoke of her intentions. "I plan to open the mine in the next week, but that decision depends on if I can hire Mr. Collins."

The girl's eyes widened, brimming with curiosity.

Amelia went on. "I've learned a thing or two about John Collins. How he knows a great deal about mine safety. How he's studied different practices just out of pure personal interest. I'd like to hire him to run the mine."

Amelia didn't add any other details she'd learned, such as how, over the years, Mr. Collins had been dismissed from several other mining operations. He'd quit some outfits on his own accord, all on account of their poor regard for safety measures. He was a stubborn fellow, that particular detail did not trouble her. Not if he was principled.

JoJo's brows lifted. "My mother wouldn't like me talking about any of this, but I understand Mr. Collins is a very smart man."

"I appreciate you saying that, but why wouldn't your mother want you to say such a thing?"

"She grouses about how everyone's gone on and on about what a fine, upstanding man he is. How he helped so many men who were trapped in the rubble. Why, he even helped my father get out of the collapsed mine shaft. Father wasn't injured but he was a mite confused amidst all the noise and mayhem."

As they walked along the trail, the girl chattered about the Collins family, Molly Collins' fine sewing and the girl who was staying at the Collins home. JoJo said she had a letter for the girl, one that looked to be from her kinfolk.

"Elsie thinks her uncle and his wife are coming back for her, but I'll bet the letter says otherwise."

"That so?"

"Yes, ma'am. The uncle was never too keen on Elsie." Amelia got the impression JoJo didn't care much for the girl either. She wanted to ask more about Elsie but couldn't get a word in edgewise. JoJo saved the best for last, finishing off her lengthy speech with the most interesting detail of all.

"I learned something about Molly," JoJo said, a blush rising to her cheeks. "Something quite surprising. Something I would have imagined she would have shared with me on account of us being such good friends."

Amelia grumbled. "Good friends will disappoint you in that way. I remember when my friend Sophie didn't bother telling me about her little fainting spells. She didn't want to trouble me or cause me any worry which, of course, only made things worse. Thankfully, it was just a matter of eating regularly, the silly goose."

JoJo gave her a sympathetic look.

"What can you do?" Amelia asked. "Friends can at times be pesky nuisances, then turn around, surprise you with some kind tender gesture that reminds you of all their fine qualities, the very reason you've loved them so long. It's the nature of friendship."

The girl blinked. Amelia sighed. "Don't keep me waiting. I can hardly stand the suspense. Tell me what you learned about Molly Collins."

"Yesterday evening, just after sunset, I ventured to the Collins house to check on Molly, seeing as she's staying there alone with that McKittrick girl for company and we just had us a fine storm."

Amelia had the distinct impression that the girl was drawing out the story for dramatic effect. She bit her tongue as the girl waxed on.

"I wanted to peek in on her to say hello, and also to bring her some peaches from our orchard."

"That was mighty nice of you."

The girl smiled with satisfaction before going on. "I was just about to knock on her door, when what do I see through the window, but Molly Collins kissing a *man*."

Amelia drew a sharp breath and turned her gaze to the girl. Was she speaking truthfully? Perhaps she was making things up.

The girl lowered her voice. "Molly kissed a stranger!"

"So you said," Amelia replied. "What happened next?"

"I couldn't see who he was, because he had his back to me, but it was clear the man was no stranger to Molly Collins."

The girl snickered at her own joke. Amelia's heart fluttered with excitement for she had strong suspicions about the stranger kissing Molly Collins. Heavens. Could this be the answer to her prayers?

She didn't say anything for a long moment as her mind spun wild, fanciful notions of her eldest son finally settling down with a sweet girl. In her mind, she imagined a wedding and a fine house for the new family, not the cramped cabin where Daniel lived.

Why, it was even possible that by this time next year, Daniel and Molly could, Lord willing, have a little one of their own. One of her boys would finally make Amelia a grandmother. The idea left her speechless with sweet anticipation.

JoJo went on. "I shouldn't say anything to anyone, of course. Molly is my friend. I wouldn't want people to tell tales. I want her to know that I'm good at keeping secrets."

Amelia nodded. "Right, that's important."

The girl went on with breathless excitement. "And I *am* good at keeping secrets. It's the folks I tell things to who don't understand how to keep secrets."

Amelia managed to suppress a smile. "I hear you. Don't you just hate that?"

JoJo nodded vigorously.

"I wouldn't want folks talking about Molly kissing strangers. They might think she doesn't have any morals. Which she does, I'd like everyone to know."

Amelia frowned. Her thoughts of grandbabies faded as a worry formed in her mind. Depending on how many people this little busybody had told, there might be all sorts of scandalous gossip about the Collins girl.

She shifted in her saddle, wishing she could give Daniel a lecture or two or three. How could he put a young lady in that position? Hadn't she raised her boys to treat ladies with kid gloves? To always protect their reputation and virtue?

The girl carried on. "Course I didn't knock on the door. I left right away, well, almost right away. I tried for a few minutes to see the man's face, but I never could, so I hurried home."

"My word! And where is Mr. Collins during all of this?"

"Oh, Mr. Collins isn't home. He traveled to Bethany Hot Springs with his two boys on account of his injuries. Mr. Armstrong invited them, hoping the mineral springs would help him mend so Molly wouldn't leave Bethany Springs to open a dress shop in Galveston."

"Augustus Armstrong?"

"Yes, ma'am. Mr. Armstrong and Mr. Collins are friends."

"Is that so?" Amelia prided herself on knowing about all manner of goings-on in Bethany Springs, but she didn't know Mr. Armstrong and Mr. Collins were friends.

JoJo spoke. "They play checkers in the livery whenever Mr. Collins brings Molly to town. He doesn't care to go shopping with her, so he just visits with Mr. Armstrong."

The girl looked very self-satisfied. Was there anything JoJo Ward didn't know? She was a veritable sleuth.

"You, my dear, are a wealth of information! I've been searching for the name of the man who helped rescue the injured miners. I asked around town to no avail. I had to hire a couple of Pinkerton agents to learn of John Collins. I believe I could have done as well if I had simply come up the trail and chatted with *you*, Josephine Ward."

"Thank you." JoJo laughed. Her eyes sparkled with pride. "Thank you, ma'am."

"I believe you might do even better than my high-priced Pinkertons. What say you? Are you willing to help me investigate a few matters?"

JoJo grew solemn. "Yes, ma'am. I'd try to do my best. I'll investigate anything you say, Mrs. Honeycutt. Anything at all."

Chapter Twenty-Three
A Man Needs a Helpmeet

Daniel

Daniel woke early, rose in the predawn darkness, said his prayers, and splashed cold water from the pump over his face. Heavens, he needed a bath and a shave. He felt a little rough and probably looked far worse.

The sun's first rays burned along the horizon. He paused for a long moment to take in the beauty of God's glory. He gave thanks for the new day.

For the first time since he could recall, he had few plans of his own. He simply waited for Molly's reply and he prayed she might accept his offer. If she didn't say yes, he was certain he'd remain a bachelor and that notion didn't agree with him at all. In fact, it left him with a heavy, painful ache in his chest.

Since breakfast was likely a few hours off, he started on various chores. There was plenty to do, probably on account of Mr. Collins being laid up. First, he repaired a corral post. Next, he mended the gate and greased the squeaking hinges. Vixen wandered over to watch.

"You'd best mind your manners," he muttered. "I'm doing all this on your behalf."

The mare nosed his pockets.

"Course I don't have sugar cubes. Heck, I haven't even had my first cup of coffee."

The mare wandered off to a grassy patch to graze.

Daniel worked as the sun rose and continued as it lifted into the clear sky. By the time Elsie called him for breakfast, he'd built up a powerful appetite. She grinned at him as they walked up the path.

"Molly has been up since before dawn."

Daniel grumbled. "I have too. Been thinking of coffee since then."

He'd been thinking of other things too, but it wouldn't be fitting to say how he'd pondered the way Molly felt in his arms, or the memory of her sweet kiss. No, he'd never speak of those yearnings. The memory of Molly's kiss, her honeyed scent, her sweet response, all of that was too closely bound to his hopes and dreams.

Elsie chattered on. "She's been busy as a hive of bees, rushing this way and that. Fussing about making a good breakfast for you."

"That so?" Daniel asked. "For me?"

Elsie stopped when she reached the porch. "Why, sure. I asked what all the fuss was about, but she told me to mind my own beeswax and set the table."

Daniel held back a smile. "I'm sure she usually makes a fine breakfast. She's not doing all that on account of me."

"Well, usually she just makes plain bread or oatmeal. This morning she made sweet rolls with extra cinnamon. I woke up to the smell of spice and sugar."

Daniel's stomach rumbled.

"She had me running to and fro, grumbling all the while. First it was a complaint about how long it took me to get the eggs from the henhouse. I told her that Pepper was out of sorts, but she didn't seem to care. Then she groused about me setting the table all wrong. I wanted to tell her it doesn't matter which side forks go on."

"Don't tell my mother that."

Elsie frowned. "Beg your pardon."

"Forks go on the left, Elsie."

"If you say so, Mr. Honeycutt. Then she got peeved because I hadn't checked in on you when I went to the henhouse."

Daniel felt a glimmer of happiness. "So, she was asking about me?"

Elsie nodded. A smile brightened her face. Her eyes sparked with amusement. "Why, sure, she asked about you."

Daniel had the distinct impression he was being mocked by a tiny, troublesome scrap of a girl. She snickered and tried to hide her amusement behind her hand. Her eyes shone with mirth.

"You're a rascally girl, Elsie McKittrick."

"I'm terribly sorry, Mr. Honeycutt." She lowered her hand but bit her lip to keep from giggling. "Really, I am. I don't mean to tease."

"I don't think you mean to tease. I believe it comes natural," he grumbled as he crossed the porch. "Pesky girl."

She followed a few paces behind him. He knew she was nearby from the sound of her girlish laughter. He had to admit, Elsie's laugh was a sweet sound. He relished the sound of her happiness and hoped he could find a way to make sure she had a good home with people who appreciated her.

They went inside the cabin and found Molly setting food on the table. She looked somewhat harried and worn out despite the early hour. Her dress was rumpled, her face flushed. Her hair, normally neatly arranged, was bound with tattered ribbon, and hung askew. Wisps of hair had sprung loose, framing her pretty face.

Despite her slightly disheveled appearance, or perhaps because of it, Molly looked especially lovely. He stopped in the doorway, removed his hat, and waited, trying his best to battle a sudden rush of awkwardness. Molly stood on the other side of the table, looking as stricken as he felt.

He prayed she didn't regret any of what happened last night.

Elsie wandered around the table, studying the food Molly had prepared. "I was telling Mr. Honeycutt how you had made a special breakfast this morning."

Molly startled. Her cheeks reddened. "It's not special. Just the usual."

Elsie snorted.

Daniel scanned the various plates. He noted the singed, yet limp bacon, the burned eggs, and the scorched potatoes. A hint of acrid smoke drifted from the kitchen. He held out hope that the sweet rolls in the basket had escaped the same fate as the rest of the food.

Clearly, the fire had burned a little hot in the oven. Molly had probably forgotten to adjust the damper. Perhaps she hadn't noticed the time. Either way, the breakfast had burned. He noted a strong urge to point this out but recalled the times he'd mentioned such obvious matters to his mother. She'd gotten a tad miffed. Over time, he'd learned to keep his observations to himself. Women didn't seem to take kindly to menfolk pointing out matters that were clear.

"Breakfast looks mighty good," he said.

Molly let out a breathless laugh. "I thank you for your optimism."

"It's fine," he said gently.

"I was a little distracted this morning," she said.

"I'll say," Elsie muttered. She lifted the embroidered linen to peek inside the basket. Steam rose from the sweet rolls tucked inside the cloth. "My, but the rolls smell good."

Daniel held Molly's gaze from across the table. More than anything, he would have liked to circle the table and draw her into his arms. He imagined holding her, kissing her lips, whispering sweet things to her, promises, hopes and dreams of a life together.

He never imagined he'd change his mind about settling down. But he had. And it had happened in a heartbeat the day he met Molly Collins, the only girl he'd ever known who seemed determined not to get married. Just his dumb luck. He prayed he might change her mind. If he could make her see things his way, the two of them would be happy together. He was sure. Not only that, but if needed, they could offer Elsie a home.

Molly gestured for them to sit and asked Daniel to say a prayer. He offered grace, thanked God for the countless blessings and asked for the good Lord's protection for family, not just his own kin but that of Molly and Elsie. Not that he thought Elsie would ever see her family again. Just the same, he knew they needed prayers as much as anyone. Maybe more.

Molly served breakfast. Daniel was about to begin eating when a knock sounded at the door. A girl peered in the window, prompting a grumble from Elsie.

"JoJo," Elsie muttered. "What does she want?"

As if to answer the question, JoJo pointed at Daniel. He rose, went to the door, and greeted her with a polite hello. "May I help you?"

JoJo recoiled, probably on account of his eye patch and fearsome scars. After a moment, the girl's surprise faded. She gulped and spoke hurriedly. "There's someone to see you, sir. Down by the corral. A lady."

Daniel knew it had to be his mother. Just the same, he didn't want to let on. Certainly not just yet. First off, he needed to find out what she wanted and then he'd introduce her to Molly.

Molly regarded him with wide eyes and waited to hear more.

"Probably family," he said gruffly. He took his leave of Molly and the two girls. He strolled down the path to the corral, bracing himself for a barrage of questions. Mama wouldn't care for him staying overnight on the property of a young, single woman.

As he rounded the shed, he came face to face with his mother.

She stood beside her horse, reins clasped in a gloved hand, her smile radiant. "Daniel, darling."

He winced. That sounded worrisome. She hardly ever Daniel-darlinged him. Only when she wanted something badly.

"I think you have a sweetheart," she proclaimed.

Well, dang. How could she know?

He decided to act dumb. "A sweetheart? I'm just taking care of our workers and their families. That and I'd heard there was a thief prowling around the hills. I felt a duty to take care of the matter. Can't have a bandit preying on innocent families."

"Don't try to change the subject."

"Ma'am?"

"I have it from reliable sources that you've been stealing kisses."

He hardly knew what to say. Every single reply that came to mind sounded bad or drifted into the territory of being a flat-out lie. He prided himself on being truthful and frank, especially with his mother. She had an uncanny ability to sniff out a fib, exaggeration or lie. Mama was like a bloodhound whenever he or his brothers tried to dance around the truth of any troublesome topic.

"Well," she asked. "Did you or did you not kiss Molly Collins?"

"Yes, ma'am." Part of him felt like a youngster about to get chastised. Another part of him realized he didn't care if Mama knew. He'd kissed Molly. He'd kiss her again the next chance he got. "I aim to marry her."

For a long moment, his mother didn't speak. Her expression softened. She drew a soft sigh as she gave him a tender look. In a choked voice, she spoke. "A mother is only as happy as her least-happy child."

Daniel couldn't imagine what she meant. "Least-happy child?"

"One day, Lord willing, you'll understand what I mean. One day when you have your own children."

His heartbeat drummed against his ribs. He'd hardly dare imagine children, not since he'd gotten injured and lost the sight of his eye. But after he'd met Molly, he'd begun to picture a family. Not just any family but one he would share with Molly. The idea warmed his heart and made him wish Molly would change her mind about marriage, sooner rather than later. He'd have to think of a way to persuade her.

Mama smiled wistfully. "Men need a helpmeet."

He couldn't agree more.

His mother went on. "A woman to greet them at the end of the day. You're my firstborn, my constant, kind-hearted son, a man who will be a fine father. You shouldn't be alone. Women can tolerate solitude, but I don't believe men do well on their own. I've prayed that you'd find a good woman to marry."

Daniel's reply remained fixed in his throat. He wanted the same. Molly had softened his stubborn heart. Since he'd met her, he had begun to pray for the very thing his mother spoke of. A family and a helpmeet, a mother for his children, the children he never realized that he wanted.

He'd considered the notion of a wife and family ever since he'd found Molly riding a runaway horse on the outskirts of Bethany Springs. In that moment, he understood why men happily discarded their bachelor ways, why they went from contented loners to lovesick menfolk. It was all on account of that moment when a fella met the one woman who fit. Perfectly.

A sweet woman who called his heart in ways he'd never imagined. The one, single woman.

The *only* one who'd called to his heart.

"I can wait to meet her," his mother said. "Best you talk to her father first."

"Yes ma'am."

"And then I'd like to visit with him a spell. I intend to offer him the job of foreman."

Daniel frowned as he considered this news. He could picture the worry in Molly's eyes. "Molly doesn't want him mining."

His mother mounted her horse. "John Collins won't be working a pick-axe. He'll manage men who wield a pick-axe."

"That so?"

"And I'll give him a percentage ownership. I'll make it worth his while."

She bid him good-bye and trotted down the road, heading back to the ranch.

Chapter Twenty-Four
An Elbow to the Eye

Molly

    Molly half-listened to JoJo's and Elsie's chatter while she tidied the dishes. She knew that neither girl much cared for the other. For that reason, she felt especially grateful to hear them talk to each other in an amiable manner.

    JoJo spoke of her upcoming piano practice that afternoon and how she'd struggled with the new piece. Elsie asked various questions about playing a piano. Was it difficult to learn so many keys? Was it enjoyable to play hour after hour? JoJo needed little prodding to chatter on about her music, her practice and how much her piano meant to her.

    "Do you ever get tired of playing?" Elsie asked.

    "Never. I get frustrated, at times overwrought while playing, but I also have my finest moments sitting at my piano. Maybe I'll show you how to play a tune when I return from music school."

    Molly could hardly believe her ears. Even Elsie seemed stunned, judging from the girl's uncharacteristic silence. JoJo didn't notice and prattled on about all her hopes and dreams being realized on account of heading off to music school. How she hardly dared to hope the school would pick her out of the hundreds of girls applying.

"After I've graduated from the program," JoJo said, "I hope to play piano for a church, either here in Bethany Springs or somewhere nearby. I don't know how my mama will take it but I'm praying the good Lord will give her a little nudge."

Elsie giggled. "I hope so too."

Meanwhile, Molly cleared the dishes and heated water for washing. The girls offered to help, but Molly waved them off. She yearned for a moment alone so she could gather her thoughts. Daniel was down by the corral. Who was this lady who wanted to speak to Daniel?

Molly wasn't exactly sure what to think of that. A lady?

Of course, it could mean anything. Maybe it was one of his tenants. She preferred to think the caller was an elderly, drab woman. Daniel had mentioned family but why wouldn't he invite the family member to the house?

She tried not to picture a *young* lady who might have, for some inexplicable reason, come to call on Daniel. She knew little about courting, but even to her thinking, that sounded untoward. A young lady would hardly seek out a sweetheart. She fretted nonetheless.

She poured the steaming kettle of water into the dishpan. After the water cooled a moment she began washing plates, scrubbing each one while her traitorous mind wandered to notions of Daniel's sweethearts.

It couldn't be, she argued with herself. Daniel told her he didn't have a sweetheart. He was honorable. Noble-hearted. He'd offered for her. Surely, he wouldn't have asked her to marry him if he already had a sweetheart. Surely not.

She scrubbed the dishes as her mind twisted back and forth between the two notions. He loved her. He loved her not. Frustration knotted inside her. She'd never intended to yearn for any man. Her every thought centered around caring for her family, but ever since meeting Daniel, he'd come to mean so much to her.

She rinsed the plates and set them on a dish towel. With a deep sigh, she went back to thinking about the lady who had asked for Daniel. Wiping a stray tear, she laughed softly, imagining how she might sneak around the back of the house to spy on Daniel as he spoke to the lady.

It was silly. Absurd. After all, she couldn't possibly marry Daniel Honeycutt or any other man. She needed to take care of her brothers and father.

Amidst her worries, she noted the silence. A moment ago, the girls had chatted. Now the house was quiet. Her heart thudded. A plate slipped from her hands and shattered. The shards slowly sank to the bottom of the basin. She held her breath as the fine hair on the back of her neck tingled and her breath caught.

The eerie silence weighed down upon her shoulders like a heavy, leaden cloak.

Something was wrong. Terribly wrong. Lifting her hands, she paused to watch the water drip from her fingers. Scarcely able to breathe, she listened intently for a word from the girls but heard nothing. A burst of strength surged through her veins. Swiftly, she moved across the kitchen and rounded the door of the parlor.

She wanted to ask what was amiss, but the question died in her throat.

The girls stood by the fireplace. A young man stood a few paces away. He looked frail, ragged, and desperate. He was young, no more than a few years older than Elsie.

"What do you want?" Molly spoke, her tone even and steady. The words sounded strange to her ear. Hollow. As though they came from someone else. Not her.

"Don't mean to bother you." He gulped. "Ma'am."

"What are you doing here?"

He licked his lips and glanced about. "I'm hungry. Can you give me something to eat?"

Molly blinked. His words gave a bit of relief since she could surely give him food. Still, she felt afraid. Not for herself so much as for JoJo and Elsie. While Elsie didn't appear afraid, JoJo looked as though she was on the verge of fainting. Molly couldn't keep from thinking the worst and wondered if more young men prowled around the cabin.

"His family left," Elsie said quietly. "They left him, and they left his brother too."

Molly watched the boy and noted the look of anguish on his face. He didn't argue the point. Instead, he cast his eyes down and remained silent.

JoJo sank to a chair and stared at the boy with a stricken look. "He's a thief. He's one of the outlaws that have been terrorizing families around the mine."

"Didn't mean to cause trouble," the boy muttered.

"That matter doesn't concern me," Molly said. "I'm happy to share what we have with others."

She returned to the kitchen and packed food in a basket. She regretted the poorly cooked breakfast. Part of it was scorched, the other part was raw. Usually, she managed a little better but had to admit that when she'd prepared the meal, she'd been distracted. To make up for the paltry, charred offerings, she tucked half a loaf of bread and the last of the strawberry jam into the basket.

She returned to the parlor to find JoJo recovered from her fright and glaring at the young man. Elsie, on the other hand, looked abashed, as if she herself had been caught stealing. Molly couldn't help wondering if Elsie had come close to finding herself in the same circumstances. That was a discussion for some other time.

"You'd best go before Mr. Honeycutt returns," Molly said quietly.

"The boy is a brigand," JoJo proclaimed, rising from the chair.

"You gave him the strawberry jam?" Elsie asked, looking at the basket wistfully. Almost as quickly, she put on a cheerful face. "Never mind, it's fine."

JoJo gave a cry of outrage. "Thief!"

"He's just hungry. That's all," Elsie said, trying to appease JoJo. "You've probably never been hungry, have you?"

"That jam was for my friend, Molly," JoJo cried. "I snitched it from Mama's pantry for Molly, not for some common thief."

The poor boy looked guilt-ridden. He could hardly meet Molly's gaze. She held out the basket and urged him to take it and enjoy the food with his brother. She wanted to add a comment about giving the food readily, that she was happy to share, but worried that her words would only add to his shame. He took the basket with a nod of thanks.

With a surprising burst of anger, JoJo rushed across the parlor. Elsie tried to stop her. Molly drew a sharp breath. The boy slipped hastily out the door and bolted from the porch.

"No, you don't," JoJo shouted, trying to give chase.

Elsie stepped in front of her. "Quit being such a danged cootie, JoJo Ward."

JoJo gave a cry of outrage and tried to shove Elsie out of her way. Despite her indignation, JoJo could not get past. For just a slip of a girl, Elsie held her own. JoJo and Elsie tussled.

Molly had never seen such a sight. She stepped into the melee, trying desperately to keep the girls from fighting. They kept on, however, fussing and carrying on like a pair of schoolgirls squabbling and scrabbling.

A chair fell with a resounding crash. A stack of fabric tumbled off the table. A box of buttons fell and scattered across the wood floor.

"Girls," Molly said, her tone frantic. "The two of you are acting like children."

Neither paid her one bit of attention. In the melee, one of the girls' elbow struck Molly's eye. The blow knocked her back. She stumbled. Stars burst across her vision. She staggered away from the fracas, nearly slipping on several stray buttons and sank to the floor with a cry of shock and pain.

Chapter Twenty-Five
Molly Hides Herself

Daniel

After his mother left the Collins' place, Daniel left the shed, intending to return to the cabin. As he ascended the path, he thought he heard a cry. Without thinking, he set off in a run. Just as he rounded the bend in the path, he saw a young man dart into the brush, a basket in hand. A surge of anger rushed over him. The boy was no dangerous outlaw. Just the same, what was he doing in the Collins' cabin?

Daniel started after the boy, and yelled at him to stop, but the boy ran like a jackrabbit. Pretty quickly Daniel realized he was not going to catch the boy, so he hurried back to the cabin to check on Molly and the other girls. The most important thing was to make sure the womenfolk were safe.

He burst into the cabin to find the parlor empty. Voices drifted down the hallway.

"You ought to lie down," Elsie urged, her voice coming from Molly's bedroom.

"There's no need," Molly argued, her voice sounding like she had a mouthful of mashed potatoes.

"I might swoon," JoJo murmured. "It looks frightful."

"It does?" Molly asked. "Let me take a look in the mirror."

Both JoJo and Elsie protested. *No. Don't look. You mustn't see.*

Daniel's heart thundered in his chest. What on earth had happened? He hastened down the hallway and stopped a few paces from the doorway.

The three girls argued about whether Molly should see her reflection. What could that mean? Rubbing the back of his neck, he debated what to do. Thankfully, the girls were safe and sound, or mostly safe and sound. Still, he wanted to be certain. For that reason, he needed to see Molly face to face.

And yet something made him hold back.

There was a nagging concern about propriety. Whatever had just happened sounded a tad grim. His mother's lessons on good manners so many years ago never covered this sort of situation.

He winced. After trying his best to protect Molly, she'd gotten hurt anyway.

"Oh, my word," Molly said. Her voice was so strange, the words sounding like she'd been drinking, which obviously she hadn't, but that's what came to Daniel's mind.

Daniel couldn't hold back any longer. He knocked on the door. "Molly?"

All three girls shrieked.

He heard some quick murmuring amongst the girls.

"Please don't come in," Elsie said hastily. "It's fine. Nothing really. Molly has a small bruise and she'd rather you not see her like this."

JoJo made gave a breathless laugh. "Well."

"Molly does not sound fine," Daniel said. "I'm coming in to have a look."

Daniel grabbed the knob and turned it and started to push open the door, but someone on the other side blocked him.

Elsie said hurriedly, "You'd best not see this, Mr. Honeycutt," as she peeked from the partially opened door.

Usually, Elsie wore a cheerful expression as if ready to share a fine joke or funny story. Instead of a happy smile, she was pale. All color had drained from her face. Her hair was disheveled, and the collar of her new dress, the one Molly had made for her, now had a small tear.

"Is everything all right?" he asked. The question was absurd. He could plainly see that everything was *not* all right.

Elsie gulped. "Yes, Mr. Honeycutt. Just fine. Molly got hit in the eye."

Daniel narrowed his gaze and pushed a bit on the door, opening it a few more inches, but Elsie pushed right back. For a tiny little gnat, she had the tenacity of a mule. Elsie quickly waved one hand as if to say, go away, and then she pushed the door and narrowed the gap back down so just her face was visible.

"Who hit her?" Daniel demanded.

"JoJo," Elsie said. "On accident."

"Wasn't me either," JoJo protested. "It was Elsie. The pesky girl banged Molly square in the eye with her pointy little elbow."

Elsie shook her head.

"It's fine," Molly announced, the words drawled out in an odd way.

Daniel heard more murmuring between JoJo and Molly, then JoJo said, "She's just going to rest a spell and see if the swelling goes down."

"Swelling?" Daniel asked, suddenly feeling a mite unwell. "Swelling?"

Elsie grimaced and nodded. "Yes, sir."

JoJo came to the door and gave Daniel a solemn look. Pushing Elsie into the hall, she drew the door closed behind her. "Molly will be fine. She just needs to rest right now."

"I don't know. It sounds pretty bad. Are you sure she's fine?"

"Of course." JoJo looked offended. "In a week or two."

Daniel's stomach clenched. A week or two? He was used to getting injured, not just the injury to his eye but day-to-day incidents. He hated to imagine Molly hurt. With a pained sigh, he wandered back up the hall and tried to picture what happened. How could he have prevented the incident?

"I saw a boy running from the cabin on my way back. Are you sure that he didn't do this?"

"No sir," Elsie said. Neither girl seemed to want to go into much explanation.

"What was he doing here?"

"Molly was kind enough to give that boy some food," Elsie offered. "And then he left."

Elsie and JoJo set about washing the last of the dishes so that Molly would have one less chore whenever she felt well enough to leave her room. The two girls bickered about whose fault it was. Elsie claimed the boy was suffering mightily. JoJo argued the scamp was no better than a common thief.

Daniel couldn't make heads or tails of their debate.

When the dishes had been washed, dried, and put away, the girls came to the parlor to tidy up. It looked like a storm had blown through the parlor. Upended chairs. Buttons scattered to the four corners. Fabric lying this way and that. While they didn't squabble anymore, the two girls scowled at each other several times while putting things to rights.

Daniel picked up the chairs and wondered about checking on Molly.

When they were done, JoJo announced she would need to go home. "Mother will be looking for me."

"You'd best be off then," Elsie replied, sounding pleased. "Don't let us keep you."

JoJo ignored the girl. Instead, she regarded Daniel with a curious gaze. "Will you be staying, Mr. Honeycutt? To keep Molly company?"

Her tone galled him. She seemed to imply something untoward. Folding her arms, she gave him a self-satisfied look and waited for a reply. His mother's words came back to him. She'd fussed at him when she first arrived that afternoon, suggesting he toyed with Molly's heart, which couldn't have been further from the truth.

I have it from reliable sources that you've been stealing kisses...

JoJo must have seen him kiss Molly. Well, that was a bit of a problem. He hated to think of anybody gossiping about Molly. He didn't want them to portray her in an unflattering light. There was the matter of honor, not to mention Molly's father. Daniel still needed to ask permission to court Molly, who from the sounds of things might have a black eye, and maybe missing a tooth too based on how she sounded.

"Yes, I'm staying to keep her company," Daniel said. "Molly's mighty important to me. I care for her."

JoJo and Elsie both stood silent, waiting for him to say more.

"I intend to offer for her," Daniel added, giving JoJo a pointed look.

Elsie sighed. "That's very romantic."

"Hm." JoJo said, the hard edge of judgment fading from her eyes. "Molly's my best friend. I need to look out for her."

A discontented grumble came from Elsie.

"I appreciate that," Daniel said gruffly. "You don't need to fret. I'll watch over her and tend to her if she needs something."

"And I'll be sure to help," Elsie said, gesturing to the door. "We'll be just fine."

A sound came from Molly's room, a sound like something small falling to the floor, and Molly grumbling. Elsie said she'd check on her and hurried to the hall.

JoJo frowned and went to gather her things. Stopping at the door, she turned to Daniel. "I just recalled that I have a letter for Elsie. Can I leave it here on the table?"

Daniel's head was spinning with the morning's events. All he could think of was Molly and whether she was really okay, like the girls claimed. He noticed JoJo by the door, looking at him like she was waiting for an answer to some question. "Sure, whatever you need."

He then headed down the hallway to stand by Molly's door to see what he could hear from inside.

Chapter Twenty-Six
Notes Passed Under the Door

Molly

Molly woke with a terrible headache, aware of a faint light outside. A few times in her childhood she'd been so exhausted from work or play that she'd fallen asleep in the afternoon and when she'd woken up, she hadn't known where she was or if it was morning or evening. That's how she felt now, confused and hurting.

Elsie must have heard her stir. The girl quietly stepped into the room and moved quickly to sit down on the edge of the bed.

"How do you feel?" she asked.

"My face hurts." Even talking hurt. Opening and closing her mouth hurt. She thought about it, and decided that breathing did not hurt, so she was grateful for that.

"What day is it?" she asked, her words almost too jumbled to understand.

"It's Thursday."

"Morning?"

"No, silly. It'll be dark in an hour."

"What happened?"

"JoJo hit you in the face with her elbow. You don't remember?"

"Not really."

"Do you remember giving that boy the last of our strawberry jam?"

Molly touched her face. It hurt terribly. Something about the thought of the jam reminded Molly of the boy and his worried look, how hungry he was. It all came back to her, JoJo and Elsie fighting, Molly trying to intervene and then an elbow to the face... maybe two elbows. She sat up on the edge of the bed next to Elsie.

"Hand me that mirror please."

Elsie handed it to her.

Peering into the small mirror, Molly wondered how she'd managed to be on the receiving end of a blow not just to her eye, but her mouth as well. Pure luck, she had to guess. Her lips had swollen to twice their normal size. The tip of her tongue had suffered a similar fate.

"My heavens." She drew a sharp breath of surprise for her words were hardly intelligible.

Daniel spoke from the other side of her bedroom door. "May I come in?"

Molly shook her head, trying to tell Elsie with her eyes to ask Daniel to go away.

"Not right now, sir," Elsie said in a sing-song way. "Molly needs a little time to..." Her words trailed off. Molly pointed at the bed and tilted her head as if it were on her pillow. The motion caused her to whimper in pain.

"Molly is resting and won't be coming out of the bedroom again today."

"Ok," Daniel said, but Molly could tell he remained just on the other side of the door. Elsie quickly pointed out the glass of water and bowl of porridge sitting on Molly's sewing table and gestured for Molly to eat and drink something. Then she hurried to the door and left Molly to eat and rest.

Molly felt a deep satisfaction to know Daniel was near. At the same time, she desperately hoped she could conceal her injuries from him. Was she vain? Possibly. She might need to add that to her list of self-improvements.

She walked over to the door and pressed her ear to it. She heard Elsie and Daniel move down the hall, and for that she was thankful.

"We'd best tend to the horses and Molly's chickens," Elsie said.

"All right," Daniel said grudgingly.

Molly let out a sigh of blessed relief when she heard them leave. She paced her room. Her thoughts went to her father and brothers. What if they returned this evening? On one hand, it would spare her the humiliation of Daniel seeing her like this, but on the other hand, he'd no longer remain there on the Collins property. In just a few days' time she'd come to depend on Daniel.

The realization came as a shock. It was true. She both wanted and needed Daniel Honeycutt.

Shortly, Daniel and Elsie returned from tending to the animals. Elsie was jabbering about the various hens. "The chickens seem really fond of Molly," she said.

"I reckon that's one thing the chickens and me have in common," Daniel grumbled.

Molly felt a bloom of warmth washing across her heart. She smiled, but it hurt to do so, and she only imagined how hideous of a smile it would be to others, the kind to make small children run away.

"I'd best check on her," Daniel said.

"That sounds nice," Elsie said.

Molly shook her head.

"Right. Maybe she'll let me talk to her a spell."

"Heafenths," Molly said, wincing at the sound of her distorted speech.

Daniel's footsteps echoed in the hallway as he drew near. He knocked on the door, a sharp rap that drew a panicked yelp from Molly. Her heart hammered against her breastbone. She could reply but he'd hear the peculiar sound of her speech. Her mouth had swelled considerably. He would likely demand to see her.

A few moments before, she'd wondered if she was vain. Now, she knew that she was. Sadly. She'd like to think it wasn't a regular transgression, just one inspired by Daniel Honeycutt.

Hastily she scribbled a note. *I'm a little under the weather.*

Shoving it under the door, she waited.

Daniel muttered. "Under the weather?"

Elsie's light, skipping footsteps sounded on the floorboards. "She's under the weather?"

Molly couldn't help wincing which hurt her lip and her eye and strangely, her tongue as well.

"Why don't you write her back?" Elsie asked. "Find out if there's anything she needs."

Molly shook her head, trying her best to somehow send the message to Elsie. Molly needed nothing. Especially not from Daniel. Not if it meant he'd see her swollen, distorted appearance.

Daniel pushed the paper back under the door.

Need something? Anything?

Molly snatched her pencil. *No. Thank you kindly.*

She cringed inwardly at her overly polite reply. Her reply made it sound as if they were mere acquaintances when, only last night, he'd held her in his arms, kissed her, and spoken of forever. Now, she was dismissing him and likely wounding his feelings.

Another note appeared at the bottom of the door. *I'd do anything for you.*

Molly closed her eyes. Such a simple message, and yet, it unraveled something inside her, a knot she'd never realized she had, bound fast around her heart. She could scarcely breathe as she rested her forehead against the wood panel.

She knew without a doubt that he *would* do anything for her.

Slowly, she gathered her wits and wrote a reply. *I know that. I thank you. I just don't want you to see me with a swollen lip and bruised eye.*

Makes no matter to me, Molly. I only have one good eye, after all.

Molly gave a soft cry of dismay. Regret and indecision wound a tight thread around her heart. She set her hand on the doorknob as she debated simply opening the door and speaking to him face to face. Her heart thudded heavily. Pain throbbed across her injuries. No, she decided. She couldn't let him see her like this. She let her hand fall from the doorknob.

She rested her palm on the door, wishing she could go to him and find comfort in his arms.

A few moments later, another note appeared by her feet.

I will let you rest and check on you later. I'll be nearby in case you need me.

Chapter Twenty-Seven
Elsie Learns the Terrible News

Daniel

Daniel spent the evening working on various chores around the Collins place. He figured Molly was worn out after the elbow to her face, so he let her rest.

He spent an uncomfortable night sleeping in a chair on the porch. At one point, Elsie had tiptoed outside and left a blanket on the arm of the chair. He muttered a few words of thanks.

To that, she offered a reply. "Mighty glad to have you nearby, Mr. Honeycutt."

He heard her lighthearted laughter as she closed the door behind her. After a restless stretch of patchy sleep, he awoke at dawn. His first thought was of Molly. How had she slept after getting injured? He scrubbed his hand down his face and wished somehow that he could have gotten hurt, not Molly.

Slowly, he got to his feet, grimacing at the knot between his shoulders.

In the forefront of his mind was the question of Molly. Of course. He fretted, wondering if she was feeling better. Beyond that matter was the topic of Mr. Collins and the foreman job. Mama wanted to hire Mr. Collins, pay him handsomely and give him interest in the mine.

Which was all fine and good.

And yet, Daniel wanted to offer for Molly. How could he ask for Molly's hand in the same breath he spoke of Mr. Collins working in the Presidio Mine? It all felt a tad off. Molly was bound to object to some part, or maybe to all the parts. Who could say?

The aroma of coffee tempted him and drew him to the door. He slipped inside without bothering to knock. Sounds came from the kitchen. Clattering pans. Dishes set on the counter. Butter sizzling in a hot pan.

He couldn't help smiling as he crossed the parlor and imagined Molly at the stove. Hopefully, she'd recovered from yesterday's tussle. They could have a regular sort of conversation instead of passing notes under the door. Not wanting to startle her, he cleared his throat as he approached the kitchen.

"Mornin'. Could I talk you into a cup of coffee?" he asked as he rounded the doorway.

To his amazement and disappointment, he found Elsie in the kitchen. Not Molly. Even more surprising, judging from the girl's red, watering eyes, Elsie had been crying.

The sight of her distress shocked him. He came to an abrupt halt. He'd never seen her cry. Shoot, he could hardly recall ever seeing her frown.

When they'd first met, she accused him flat-out of being a thief. She was frightened. Once they'd cleared up that misunderstanding, Elsie quickly changed her entire demeanor. From that point on, she was as kind and cheerful as the day was long. Aside from her feud with JoJo, Elsie was a ray of warm sunshine. He could have hardly imagined Elsie ever cried.

And yet, here she was. Her eyes were pools of unspent tears. Her slim shoulders lifted with a loud, pitiful hiccup. Her hands trembled.

"Molly's okay?" His heart sank. "She's well?"

"Yes, sir."

The girl kept her attention on her work. She sliced onions and slid them into the pan where they crackled and hissed as they hit the hot fat.

Daniel crossed the kitchen, took a cup from the shelf, and poured himself a cup of coffee. He leaned against the doorframe and regarded the young girl as he tried to form a proper question. She wasn't a child, not really, but she was nowhere near to being an adult. Making matters worse, he wasn't accustomed to dealing with tears and tender feelings. Mama certainly never indulged in such things.

Which meant Daniel had no practice. None whatsoever. He was better at roping and working cattle than finding kind words of comfort.

Elsie gulped as she cracked eggs into a bowl. A sniffle followed.

"You seem upset," he said. Instantly, he regretted his words.

Just swell, Honeycutt. Mighty observant.

"Seems like you've been crying this morning," he said gruffly. "Is that right?"

Even better...

He grimaced, took a swallow of coffee, wishing he could be anywhere else, maybe riding the pasture. Alone. Anything had to be better than trying to console an overwrought girl. He tried once more to find out what troubled the poor girl.

"Something's upsetting you. Clearly."

"Yes, sir," Elsie said. "I've received a letter from my uncle. I found it on the table this morning."

"Seems it wasn't the news you were expecting."

This question seemed to miss its mark. Elsie sniffled. She stirred the eggs more vigorously.

He lowered his gaze, studied the coffee in his cup and considered setting it aside. Maybe he could just walk out the door, turn around and come back to the kitchen and try anew. A fresh start might be just the thing. Could be a good idea, but only if he could come up with a few questions that had a lick of sense. So far, he sounded like a danged fool.

"Not the news you hoped for?" he asked gently.

Elsie shook her head. Softly, she said, "no, sir."

"You want to tell me more?"

"My uncle's not coming back. He hadn't planned to tell me."

"That so?" Daniel growled. "What made him change his mind?"

"He fretted."

"Did he now?"

Elsie nodded. "He feared my grandma's ghost would come after him."

Daniel snorted.

Elsie went on. "His conscience troubled him, kept him awake at night. Gran came to him and told him he needed to let me know."

Daniel didn't believe in ghosts or visions but kept his opinions to himself.

"And his wife agreed on matters," Elsie finished.

"Agreed on what matters?" Daniel was pretty sure he didn't want to know the answer.

"I'm a burden."

She stirred the eggs and poured them into the pan.

Daniel shook his head. "He doesn't know squat, Elsie. You forget about what he said."

She didn't reply. Instead, she kept her gaze fixed on the pan as she scrambled the eggs. He moved to the stove and set his coffee cup down.

Elsie sniffed. A soft, sad murmur escaped her lips as a tear rolled down her cheek. Daniel gritted his teeth, imagining the uncle and what he would like to say to the man. If he had the chance, Daniel would teach the man a lesson. What kind of man tricks an innocent, vulnerable child? He didn't want to know the answer to that question.

"I mean it, Elsie. You deserve better."

She said nothing.

A tress of copper hair had sprung loose from her arrangement. He gave it a gentle tug, folded his arms across his chest and leaned a little closer. "You hear?" he asked. "I won't speak ill of your kin. Now's not the time, but, that uncle of yours isn't worth one single moment of your trouble. You're better off without him. Why, he wouldn't know a fine, wonderful thing if it bit him right-"

Elsie stopped stirring.

Daniel cleared his throat, reminding himself he wasn't talking to one of his trail hands. "If it bit him right on his *elbow.*"

She looked up at him, her eyes awash with heartache. Daniel could hardly stand to see Elsie in such a state. Her skin was blotchy. Her eyes brimmed with tears. She hiccupped once again.

He reached into his pocket to retrieve a handkerchief. "Here you go, little bit."

She took the hankie. "Thank you, sir."

He drew a long, weary sigh and took a drink of his coffee. Land sakes, he wasn't used to so much effort first thing in the morning. He refilled his cup, noting a heavy stream of clumped grounds. He stopped his pour when the cup was half full.

"You like the coffee?" Elsie asked, wiping a tear from her cheek.

"Mighty fine coffee," he replied as his stomach tightened.

"Truly?"

"Why, sure. It hits the spot." He grimaced as he rubbed his chest.

"Want more?"

"No. Thank you. Probably won't need any for the rest of the month."

A smile tugged at her lips. "I'm so glad you like it. I was worried I'd make it wrong."

"You made it just right," he said. "I'd best check on Molly. See if she's accepting callers this morning."

Elsie knit her brows, making him doubt his chances as far as Molly was concerned. Just the same, he intended to learn if she was feeling better after yesterday's scuffle. He strolled out of the kitchen as he considered what to say as he knocked at Molly's door. Maybe he ought to send her a note instead.

He raked his fingers through his unkempt hair. Everything seemed wrong somehow. Mighty improper, truth be told. It all amounted to the sort of situation his mama had warned him against if he wanted to be a gentleman. If Mama were about, she'd caution him against stepping one foot closer to Molly's door, but he couldn't hold himself back.

He could almost hear her fussing.

So be it.

If she ever found out about his various transgressions and bad manners, he'd confess and make amends. He'd explain why he called on an injured lady first thing in the morning. He might even tell his mother about Elsie's uncle, a man who cast aside his own kin because they were too much of a bother.

Daniel curled his fist. More than anything, he'd like to take matters up with Elsie's uncle. Now, that would be mighty satisfying. He'd give the man a lesson. Teach him the meaning of a burden. Make him regret casting off a sweet, innocent child.

He wasn't a brawler, but he'd take on that battle. Gladly.

It didn't matter so long as things turned out right. At the end of the day, he might have a few missteps he'd have to atone for, but in the meantime, he'd take comfort in the simple fact he'd tried his best. Done the decent thing.

Coming to a stop a short distance from Molly's door, he lifted his hand and knocked.

Chapter Twenty-Eight
A Visitor At Dawn

Amelia

Amelia had been up since the wee hours of the night. Thoughts of Daniel, and Miss Collins, and notions of grandbabies teasing her mind. Unable to sleep, she dressed and went to the study to catch up on paperwork.

It wasn't long till she was absorbed by the various tasks. She worked steadily, hardly noticing the passing time. When a knock at the door drew her from her work, she wondered if her mind played tricks. The brass knocker thudded once again, only this time louder.

She startled. A blotch of ink sprayed from her fountain pen, marring the paper of her ranch ledger. Setting her pen aside, she muttered a few words of exasperation.

Who on earth would call on folks at this hour? It wasn't even six in the morning. The sun had not risen. Stars still twinkled in the sky outside the window.

"It's got to be Sheldon," she said to the empty room. "Must be."

She left her study and walked the length of the long hallway. Her footsteps echoed in the empty house, giving her a lonesome pang. For an instant she forgot about the visitor.

Instead, she wondered why she'd built such a large house. Probably to show everyone that she'd done well for herself, despite the naysayers. Now that she was stuck living alone in the sprawling, empty home, the big house didn't seem like such a fine idea.

The family's old house stood empty. She'd raised the boys in the limestone home. The wraparound porch had a fine view of the Bethany River. The dear, old house had been full of bittersweet memories.

Now it was vacant.

Homes didn't like to be empty. She'd decided as much shortly after she moved into the new house. By then it was too late. She couldn't go back. Not without admitting her mistake.

Another knock sounded at the door.

"I'm coming, dang it."

She swung the door open to find Sheldon standing at her threshold, hat in one hand, a lantern in the other.

"Sheldon," she exclaimed. "It's a little early. Even for you. Can't this wait till I've had breakfast?"

"Sorry to trouble you, Mrs. Honeycutt. I know it's early. I saw light coming from the study window and figured you were up. I would never knock on your door at this hour unless it was important."

"What's the trouble? Is everyone all right?"

"Everyone's fine, Mrs. Honeycutt. Well, mostly fine. Simon and Zach were in jail."

Her breath caught. Her blood turned cold. The words twisted in her mind. *Jail. Simon and Zach.*

Thankfully, Sheldon used the past tense and not the present. They *were* in jail. But not anymore. She let out a weary sigh. She might have guessed they'd get themselves into some sort of scrap. They were supposed to be back at the ranch already but had written to say they intended to visit some friends for a spell.

Amelia sighed. "Go on. Where?"

"A little town called Galisteo. I believe they were looking for your mining foreman. The one who skedaddled after the explosion."

"Thank you, Sheldon. I know the man. I only have one mine. Thank heavens."

"They wanted to search the saloon. The sheriff warned them not to set one foot inside."

"A man after my own heart. He'd probably heard of some prior tomfoolery. Sounds like his threat fell on deaf ears."

Sheldon shrugged. "Suppose so."

"Those two boys are a pair of no-good rascals."

"I found out about their trouble last night," Sheldon said. "The postmaster sent a telegram late. I didn't want to trouble you till after I'd arranged to pay their bail."

"Any idea why they were tossed into jail?" Amelia winced. "Almost afraid to ask."

Sheldon reddened. He hesitated, searching for a proper explanation. Finally, he chuckled awkwardly and spoke. "They caused a ruckus when they went into the saloon looking for that foreman. Nothing too serious, of course. No one got hurt. So, all's well that ends well, wouldn't you say?"

He wanted to leave it at that, but Amelia wouldn't let him get away just yet. "Why'd they get in trouble with the law. Causing a ruckus isn't a crime, last I heard."

"Well, no, ma'am, but the sheriff of Galisteo lost a poker game on account of the disturbance. Seems one of the horses upset the card table. Purely on accident, you see. Can't hardly blame the horse."

"Sheldon, you're not making a lick of sense. Are we talking about Simon and Zach or a horse?"

"All four, ma'am."

Amelia closed her eyes and drew a deep breath before going on. "Let's see. We have Simon, Zach and a horse." She counted off the three culprits on her fingers. "Mind telling me who counts as the fourth in this story?"

"The other horse."

Setting a hand on her hip, she studied Sheldon. If she were having this conversation with any other man, she might ask if he'd been drinking. Her foreman never drank, however. This morning, as always, he was sober as a judge.

"Why were the horses in the saloon?" she asked slowly. "Not playing cards, from the sounds of things. Seems they'd avoid upsetting the table if they were in the middle of a game."

Sheldon's lips quirked. "Unless they got dealt a bad hand."

Amelia narrowed her eyes.

He cleared his throat. "Sorry, ma'am. After the sheriff told them not to step one foot into the saloon, Simon and Zach rode their horses into the saloon."

She blinked. The breeze blew across the porch, rustling the branches of the two magnolias. When she was a new bride, George had planted the trees for her. He knew how fond she was of magnolias. The whispering breeze made her wonder if George was enjoying a fine laugh about their boys.

Not funny, darling. I'll be the one to get the last laugh when I give our three sons an ultimatum.

She gave Sheldon a faint smile. "I hope the horses didn't suffer any mishap in the saloon."

"No, ma'am. The horses are just fine. The boys too, mostly."

"Mostly?" She gripped the doorknob.

"It's fine, Mrs. Honeycutt. I wired them some money from the ranch account. They needed a little extra to visit a doc in town to get Zach a couple of stitches on his shoulder."

"Sheldon, I don't believe you. My sons have never bothered with a couple of stitches. It must have been more than that."

He set his hand over his heart. "It's the truth, ma'am. Lord strike me down if I'm lying."

Amelia loosened her grip on the door. "Sometimes I think we ought to let them stay in jail a spell. Might teach them a lesson. You catch my meaning?"

Sheldon frowned. "Yes, ma'am."

Her foreman didn't look like he agreed at all.

"Next time, talk to me before you send money."

"Yes, ma'am."

She shook her head. "Listen to me, speaking about the next time. I'm plum worn out with worrying over my boys. They need to grow up." Amelia lowered her voice. "I'm tired of their brawling and carousing. I mean to call an end to their revelry."

Sheldon gave a slight nod. "Yes, ma'am. Sounds perfectly reasonable. Only I believe they were looking to bring that foreman to justice."

Amelia narrowed her eyes, trying to gauge his sincerity. She often wondered if his loyalties might lie more with her boys than her.

He lowered his voice. "You know the rumors. Some of the fellas around these parts sometimes take the law into their own hands since we don't have any Rangers or lawmen of our own."

Amelia found the topic too upsetting to dwell on at this hour. Instead, she put on a mask of stern resolve. The time had come to show her mettle.

"Wait till they get back," she said, her tone icy. "Soon as I see the whites of their eyes, I intend to lay down my version of the law."

"Your version?"

"Right. They need to marry. This year. Women have a civilizing influence."

"You believe that a wife can civilize those boys?" He sounded more than a little skeptical.

"I'm depending on it."

"All three boys?"

"All three."

Sheldon swallowed. "Yes, ma'am."

"I'd best get back to my work, Sheldon. Thank you for stopping by."

He nodded, wide-eyed and too astonished to say much more than a polite goodbye. She shut the door and slowly turned around. Folding her arms across her chest, she leaned lightly against the wooden door panel.

This time the boys had gone too far.

Up till now, she'd been cordial. She'd asked politely, bargained, and even offered thinly veiled bribes, all in hopes of keeping them out of trouble. Despite her efforts, they continued with their foolish pranks.

Only Daniel showed any promise. He seemed sweet on the Collins girl. Amelia was pleased with his choice. The Collins girl was a fine, upstanding young lady. Amelia's darling eldest boy seemed as though he *might* abide by her wishes. Maybe.

Then again, she'd best not assume anything. After he got injured, he kept to himself and spoke of enjoying the solitude. What if he merely stole a few kisses from the Collins girl? He might simply indulge in a short flirtation, cast the girl aside and retreat to his quiet, remote cabin.

Amelia fretted. She couldn't get her hopes up. After all, she'd already ventured down that path and met with disappointment when she'd persuaded Daniel to court that empty-headed Cordelia.

No. She'd need to have a come-to-mercy chat with each boy. Better safe than sorry.

She knew how to manage ornery, obstinate menfolk. She'd brought dozens of powerful men to heel over the years. Up till now, all those dealings pertained to business.

This was far more important. This concerned her precious family, which was exactly why she needed to get tougher. She'd resisted making threats about money up till now, but one thing was clear.

The time had come.

Chapter Twenty-Nine
Elsie Leaves a Note

Molly

When Molly heard the knock at the door, she had no doubt who waited on the other side. It could only be Daniel. Elsie rarely remembered to knock, or if she did remember, never waited for Molly to respond.

She gazed at the door as her heart sank. All morning, she'd dreaded this moment, the moment she'd have to come out from hiding. It wasn't possible to hide all day. Sooner or later, she'd have to face both Daniel and Elsie.

With a tentative step, she edged closer to the door. She knew perfectly well that her eye looked terrible, and her lips looked crooked on account of being larger on one side than the other. While her eye was no longer swollen shut, the entire side of her face was varying shades of blue and purple. Even Jack and Will had never ended up with such a black eye.

"Come on, Molly," Daniel said. "Let's take a look."

She groaned softly and pushed the door open. Keeping her gaze averted, she kept her eye on the very middle of Daniel's broad chest. He wore a new shirt. Where was the shirt she'd given him, she wondered distantly.

He lifted his hand to her chin and tilted her head back gently so he could examine the injury. His touch sent a shiver across her skin. He held her gaze with a look that wrapped a sense of warm comfort around her.

"My, my," he murmured. "Either Elsie or JoJo, whichever of the two girls, sure managed to give you a wallop."

The soft comfort of his touch vanished. She tried to pull away, but he set his other hand on her shoulder. He studied her injury a moment longer.

"Does it hurt as much as yesterday?" he asked.

"A little less."

"Good."

"I look frightful."

He dropped the hand that held her chin, but let his other hand lingered on her shoulder. "You look very pretty. Not even a black eye could make you look bad."

"Aren't you the charmer."

"It's true. You look beautiful even with a prize-winning shiner."

Elsie tip-toed down the hallway and peeked around the side of Daniel. Her eyes widened. She shrieked and clasped a hand over her mouth. After a moment, she let her hand fall to her side.

Daniel gave the girl a look of mild reproach.

Elsie pressed her lips together as her eyes filled with tears. "I suppose there's a chance it was my elbow. I can hardly bear to think I hurt you, Molly."

"Oh, Elsie," Molly said gently. "It will heal before we know it."

She stepped past Daniel and held out her arms to the girl. Elsie dropped her gaze and retreated. Try as she might, Molly could not induce the girl to embrace her. Elsie backed away and darted into the kitchen.

"You sit down, Molly. And Mr. Honeycutt too, please. I'll have breakfast out shortly."

Daniel and Molly went to the table and took their seats to wait for the meal. Molly didn't like to sit idle. She started to get up to help Elsie, but Daniel stopped her from going to the kitchen. Elsie clattered spoons and banged pots. The oven door opened and closed. Molly shifted uncomfortably. Daniel smiled at her and patted her hand.

After a short while, Elsie brought breakfast. She'd made fried eggs and potatoes. Aside from slightly undercooked potatoes, the breakfast was tasty. Both she and Daniel complimented Elsie on her cooking skill.

"We'll have to put you to work in the kitchen more often," Molly teased.

Elsie looked startled. "Your family will be home in the next few days. I'll be on my way when they return."

"We'll see about that," Molly replied.

Elsie shook her head. "I couldn't bear to be a burden. Not again."

Molly was taken aback. She wanted to tell Elsie that she would always be welcome in the Collins home. Even though Molly's father had never met Elsie, Molly knew he would insist on taking the girl in.

Daniel spoke before she could say a word.

"Elsie received a letter from her uncle saying they would not be back for Elsie. I've been thinking, though, my mother's a widow. She lives all alone in her big house. I've always thought she'd do well with a companion."

Elsie hardly listened. Instead, she stared out the window at a distant point on the horizon. She murmured a few words of half-hearted agreement.

For the rest of the day, Elsie seemed lost in thought. Molly tried to draw her into conversation to no avail. The girl kept busy but hardly spoke. Daniel kept busy as well. He trimmed Vixen's hooves, mended her halter, and sharpened Molly's scissors and kitchen knives.

Molly fretted about Elsie's plight. She also fretted about her father and brothers returning. According to the letter she'd received, they would come home in the next day or so. She tried to imagine her father's response to finding she had not one guest but two. The girl would hardly cause any concern, but what would her father think of Daniel Honeycutt? A stranger who'd stayed overnight in the shed. And what would they say about her bruised face? Papa would never leave her alone again.

She missed her brothers and her father. At the same time, she'd enjoyed Elsie's company. And Daniel's too. Elsie inspired a protective feeling inside her heart. Daniel stirred a yearning she'd never known.

He alluded to speaking to her father but didn't elaborate. Would he ask for permission to court her? Or would he ask for her hand in marriage? She recalled the afternoon by the river when he spoke of marriage. His proposal had taken her by surprise, to say the least. She'd felt slighted by his suggestion of doing a good deed. And yet, he'd looked at her with tenderness, then and several times since that day.

Her heart summersaulted. She felt a gentle thrill wash over her despite her efforts to set romantic notions aside. She had no business dreaming of a life with Daniel. She could never have a place beside him. How could she be a wife to any man when she had a duty to her family, especially her father?

After the meal she washed dishes and tidied the kitchen. Daniel busied himself outside as he often did, tending to a list of tasks that kept expanding. When Molly finished her chores, she looked for Elsie. She wanted to make sure the girl wasn't still distressed about her uncle's letter.

Molly looked for the girl outside. When she couldn't find her, she continued her search inside. She went to her brothers' room where Elsie had been sleeping. The girl had made her bed as she did every morning. A window was open to allow fresh air inside. The curtains moved gently in the breeze. Molly's gaze was drawn to the bedside table. A note had been tucked next to the stack of books.

Molly's heart tumbled. She crossed the room and hastily read the note. She tried to understand the meaning of Elsie's message but struggled to make sense of the words. Her mind rebelled, refusing to believe. She read the note several times in hopes she'd misunderstood. Finally, she allowed herself to accept what the girl had written.

"Oh Elsie," she whispered.

Chapter Thirty
The Search

Daniel

Kneeling beside the gate, Daniel oiled the hinge he'd repaired. He got to his feet and tested the gate. It swung freely and without any squeaky complaint. He brushed off his hands and headed back to the shed to put the oil can where he'd found it.

He was thinking about Mr. Collins and how he thought he'd probably like the man. Molly was a good woman, he knew that, but there was more. He'd heard how Mr. Collins had gone into the mine on the day of the accident and helped a fair number of his fellow workers get out. Only a man of the highest caliber would do that.

He heard Molly's voice from the house. She called his name with a panicked tone. He hastily set the oil can on the shelf and hurried to meet her.

"Elsie's gone." She waved a note. "She's gone to the mine."

Daniel tried to make sense of her words. Elsie was gone? To the mine? After a moment's confusion, he recovered his senses. "Why would Elsie run off to the mine?"

Molly showed him the note. Daniel read the girl's message, his heart filling with dread. Elsie had written that she intended to search a small, obscure mine passage for the hidden silver.

The treasure would be the answer to her troubles. She'd have her own money and never again be a burden to anyone.

"She can't wander around the mine." Daniel gave the note back to Molly.

"I'm going after her." Molly's voice trembled. She looked pale and shaken by the turn of events. He wanted to tell her to stay home and that he'd find Elsie. He knew it would be no use. Molly was afraid, but she'd never agree to wait at home while Elsie was lost and possibly in danger.

"We'll go together." He set his hands on her shoulders.

When Molly offer a ready reply, he spoke again. His words came to him from a distant childhood memory. "When me and my brothers quarreled, Mama used to quote the Bible. She told us that two are better than one, because together they can work more effectively. If one of them falls, the other can help him up."

Molly nodded. "Ecclesiastes."

Without further discussion, they prepared to ride to the mine. Daniel brought the saddles from the shed while Molly bridled Vixen. When they finished tacking up the horses, Daniel went to the shed for a lantern. He tucked it in his saddle bag. A moment later, they were on their way.

Much of the road was smooth and even. They loped along the good part of the road, but as they neared the mine, they had to slow their pace and ride single file. The road narrowed to an uneven path as it ascended the ridge. By the time they reached the mine, the horses were lathered, their flanks heaving with exertion.

Daniel dismounted and tied his horse to a hitching rail near the mine office. He took out the lantern and set it down. Turning to help Molly, he found her staring at the mine entrance. Her complexion was ashen. Her eyes wide and fearful.

"Molly?" he said quietly.

She said nothing.

He approached her horse and spoke again. "Sweetheart, are you all right?"

Startled, she turned her gaze toward him. She swallowed hard and nodded. "I'm fine."

He helped her down, took Vixen to the hitching rail and tied her beside his gelding.

When he went back to Molly's side, he touched her arm gently. "Why don't you let me go find Elsie?"

"When I came to Bethany Springs with my family, I'd already lived in a number of mining towns. Over the years, I've seen all manner of mining accidents. Menfolk aren't meant to toil inside the earth. The accidents are something awful to see."

"I know," Daniel said. "Especially when careless men use explosives inside the mine."

Molly bit her lip.

Daniel lowered his voice. "That little Elsie didn't take any dynamite, did she?"

Molly turned her gaze toward him, her brow drawn together with bewilderment. He smiled.

Slowly, her confusion faded. A hint of a smile tugged at her lips. "She better not have found any dynamite."

Daniel's smile widened.

Molly shook her head. "JoJo warned me about Elsie McKittrick. She said I should be careful who I invite into my house. Maybe she was right, but not for the reason JoJo said... she worried about the girl having cooties. If only that was the worst of it."

With a determined step, Molly walked down the path to the mine entrance. Daniel followed, carrying the lantern. He could see that she wasn't entirely steady on her feet but knew it would be no use telling her to sit and wait.

As they neared the entrance, the damage from the blast grew visible. Rocks littered the ground. Several large boulders blocked one side of the opening. Daniel paused to light the lantern. Molly called for Elsie. Silence followed. She called twice more. Finally, a soft cry came from the darkness.

Molly stared into the murky darkness. Once again, a look of terror came over her features. Daniel was about to speak, but before he could say a word, Molly took his hand in hers. She closed her eyes.

"Merciful Father," she whispered. "Help…"

Daniel stood with his eyes closed. When she didn't say more, he opened them. Molly looked at him with a panicked expression. She shrugged a shoulder helplessly.

"It's all right, sweetheart," Daniel said. "I'm sure the good Lord knows what you want to say. You pretty much summed it up anyway."

"Okay. Thank you, Daniel."

He lit the lantern, squeezed her hand. Holding the lantern aloft, he led her into the pitch-black mine.

Chapter Thirty-One
Amelia Eavesdrops

Amelia

Late afternoon sunshine shone through the open window. Amelia brought the mare and foal into the stall and their movement sent wisps of dust swirling in the soft, buttery sunlight. After the foal went to Mandy's side to nurse, Amelia drew the door closed.

"You're a fine mama," Amelia murmured as she unhooked the mare's halter.

The mare stood quietly as the baby fed. Amelia stroked her neck, admiring the colt.

A movement caught her eye. Zach and Simon rode into the barnyard. Amelia frowned. Ever since she'd heard of their little stint in jail, she'd rehearsed her lecture. She was more than ready to lay down the law with her two boys.

They stopped to talk to Sheldon. Amelia couldn't hear the conversation but could tell the three men were having a lighthearted chat. Zach and Simon both dismounted. The three men talked more. One of them said something that made them all bust out laughing. As their laughter faded, Zach and Simon glanced toward the house before they resumed talking.

The two boys unsaddled their horses. Sheldon offered a few parting words, took the reins of both horses, and led them to a corral. Zach and Simon carried their saddles toward the barn door.

Amelia gave the mare a knowing look. "Those two rascals aren't going to know what hit them."

Mandy began to eat the hay in the manger. Amelia waited. Sheldon hadn't seen her in the barn which meant he couldn't have warned them. Which he would have done to be sure.

The door opened. Amelia cleared her throat, preparing to give the boys a stern talking-to.

"We need to make sure none of this gets back to Mama," Zach said.

"You know it," Simon replied.

Amelia snickered. She set her hand on the stall door. This element of surprise always pleased her. It had when the boys were young, and it still brought her a fair bit of delight. The looks on their faces made it so enjoyable. Her sons would startle and stammer. The last time she'd surprised them, Simon had given a high-pitched yelp. Zach and Daniel still talked about the sound of terror that had come from their brother.

The way Amelia saw it, over the years, her boys had scared her plenty. Turnaround was fair play.

They walked down the aisle, heading to the tack room.

"We'll call a meeting of the brotherhood next week," Simon said.

Amelia's breath caught.

"What about Daniel?" Zach asked.

"We'll send a note to his home to let him know."

"Is he back from the ridge?"

Simon scoffed. "You think *our* brother stayed away from his home one minute longer than absolutely necessary?"

"Nah, I wasn't thinking."

As the boys neared the tack room, Simon's gaze traveled across the barn. Amelia ducked down. She crouched by the door, trying to be quiet as possible.

The foal, finished with nursing, wandered over to investigate. He started by sniffing her hair. She tried to swat him away, but he persisted. His velvety nose brushed against her ear. Warm breath fanned across her cheek. He puffed soft breaths, drawing in her scent.

He was gentle and inquisitive. His antics amused her, and she had to bite her lip to keep from laughing. When he nibbled her hair ribbon, she tried to push him away. He persisted, nosing her shirt collar, down her sleeve and paying special attention to the delicate lace on her cuffs.

While the colt inspected her attire, Amelia tried to hear what the boys discussed. What was this about a brotherhood? They didn't use that term when they talked about themselves. Usually it was *dang brother*, or *no-good brother*. At times they might even resort to *useless brother*, but she'd never heard them mention a brotherhood.

"Of course, we could just take care of matters on our own," Simon said.

"We could. But what if it's more than one troublemaker?"

Amelia drew a sharp breath. She thought of the rumors she'd heard about the men around town who took the law into their own hands. Maybe it was true, and maybe her boys were part of the vigilante group.

"Then Daniel will want to ride along to lend a hand."

The men's voices faded as they went into the tack room. Amelia's heart hammered against her ribs. She remained very, very still as her mind fell into turmoil. The foal grew bored and returned to his mother's side.

"How 'bout we see if Mama will serve us some supper?" Simon asked as he came out of the tack room.

Zach followed behind. "Well, she might, after she serves us a big ol' helping of fussing."

Amelia grumbled under her breath. "You boys don't know the half of it."

"She can fuss all she wants," Simon said. "I'm not getting married. Even if it means she cuts me off. I don't mind cowboy wages. She won't hold out too long. She's too tender-hearted."

Amelia blew out a huff.

Zach responded but Amelia couldn't make out his words. She pressed her lips together and shook her head as her ire burned. Pesky boys. She'd serve them dinner and then some. And Sheldon, he might get a helping of fussing too, for telling the boys her plans, the turncoat.

When the boys left the barn, Amelia got to her feet. She groaned and rubbed her lower back as she straightened. She was getting too old to be sneaking around.

Mandy stopped chewing and regarded her with mild interest. The colt nipped the mare's shoulder, trying to get his mother to pay attention to him. Mandy flicked her ears and shook her head. The colt side-stepped handily.

"You see, Mandy. That's the trouble with males. All males. Doesn't matter if they're young men or colts. They're a world of mischief. Nothing but trouble. Sometimes I think it's me against a whole passel of bothersome menfolk. My boys, my ranch hands, my workers."

The colt watched her with keen interest and moved closer. Amelia stroked his head. "Well, maybe not *all* males. You're a pretty sweet little fella."

She sighed as she closed and latched the stall door. Her mind returned to Zach and Simon's conversation. Tonight, when she said her prayers, she'd need to beg the good Lord for help. She'd need His help if she ever hoped to marry off her ornery boys.

Chapter Thirty-Two
The True Treasure

Molly

Once they'd gone a little way into the mine, the only sound came from their footfalls. Molly wondered how far Elsie had gone. The dark, dank air pressed in on her. She clung to Daniel's arm, closed her eyes and prayed that God would help lead them to the girl.

A sound came from a distant point. Molly couldn't tell what it was. Her heart thundered inside her chest. Daniel stopped and turned to her.

"Maybe you ought to try calling her," Daniel said.

"Yes. You're right," Molly said. "Elsie," she called. "Are you there?"

"Molly?" came the answer.

"Yes! It's me. Are you all right?"

"I'm fine."

The girl's voice echoed along the passage. The sound struck Molly as odd. She couldn't tell if the girl was around the corner or some distance away.

"Well, mostly fine," Elsie grumbled. "I've searched and searched, and I still haven't found any of the missing silver."

Daniel snorted. "The girl doesn't sound too scared."

"I'm not scared at all, Mr. Honeycutt." Elsie replied cheerfully.

He muttered a few choice words that Molly couldn't make out.

Molly had to marvel at Elsie's reply. How was it possible that such a small girl had no fear of such a frightening place? While Molly had always been afraid of mines, nothing had prepared her the experience of being inside a mine. She almost envied Elsie's pluck.

"Stay where you are," Daniel said. "We'll find you."

"Thank you, Mr. Honeycutt. I'm certain I could find my own way."

"I'm telling you stay put," Daniel snapped.

"All right," Elsie replied, her feelings hurt.

The girl was quiet for a few moments. Daniel told her to keep speaking so they'd locate her more easily. She resumed her chatter, talking about hidden passages and lost treasure and all manner of things that came to her mind.

Clutching Daniel's arm, Molly did her best to avoid stumbling as they walked along the shadowed passage. With each step they got closer to Elsie. While Molly felt relief, she also felt her nerves grow taut. She struggled to remain calm. They got closer to the girl, but they also moved deeper into the mine and further from the entrance.

After a wrong turn, Elsie's voice grew more distant, and they had to double back. Molly's throat tightened. Her breathing grew faster as she struggled to hold back the panic. To her relief, Elsie's voice began to sound closer. Thank heavens they were back on the right track. Elsie chattered on about the rocks and hidden passageways.

"Molly," Daniel said quietly. "You're doing fine. We'll be out of here in no time."

"Could we go a little slower?"

"If that helps, we can go as slowly as you like."

He reduced his pace. Molly wasn't sure if it helped or not, but she appreciated his willingness. Her breathing grew a little steadier.

"I don't know why my father enjoys this sort of work," she said.

"Maybe because it's so interesting," Elsie offered. "It helps if you don't think about being underground."

"Heavens," Molly whispered, her fretfulness rushing back. "We are underground. Aren't we?"

Elsie answered. "Pretty deep too. If I recall your father's sketch, the passages really slope down. Some of the tunnels even have ladders for the miners to use. It's interesting. Sort of makes me think-"

"Elsie, talk about something else, would you?" Daniel suggested. "Molly's not feeling well."

"Molly's not well? Oh, I'm sorry. I didn't think about how scared she is of mines. Especially ever since the explosion and her father got hurt. I'm going to start making my way to you."

Before either Daniel or Molly could insist the girl remain where she was, they heard a strange sound. It sounded like a soft cry. The noise came from Elsie's direction. When she didn't resume her chatter, Daniel called her name. Silence.

"What happened now?" Daniel muttered.

"I don't know. But it can't be good."

"Right. Elsie's never quiet for this long."

Molly winced. Any other time, his words would have made her laugh. Now, all she could imagine was that some terrible disaster had befallen the child. What if she'd tumbled down a hole, off the side of a cliff? Did mines have cliffs? She dared not ask.

"We need to go faster, Daniel."

"All right."

They moved down the passage, but instead of Daniel leading Molly, she tugged on his arm. Silently, she urged him on. He said nothing but quickened his step.

"Don't be afraid, Elsie," Molly said, feigning cheer instead of dread. "We're almost there. As soon as we find you, we'll have you out of this mine in two shakes of a lamb's tail."

They went a few paces more to find the passage split into two. The stopped. Molly's heart skipped a beat. What now? Her first inclination was to pray and ask God's help. Before she could form the words, she felt drawn to the right-hand passage. She lifted her hand and pointed. Daniel nodded.

Molly hoped that the Lord had, in his mercy, led her the right way even without her asking for guidance.

They rounded a sharp corner and saw their first glimpse of a light. A few paces ahead, Elsie lay on the ground, a softly burning lantern on the ground next to her. Daniel lifted his lantern to cast a light over the child. They hurried to her side and found her unconscious. In the flickering light of the lantern, Molly could see the girl must have hit her head on the low hanging roof of the passage.

Molly stroked Elsie's head. "She's got a goose egg. She's bleeding but not too much, thank heavens."

"Let's get her out of the mine." Daniel lifted the girl in his arms. Molly carried the lantern and walked at his side. Elsie lay motionless in Daniel's arms. To Molly's surprise and relief, Daniel recalled each twist and turn of the various passages. At last, Molly knew they were near the mine entrance, the light at the end of the tunnel.

Elsie stirred in Daniel's arms. "Grandma, I don't want to go to school."

"Hush Elsie," Molly said. "Don't fret, child."

Elsie's eyes fluttered. "I wanted to go to the Presidio Mine. I need to find that s-silver. In the mine."

"We just found *you* in the mine," Daniel said. "You must be the lost treasure folks talk about."

Molly laughed at Daniel's sweet words.

Elsie smiled, suddenly shy.

"Well it's true," Daniel insisted.

Elsie squinted as they neared the entrance. "The sunshine is so bright."

"It is," Molly agreed. "We all need to let our eyes adjust."

A few paces inside the entrance, Daniel set Elsie on a low ledge of rock.

"Let's sit here a bit. If we walk straight out there, we won't be able to see anything for a few minutes."

The sunshine lit the area with a dull muted light. Daniel inspected Elsie's wound. He spoke of his thanks that she hadn't been more seriously hurt. Elsie looked remorseful. Her eyes filled with tears. Daniel soothed the tearful child. "Never mind, Elsie. You're safe. That's the important thing."

"I didn't mean to be a nuisance. I know how much Molly dislikes the mine." Elsie hiccupped and scrubbed her hands across her face. Tears mixed with dust, leaving the girl's pretty face a grubby mess.

"It's fine." Molly wished she had something more comforting to say but couldn't think of anything better. She could feel her own tears gathering much to her astonishment. "It was very interesting. Down there. Deep below the ground."

Daniel raised a brow.

"It was." Molly said to his unspoken question. "I never realized that the dark was so..."

Her words trailed off.

"Dark?" Daniel offered.

Elsie hiccupped again. "I didn't expect anyone would bother to look for me."

Molly drew a sharp breath. She set her hand over her heart. Elsie's words struck a pang of sorrow in her heart. How could any child think such a thing?

"Elsie," Daniel said. "I don't know what the future holds exactly, but I will always make sure you're safe and cared for. Maybe with Molly and me."

Elsie's eyes widened. Her lips parted with surprise, but she said nothing.

Molly too, remained silent. Up till this point, Daniel hadn't spoken of their marriage in front of anyone else, just her. He turned his gaze toward Molly. "I intend on doing things properly. When I finally meet your father, that is."

His gaze drifted to her injured eye. He winced. "I hope you're all healed up by then. Can't stand to see you hurt, sweetheart."

She nodded. The soft tender look that she saw in his eyes stole her breath. His kind, loving words left her speechless.

For Elsie, his words had the opposite effect. "Mr. Honeycutt, do you mean to say you're really going to ask Mr. Collins for Molly's hand? It sounds like the real thing, like how it happens in storybooks."

Daniel smiled at Molly and she gave him an answering smile.

"That's just what I mean," Daniel said.

"That is so romantic!" Elsie exclaimed. "Can I be in the wedding? Will I need to call you Mr. and Mrs. Honeycutt? Are you going to have a lot of children? Will they call me Aunt Elsie?"

Molly blushed. Daniel's smile widened to a broad grin.

Elsie's excited chatter went for some time as usual. After a spell, she ran out of words or perhaps needed to catch her breath. The silence stretched between them as Elsie smiled happily.

A sound came from outside the entrance. Men's voices echoed against the rocks of the mine entrance. They grew louder, more agitated. Molly recognized her brothers and her father too. She gasped. Before she could speak, her father appeared.

"Molly!" he shouted.

Molly took Elsie's hand. Daniel took the other. They walked the rest of the way out of the mine.

Papa stared, first at Molly and then at Daniel and Elsie. His gaze darted back to Molly and he recoiled. Molly could only imagine the sight. Papa went pale with anger as he turned back to Daniel.

"Who are you?" He thundered. "And what in tarnation are you doing with my daughter?"

Chapter Thirty-Three
Convincing Mr. Collins

Daniel

Mr. Collins and his two sons regarded Daniel with a full measure of indignation and outrage. All the way back to their home, Molly tried to explain matters. She began with Elsie's arrival. None of the menfolk much cared about the girl. They all waited for answers about Daniel Honeycutt.

Molly told them about what had happened since they'd left, but Daniel could tell her words fell on deaf ears. When they arrived at the Collins home, Mr. Collins dismissed Daniel. He instructed the boys to "help" Mr. Honeycutt with the horses while he "visited" with Molly.

Molly gave him a small apologetic smile and told Elsie to come with her to the house.

Daniel tended to the horses. Will and Jack trailed behind. From the way they glared at him, Daniel guessed they intended to make sure he didn't slink away. When he finished unsaddling the horses, he returned to the shed and gathered his few possessions. The sun was descending and in a couple of hours it would be dark. It was time for him to go, but he wouldn't leave without speaking to Mr. Collins.

"You really slept here in the shed?" Jack looked skeptical as he leaned against the shed doorway.

"I did sleep here."

"Because there was an outlaw in the area?" Will asked. His tone was a tad more stern than Jack's tone. "You expect us to believe that?"

"You can believe whatever you please."

Will directed his attention to Daniel's eyepatch. Without waiting for the question, Daniel offered an explanation. He pointed to the injured side of his face. "Knife fight with a cattle rustler."

The boys regarded him with a tad less hostility, or so it seemed to Daniel. He made light of the matter. "The scars help scare off troublemakers. They're handy at times. Especially when protecting a vulnerable young lady."

The boys shifted with clear discomfort. They didn't care for the idea of their sister needing protection. Especially from a stranger. It didn't sit well with them. Daniel had to give them credit for their response.

"Papa wanted Molly to come along." Jack shook his head. "He's going to blame himself for leaving her here. Even though he's mended, he won't be happy he went on the trip and left Molly alone."

Daniel nudged the subject a different direction. "Your father's feeling better, is he?"

"He is," Will replied guardedly. "The mineral springs did him some good."

"The water was fine." Jack snickered. "The company was even better."

Will glowered at his brother. Jack's smile faded. He shrugged and looked away.

Daniel lifted his saddle from the ground and set it on a rack. He imagined Mr. Collins had met a lady friend at the springs and that it might mean more than just a flirtation. Mr.

Collins had a serious air about him. Perhaps the springs healed his injuries and the lady friend had mended his spirit.

"I've heard a lot about your father," Daniel said. "If he's willing to remain in Bethany Springs, I'm certain he could have any job he wanted at the mine."

Both boys stared at him, eyes wide with a mix of doubt and surprise. Footsteps approached and a moment later Mr. Collins came around the corner of the shed. He looked flustered but nowhere near as furious as he'd been at the mine.

He was about to speak when he stopped abruptly and looked around the shed. "Who did all this?"

Daniel followed his gaze. "What do you mean?"

"The shed's been tidied up." Mr. Collins scowled. "You did this?"

"I did a few things around the place. I hope I didn't overstep," Daniel said. "I only meant to be of service to Molly and her family."

Mr. Collins scratched his jaw as he eyed the changes. Daniel had removed every tool and canister, cleaned them properly and the shelves too. After, he'd organized everything. He sharpened and oiled the tools and mended those that needed repair.

"I wanted to help out, seeing as you'd been recently injured," Daniel added.

"Appreciate it," Mr. Collins said quietly. "I'm feeling almost back to my old self."

"Papa, Mr. Honeycutt said he'd offer you a job at the mine. Any job you want." Jack's eyes sparked with excitement. "Imagine that. If we stayed in Bethany Springs, you could court Ingrid."

Mr. Collins looked stricken and then sheepish. He reddened, turned away to examine the orderly state of the shed. He muttered under his breath. Daniel waited, turning his attention to Jack, then Will and back to Jack. Both boys pretended not to notice. Jack studied his thumbnail. Will paced along the open side of the shed, gaze downward.

Finally, Mr. Collins broke the silence. "Certainly, hope you're not the sort of man who'd toy with a girl's heart. Or make insincere offers about a man's livelihood."

"No sir. I'm not offering you a job. My mother is making the offer. I'm only interested in marrying Molly. I don't much care about the Presidio Mine."

"Well, I care about the mine!" Mr. Collins cleared his throat. "I care about my daughter too, of course."

"The word is you know more than anyone else in these parts, about mining, and about the Presidio Mine in particular."

Mr. Collins narrowed his eyes. "Maybe I do."

"Tell me something, Mr. Collins. Do you think if the Presidio Mine were run right, by an honorable man who put the safety of all the miners before profits, do you think it could earn a little money?"

Mr. Collins shrugged. "Don't know. Maybe. Molly has nothing to do with my work, understand?"

"Yes sir."

"You best be on your way then, Mr. Honeycutt. I'd like to talk things over with Molly. She's a little hot under the collar right now."

"What do mean?" Jack sounded fretful. "Is she making threats?"

Will grimaced. "The threat about cooking?"

Mr. Collins gave a slight nod. Both boys muttered, their expressions taut with dread.

Daniel tried to suppress a smile. His Molly, his sweet Molly was putting up a fight for him. He shouldn't be happy about the potential family turmoil. But he was pleased. Mighty pleased.

He addressed Mr. Collins. "The business about the Presidio Mine is between you and my mother. The matter of Molly and me has nothing to do with the mine. I'd like to return in two days' time to ask for permission to marry your daughter, Mr. Collins."

Mr. Collins nodded. It was a grudging gesture. The bare minimum of agreement. But Daniel didn't care. Molly's father had given him the answer he'd prayed for and that was the only thing that mattered.

Chapter Thirty-Four
No Objections

Amelia

Amelia sat in the front pew and waited for the wedding of Daniel and Molly to begin. As the music filled the chapel, she looked about in disbelief. Was she dreaming?

For as long as Amelia could recall, she'd hoped and prayed that her boys would marry. Most of her prayers had concerned Daniel. After he got injured, she'd doubled her prayers several times over. If only one son got married, she asked the good Lord to let it be Daniel.

Every so often, she'd allow herself to dream of the day he wed. She could picture him, tall, strong and handsome, saying his vows before God and the world. The bride would, of course, be some sweet dear girl who only wanted to make Daniel happy. She'd be radiant. Her face would fairly shine as she looked up at him and promised to love, honor and obey.

The scene would be the most joyful sight Amelia had ever witnessed.

What Amelia hadn't imagined was how she'd cry buckets of mortifying tears when the bride walked down the aisle on her father's arm. Mr. Collins looked a little misty-eyed too, or so she thought. It was hard to see through the teary deluge.

Robert McCord moved from the other side of Sophie to a spot beside Amelia. He patted her hand while Sophie patted the other. By the time the preacher began, Amelia felt a little better.

The preacher spoke about objections to the marriage. His voice droned slowly. Amelia silently urged him to pick up the pace.

"Therefore, if anyone can show…" The preacher paused to clear his throat. He coughed a time or two and started over.

Amelia, meanwhile, silently ran through a list of possible troublemakers. She leaned forward to look at Mr. Collins in the pew across the aisle. He looked amenable enough. She reassured herself that he wouldn't cause any trouble.

The man had driven a hard bargain before accepting the foreman job. Amelia hadn't minded one bit. John Collins was the man she should have hired to begin with.

His young, strapping sons sat beside him. No worries there. The boys were stellar young men. Amelia had hired them to build new cabins for the miners, and to repair those that were still in good shape.

"Let's see, now." The preacher frowned at his prayer book. "Therefore, if anyone can show. Oh dear. I already read that part."

"Land sakes," Amelia muttered. She turned her attention to Simon, standing at the front of the church next to Daniel and Zach. His shoulders were hitched a notch. Never a good sign. Simon was still sulking about her ultimatum. She watched him intently, silently willing him to hold his tongue. Simon liked to stir trouble just for trouble's sake.

The preacher mumbled a few words and resumed the marriage vows. Amelia was tempted to whisper some encouragement, loud enough for the aged minister to make out, but not loud enough for the rest of the church to hear.

Earlier that morning, over breakfast, Amelia had spoken with Elsie. She confessed her concerns about Simon making some sort of fuss at the wedding.

"Simon could object to the marriage," Amelia told Elsie.

"I'd never heard of such a thing." Elsie's eyes grew round as plums as she considered the outlandish notion.

"He won't object. He wouldn't dare. Of course not." Amelia said the words to reassure Elsie as much as herself.

"It'll be fine, Mrs. Honeycutt. I promise."

Amelia had thought about the matter a dozen times or more over the course of the day. Now that the moment had arrived, her heart drummed fast. Holding her breath, she kept her gaze fixed on Simon. The minister labored through the passage.

"...just cause why they may not be lawfully joined together, let them speak now or forever hold their peace."

Silence stretched interminably.

Finally, the preacher continued. Amelia let out a deep sigh. Sophie did too. Robert chuckled softly.

Sweet little Elsie, standing beside Molly, glanced over her shoulder, and smiled at Amelia. It was an I-told-you-so smile. Elsie's sweet, youthful smile brightened everything. JoJo Ward looked back and smiled as well even though she likely didn't know anything about Amelia's concerns.

The rest of the ceremony went smoothly. When the preacher allowed Daniel to kiss his bride, Amelia thought her heart might burst with happiness. Daniel gazed down at Molly with such tenderness. Molly looked back at him with love-filled eyes.

Daniel and Molly kissed. They shared a smile before turning to face their guests. The preacher presented Mr. and Mrs. Daniel Honeycutt.

"Thank the merciful heavens," Amelia said. She lifted her gaze to the rafters out of habit. Moments such as this one were meant to be shared with the boys' father.

Sophie leaned closer. "Are you speaking with George?"

Amelia sighed. Sophie thought Amelia's habit of talking with her late husband was odd and perhaps even a little troubling. In her opinion, Amelia needed to put the past behind her and spend time with real, living men. Lately, Sophie had gone so far as to recommend her brother-in-law, Wade. Amelia didn't care for Sophie's match-making notions.

"I might have chatted with George just now," Amelia said, her tone cool. "Briefly."

Sophie's brows lifted. "He likes the wedding, yes?"

"He likes the wedding, yes." Amelia liked to poke fun at Sophie's manner of speech. "He wants me to tell you to mind your own business."

Sophie gasped and shook her head. "George used to have such lovely manners. Please tell him I am offended. Did he, at least, approve of the dress I lent you?"

Amelia smiled and patted Sophie's arm. "He did approve. He said you're a good friend. Most of the time."

Sophie had found the perfect dress for Amelia. Molly wanted to make a new dress for Amelia, but Amelia couldn't bear the notion of the girl having another thing to do before her own wedding.

The wedding party stopped at the front pews. Daniel kissed his mother and Sophie. Molly kissed the ladies as well as her father. Daniel shook Mr. Collins's hand. The wedding party continued up the aisle and Robert ushered the two ladies toward the church door.

After they left the church, the guests and wedding party traveled to the Honeycutt ranch for a luncheon. Sophie had made all the arrangements, thankfully. The dining room buffet table was laden with dozens of heaping platters.

Daniel held Molly's hand and asked the guests to join him in prayer before they ate. They bowed their heads. Daniel gave thanks for God's blessings. He thanked Him for Molly as well as his mother, his brothers, his father-in-law, and brothers-in-law. When he mentioned Elsie, Amelia thought she heard a soft murmur of surprise from the girl.

Everyone loved Elsie. Despite how much people cherished her, Elsie seemed continually amazed by their affection. Amelia would have liked to find the folks who discarded the child. She had no inkling what she'd do if she ever found them. No matter. She indulged in notions of meting out some punishment. Something uncomfortable and humiliating would do nicely.

Amelia sat with Sophie and Robert to eat lunch. Mr. Collins sat a spell too and chatted with Robert about cattle prices.

Elsie sat beside Amelia. The girl ate a prodigious amount, complimenting Sophie on the delicious food. "I think I like French cooking," Elsie exclaimed.

Sophie beamed at the child. "You should come to visit me. I will feed you French food morning, noon and night."

Amelia frowned. "Don't you listen, Elsie. Molly said you're all mine till they get your room ready. She promised a month. Between ordering furniture and making curtains, she'll be busy on the old homestead."

Elsie nodded. "Yes, ma'am."

Sophie waved a dismissive hand. "Poo! A month you have the child. She can come stay with me for a few of those days."

Amelia directed her attention to Elsie. "Sophie already has a daughter *and* a granddaughter. I'm not sharing you. A month is a month. Not a day less."

Sophie pouted. Elsie looked incredulous. Amelia knew why. The child couldn't imagine people arguing and vying for a chance to spend time with her. A shy smile curved her lips. "All right, Miss Amelia. I'll stay a month. Maybe we can go visit Miss Sophie a few times."

Sophie laughed with a broad smile of triumph.

Molly came to the table looking as lovely as ever. She invited Elsie to help serve the cake. Sophie sighed and murmured something in French, a compliment, judging from the appreciative tone.

Both ladies sat silently, watching Molly cross the room with Elsie. "What a lovely girl Daniel found," Sophie murmured. "I would like three just like her for my boys."

Amelia couldn't resist boasting about Molly. "Daniel asked for her hand less than a month ago. And yet, she still managed to sew her own wedding dress and Elsie's frock too. Molly is a darling girl. I can't recall the last time I saw Daniel so happy."

Sophie took Amelia's hand in hers. "You're on your way. One down and two to go. Hopefully, the next two will be easy, non?"

"We'll see about that." Amelia hadn't told Sophie about Simon. Not yet.

"You give me hope that my boys will marry one day," Sophie said wistfully.

"Won't that be something? If we end up with all seven of our children settled in happy marriages? I'm so pleased Daniel decided to take our old house. I couldn't bear to finally get a sweet daughter-in-law only to have her on the other side of the ranch."

Sophie nodded.

Amelia went on. "I'll be able to see them often."

Sophie's lips quirked. "It's very nice. I want my boys to marry, but perhaps remain at the McCord Ranch. Not Bethany Springs."

Amelia smiled. "Having three boys living next door might prove too much of a good thing?"

"*Oui, exactement.*" Sophie offered an answering smile.

Epilogue - The New Schoolhouse
(Two years later)

Elsie

Mrs. Honeycutt stood on the top step of the newly-built Presidio School. She wanted to say a few words to the people who had come to celebrate. It was a small group, mostly family, but a few friends too.

Daniel and Molly held hands as they stood in the shade of a nearby pecan tree. Mr. Collins waited, hat in hand, his new wife, Ingrid, standing beside him. Also in attendance was Mr. Whitson, the ranch foreman, along with his wife, Franny. Mr. and Mrs. McCord arrived after everyone else but before Mrs. Honeycutt began speaking.

Mrs. Honeycutt had promised to keep the speech brief. She told Elsie how it was bad manners to keep hungry folks waiting. Another reason to keep the address short and sweet was the fact that she held a young boy in her arms, her grandson, George Honeycutt.

Elsie stood nearby, ready to take the boy if he started to fuss. For the moment, he appeared content to be with his grandmother. That could change in an instant. The moment he spied the picnic baskets on the tables, he was likely to protest. Loudly.

"I wanted to say a quick word of thanks to the two Collins brothers for their hard work," Mrs. Honeycutt said.

The group offered a round of applause and turned to where the boys stood at the back. Will and Jack both grew flustered. It was clear they would have liked to skip this part. With their hands shoved in pockets and tight smiles, the two boys looked a tad uneasy.

Elsie tried to conceal her amusement. The boys were uncomfortable? Served them right. Will and Jack were a pair of rascals. The prior week, she'd spent a day in their company, helping them paint the new schoolhouse. Lately, the two boys had taken to teasing her every chance they got, and she couldn't decide which boy was worse.

Probably Jack.

When he wasn't bossing her, he complained about her painting. The paint was either too thick or too thin. She missed a spot here. Dripped paint there. Had she ever painted *anything* before?

Will mostly ignored her that day. But he'd laughed at Jack's comments. To Elsie's thinking his laughter made him equally guilty.

Mrs. Honeycutt went on. "The two boys proved themselves time and again with their work on the cabins. But this project was a great deal more complicated. Aside from a few skilled laborers, they built this school by themselves."

Elsie rolled her eyes. There'd be no end to the boasting now. The boys already had grand plans for a carpentry shop in Bethany Springs. They intended to make custom pieces as well as ready-made furnishings.

The prior week, they'd debated endlessly. Neither could agree on what to name the shop. Collins Brothers or Collins and Collins. Back and forth they went, discussing the merits of each name.

"I tried for an entire year to get the state to fund the school," Mrs. Honeycutt explained to the group. "They passed a law back in 1870, meant to give our children an education up till eighteen years of age. But they didn't bother building more schools in many of the smaller communities. Up till now, we only had one school that went to sixth grade. I intend to change that, starting with this very school."

Elsie noticed George growing impatient. He squirmed. He'd spied the picnic baskets and knew they held plenty of tasty treats. He pointed and protested.

Mrs. Honeycutt nodded. "That's right, George-darling. I don't care for those fat-cats in Austin any more than you do."

Everyone laughed and many nodded in agreement.

George's face reddened. Elsie knew he was getting ready to fuss even louder. She edged past the by standers to get closer to Mrs. Honeycutt. If she could take George, Mrs. Honeycutt could finish her talk. Otherwise, her words would be drowned out by George's fussing. Everyone knew Elsie's special gift at calming the toddler.

Mrs. Honeycutt gave her the child as she spoke more about the schoolhouse. George quieted. Elsie turned to make her way down the steps, but Mrs. Honeycutt stopped her.

"And before the blessing and the meal, I'd like to commend this young lady for her help. Elsie's always ready to lend a hand. Whether it's to help soothe a fussy child or paint a schoolhouse. She's always cheerful."

Elsie winced. Heavens, how she disliked this sort of attention. Heat rose to her face. She cringed inwardly, desperately hoping she wouldn't flush a bright red. She turned her attention to George, praying that Mrs. Honeycutt would tell the crowd to go enjoy the picnic. George sucked his thumb.

Mrs. Honeycutt wasn't finished yet. "Sophie McCord calls Elsie a helper extraordinaire. And I couldn't agree more."

The group murmured a collective agreement along with polite applause. Mrs. McCord nodded and waved at Elsie.

Now it was Will and Jack's turn to roll their eyes at her. She studiously ignored them. Any response only encouraged them to tease her more.

"I won't keep you any longer," Mrs. Honeycutt said. "Let's gather in a circle so Daniel can say the blessing."

Molly came to Elsie's side and offered to take her son. George shook his head and nestled in Elsie's arms. Molly chuckled. Daniel gave thanks for the fine day, the delicious food and their good health. When he finished and they all joined in saying 'amen', lunch was served.

Ingrid Collins poured glasses of cool lemonade. People fixed their plates and sat down at the picnic tables. Molly took George, telling him that he needed to eat with his mama and papa. Elsie served herself some food and joined Mr. and Mrs. Whitson.

"I heard you helped paint the school," Mrs. Whitson said, kindly. "You wear a number of hats around here, don't you?"

Mr. Whitson's eyes twinkled. "Maybe the Collins boys can hire you when they start their shop."

"Oh, Sheldon, hush," Mrs. Whitson chided. "Don't tease the poor girl."

The Collins brothers sat at a nearby table. They grinned. She instantly felt every bit as aggravated as last week. She narrowed her eyes.

"I'll only work there if I can name the shop," Elsie said primly.

Jack and Will looked intrigued.

"You have an idea for our business?" Will asked. "How come you didn't say?"

Elsie took a sip of lemonade. "It didn't occur to me until now."

Jack snickered. "Tell us, why don't you?"

"I like the sound of Cantankerous Collins Carpentry."

Elsie heard the unmistakable sound of Molly's laughter from another table. The boys scoffed, dismissed her suggestion and went back to eating their lunch. They filled their plate three more times.

She tried not to notice. Franny Whitson chatted about the various desserts. Elsie explained Molly's recipe for the meringue pie. The conversation drifted to other matters, when from out of the blue, Mrs. Whitson asked what Elsie would like to do when she was older.

"I'd like to be a teacher," Elsie said shyly. "My grandmother told me she thought I'd do well instructing children."

Mrs. Whitson's eyes sparkled. "Maybe you'll teach in this very schoolroom. Wouldn't that be something?"

"Yes, ma'am." Elsie felt her face grow warm. She had no business thinking about going off to school. The Honeycutt family treated her as one of their own and she lacked nothing, but two years at a teacher's college or normal school as they were often called, would likely cost a pretty penny.

She turned to find Will looking at her appraisingly. Cringing inwardly, she awaited some teasing comment. Instead of saying something unkind, he turned his attention back to an immense slice of pecan pie. Jack was returning from the dessert table with an astonishing array of sweets. Will and Jack's appetite seemed to have no end.

How long before Will told Jack all about her silly hope of becoming a teacher? She sighed and excused herself from the table. Molly seemed content tending to George and told her to enjoy the afternoon.

Elsie wandered to the door of the schoolhouse. It stood partway open. When she helped paint, she hadn't ventured inside. She ascended the steps and peeked past the door. To her surprise there was some furniture inside the schoolroom, a few chairs and tables, shelves, and cupboards. At the front of the room sat the teacher's desk.

Unable to resist, she stepped inside. The wood floor creaked under her feet as she walked to the front of the room. She smiled to see that the blackboard ledge held chalk and erasers. She circled the desk, pulled back the chair and sat down.

If anyone came inside, they'd probably be mighty surprised to see her sitting at the teacher's desk. A wave of mischievous amusement made her laugh. Straightening, she regarded an imaginary group of pupils, awaiting her instruction.

"Good morning, class," she said. "I hope everyone brought their assignments this morning."

The door opened wide. Elsie yelped. She clapped her hand over her mouth.

Will stepped inside. He looked remorseful. "I'm sorry. I didn't do my homework. Hope I'm not in trouble."

Elsie grumbled under her breath. It could have been worse. The unwelcome guest could have been Jack.

Will strolled around the classroom, inspecting various details. Elsie couldn't imagine why he'd bother. Hadn't he and Jack built the schoolhouse? They'd had help, of course. Mr.

Collins acted like a supervisor on some tasks, but most of the responsibility rested on the shoulders of the boys.

She waited for him to finish and leave. Drumming her fingers, she sat patiently. If he knew she wanted him to go, he'd make a point of lingering. She ignored him as he wandered behind her desk. The scratch of chalk on the board sparked her curiosity but she refused to give into the urge to see what he wrote. Probably something rude.

She heard him set the chalk down and brush off his hands. With a leisurely pace, he ambled back to the center of the class. He wore a smile. Will didn't smile too often. He was too busy trying to fit in with the menfolk.

When he smiled, she noted with surprise, he got a dimple. Just on one side. Somehow, she knew he'd hate for her to point it out. She said nothing. Instead, she tucked the detail away and made plans to torment him some other time.

"I wrote your name on the board, Elsie."

She blinked. Her name? Likely story. He'd probably written something insulting to get even for the suggestion of *Cantankerous Collins Carpentry*.

"Go on," he urged. "Take a look."

"No thank you."

"It's not anything unkind." He set his hand over his heart. "Promise."

His tone was sincere. She considered how Jack and Will were bothersome and impossible most of the time. While they both enjoyed playing pranks, they didn't tell outright bold-faced lies.

She got up and slowly turned to the blackboard. It was true. Will hadn't written anything unkind. Across the top of the board, he'd written, *Miss Elsie McKittrick. Teacher*

Extraordinaire. To her surprise, his words were sweet and thoughtful.

Will's smile widened. He still only had a single dimple she noticed.

"Thank you, Will." She pushed the chair under the desk.

"I'm not teasing, Elsie. You'd be a very good teacher. You're patient. And smart. Children would be lucky to have a teacher like you."

Elsie crossed the schoolroom, heading to the door. His words were indeed kind, but they troubled her, nonetheless. They made her yearn for something she could never have.

Will trailed a few paces behind. "I thought that might make you happy, or at least smile."

She stopped in the doorway. "I don't have the means to become a teacher."

"Maybe none of that matters."

Elsie waited, wondering what he could mean.

"The official education folks in Austin paid us a visit just before we broke ground. They issued us a charter for the school. One of them talked about state scholarships. Kids take an exam and those with the best scores win the scholarship. They study at Austin College."

"I never heard of such a thing," Elsie said. "Where is Austin College?"

"Somewhere around Houston."

It seemed like an impossible dream. "I only went to school till the sixth grade," Elsie said. "Like the rest of the kids around here. I'm sure they give scholarships to students who have gone to school longer than me."

"You've got a couple of years to catch up. I had to study back when I'd planned on going to the academy. I'll help you if you like."

To Charm a Scarred Cowboy

Elsie drew a sharp breath. "Oh, my goodness."

Will looked sheepish. She half-expected him to say something flippant. His cheeks colored.

"Thank you," Elsie said. "That's a very kind offer."

Will coughed. Next, he raked his fingers through his hair. After a moment, he composed himself and nodded towards a spot behind her. "Maybe you'll teach here one day. We might have the bell fixed by then."

Elsie noticed a thick cord hanging near the door. It was attached to the bell atop the schoolhouse.

Will gripped the cord and tugged. He tried with all his might, to no avail. "Guess it's still stuck," he muttered.

"Stuck? Are you certain?"

Will stepped aside and gestured to the rope. Elsie slowly wrapped her fingers around the cord. She imagined her work as a teacher. Each morning, she'd ring a bell like this one. The sound would summon her students. They'd come running, brimming with excitement, eager for her lessons.

Without thinking, she tugged the cord. To her shock, it gave easily. She, gasped, dropped the cord and retreated several steps.

The bell rang. The clamor rent the air and echoed across the schoolhouse. One clang followed the next. Elsie stood helplessly as the bell sounded a dozen times or more. The clangs faded and finally, it grew quiet.

Will grinned. Elsie was speechless with astonishment. With an outstretched hand, he ushered her out the door. The crowd greeted her and Will with laughter and applause.

"Wasn't me," Will said, sparks of mischief dancing in his eyes. He pointed to Elsie. "It was Miss McKittrick."

Elsie was too mortified to utter a response.

* * *

Molly

The picnic had exhausted George. Molly gave him a quick bath, dried him off and dressed him in his sleeper. With each yawn, the small boy grew more and more sleepy. By the time Daniel came to the nursery to say goodnight to his son, little George was already fast asleep. Molly tucked the blanket around the child and silently beckoned Daniel out of the room.

"I didn't even have to rock him or sing any lullabies," Molly whispered.

"The boy's plum worn out," Daniel replied.

"He had a fine time today. I think he especially enjoyed searching the schoolyard for pebbles. You've never seen such a grubby child. The bathwater looked like a barnyard puddle."

Daniel smiled as he followed her down the hallway. They stopped at Elsie's room to say goodnight. She sat on the edge of her bed, holding a hairbrush, lost in thought. Molly winced. She wondered if Will and Jack had hurt Elsie's feelings during the picnic that afternoon.

It wouldn't have been the first time. The two boys delighted in teasing the poor girl. Neither of Molly's brothers seemed to appreciate Elsie's tender heart. She was a good four years younger than them and wasn't used to being pestered.

Molly knocked gently on the door frame. "A penny for your thoughts."

Elsie startled. "Oh. I'm sorry. I didn't hear you."

Molly smiled. "I must say, your new dress looks very pretty on you. The blue is so becoming."

Elsie ran her hand down the skirt. "Thank you. I had a fair number of compliments."

Daniel spoke. "The schoolhouse looked mighty pretty. You and the boys did a fine job. I was sort of surprised you wanted to help the boys paint."

"I admit I was surprised too," Molly said. "My brothers can be exasperating."

Elsie turned the brush over in her hands. "I wanted to help with some small part of the new schoolhouse. It seems so important."

Before Molly could reply, Elsie went on. "Will told me about a scholarship for teachers. He said I could take an exam. If I scored well, the state of Texas would pay for my school."

Molly drew a sharp breath.

"School?" Daniel asked. "This is the first I've heard of you wanting to go to school."

Elsie nodded. "Maybe."

Molly went to Elsie's side and took the brush. She began to brush Elsie's lovely, coppery tresses. A pang struck her heart. Elsie was growing up. She was becoming a young lady. Gone was her girlish chatter and in its place was a quiet thoughtfulness. Elsie still liked to talk with her and Daniel, but some things, like her ideas about school, she kept tucked away.

"If that's what you want, Elsie, you don't need a scholarship." Daniel leaned against the doorway and folded his arms. "We've told you that we consider you to be our daughter. We'll take care of any expense. No need to worry about the cost."

"Thank you," Elsie said softly. "I still need to take an exam. Part of me likes to think I'd be able to earn a scholarship. It's silly, I suppose."

"Why is it silly? Daniel asked.

"I haven't done any book learning since I finished sixth grade." Elsie winced. "I'm not sure if I can even pass the exam, much less get a scholarship."

"We'll get what you need," Molly said. "Textbooks and whatnot."

Elsie sighed. "I figure I have a couple of years to get ready. Will offered to help."

Molly stopped brushing Elsie's hair. Had she heard correctly? Will and Jack had gotten on her last nerve. And now, she talked of Will helping her?

Daniel's brows lifted. A smile tugged at his lips despite his best efforts. His expression made clear he would not go near that prickly topic, not for love or money.

"That's a nice offer," Molly said slowly. "Will is probably a better tutor than Jack."

Elsie snorted inelegantly.

Molly set the brush on the bedside table. "What an exciting idea, Elsie. We'll talk more in the morning."

She bent to kiss the girl on the forehead. Daniel followed suit and bid Elsie goodnight.

Inside their room, they talked about the surprising development. Molly had to laugh as she recalled how Will and Jack always resisted their lessons. How things change. Now Will was offering to help Elsie with her schoolwork.

"Elsie will be an eager learner." Daniel sat down to take off his boots. "And a quick learner too."

"She will. Indeed."

Molly removed her hair pins and took down her hair. She tried to imagine the house without Elsie. Sometimes the girl stayed with Amelia for a few days. Still, Elsie was never gone long. By the time she left, George would be old enough to miss Elsie.

Lord-willing, George would not be alone when Elsie left. Molly's hand drifted to her waist and wondered if she'd soon be blessed with another child. Elsie was such a help. Molly felt fortunate that she still had a few years before the girl set her course for a new venture.

Molly donned her nightgown and slipped into bed. Daniel got into bed and took her hand in his. He lay on his side and offered a gently teasing smile. "You're missing her already, aren't you?"

"I am."

"Me too. But we can't let our feeling sway Elsie's decisions."

"I won't. I promise."

Daniel kissed her hand. "Mama's going to fuss about Elsie leaving us."

Molly nodded.

"She'll be fine." Daniel rolled to his back and tucked his hands beneath his head. "Not right at first, of course, but eventually."

"I reckon she'll come home in the summertime. But two years is an awful long time."

"Two years?" His voice was gruff and a tad loud for this time of the evening. He propped up on his elbow. "Two *years?*"

"Why, I believe that's what I've heard."

Grumbling, Daniel turned to his bedside table. He darkened the lamp and reached for her hand to say nighttime prayers. He gave thanks for their blessing and for the fine day, asked the Lord's guidance for the morrow. After they said amen, they lay in the darkness, neither of them speaking.

Molly smiled as she patted his hand. "You'll be fine, Daniel. Eventually."

Daniel scoffed. "Eventually? Nothing doing. I'm going to tell her I changed my mind. She can't go off traipsing across Texas for two years. It's ridiculous. I won't stand for it."

She edged a little closer to him. He grumbled and drew her into his embrace. "Two years! The house will be so quiet. How can the little chatterbox leave us for two years?"

Molly rested her head on Daniel's broad chest and listened to the steady beat of his heart. With a sigh of contentment, she closed her eyes. "I don't have the answer to that question, Mr. Honeycutt."

Sensing his unease, Molly waited for her husband to set aside his worries of the day and drift off. Little George went to sleep from one moment to the next. Not Daniel.

Daniel always fell asleep in stages. First, the tension in his shoulders eased. Next, he'd sigh. His breathing would deepen. The final step was a slight twitch. Held in his embrace, she'd feel the movement along his arm. With that, her husband would surrender to a deep, restful sleep.

She could tell that her husband wasn't drifting off to sleep anytime soon. He fretted about Elsie leaving. Even though it would be several years before Elsie might attend school, the notion troubled him.

"Elsie might change her mind," Molly said quietly.

"I don't believe she will. And I want to encourage her, of course."

Molly smiled. He didn't sound too encouraging. If anything, he sounded a little resigned.

Daniel spoke. "I never imagined getting married. When I met you, I changed my mind. Didn't take more than a blink of an eye. Same with taking in Elsie. There was something right about that too. I hope she knows. Not sure if I ever told her."

"I think she knows."

"I ought to tell her more often how I love her. That I'm glad she's part of our family."

Daniel rarely spoke of such things. His words warmed her heart. She was certain that Elsie felt loved and cherished, but perhaps the girl needed to hear it more often.

"I ought to tell her too," Molly said.

He tugged her closer into his embrace. "And I love you, Molly Anne. Everything about you. Your laugh. How you make our house a home. The way you love George and Elsie. And me."

His words took her by surprise. She knew he loved her, of course. He'd told her time and again, but rarely with so much fervor. Tears stung her eyes. "I love you too."

Warmth washed over her as she basked in his tender, heartfelt admission.

He kissed the top of her head. "Land sakes. I got to round up a hundred head tomorrow. Sheldon and me and a few men are heading out at first light."

She smiled. "You best get a little sleep."

"I'm trying," he grumbled. "If folks would quit carrying on."

She laughed softly. He kissed her once more. Tucked close in his embrace, Molly fell into a peaceful slumber.

The End

Book Two of Brides of Bethany Springs
Kiss of the Texas Maverick

Simon Honeycutt needs the help of a girl he knew as a child, a girl he teased. A lot. That was a long time ago, and he's sure by now she can look past his poor manners to help his friend avoid jail time. Virginia remembers Simon. She remembers all too well, and vows not to fall for his tricks ever again.

Books by Charlotte Dearing

Mail Order Providence
Mail Order Sarah
Mail Order Ruth

Brides of Bethany Springs Series
To Charm a Scarred Cowboy
Kiss of the Texas Maverick
Vow of the Texas Cowboy
The Accidental Mail Order Bride
Starry-Eyed Mail Order Bride
An Inconvenient Mail Order Bride
Amelia's Storm

The Bluebonnet Brides Collection
Mail Order Grace
Mail Order Rescue
Mail Order Faith
Mail Order Hope
Mail Order Destiny
Love's Destiny

Sign up at www.charlottedearing.com to be notified of special offers and announcements.